THE LOVED
AND THE LOST

D0899728

YG

THE LOVED
AND THE LOST

Morley Callaghan

Introduction by
David Staines

Exile Editions

Publishers of singular
Fiction, Poetry, Translation, Nonfiction and Drama

2010

Library and Archives Canada Cataloguing in Publication

Callaghan, Morley, 1903-1990.
The loved and the lost / Morley Callaghan ; introduction by David
Staines.

(The Exile classics series ; no. 17)
ISBN 978-1-55096-151-5

I. Title. II. Series: Exile classics ; 17

PS8505.A43L6 2010   C813'.52   C2010-907052-6

Design and Composition by Digital ReproSet
Cover Photograph by Valentin Casarsa
Typeset in Garamond and Bembo at the Moons of Jupiter Studios
Printed in Canada by Imprimerie Gauvin

The publisher would like to acknowledge the financial assistance of
The Canada Council for the Arts and the Ontario Arts Council.

 Conseil des Arts   Canada Council
du Canada   for the Arts

 ONTARIO ARTS COUNCIL
CONSEIL DES ARTS DE L'ONTARIO

Published/Produced in Canada in 2010 by Exile Editions Ltd.
144483 Southgate Road 14 – GD
Holstein, Ontario, N0G 2A0
info@exileeditions.com / www.ExileEditions.com

Canadian Sales Distribution: U.S. Sales Distribution:
McArthur & Company   Independent Publishers Group
c/o Harper Collins   814 North Franklin Street
1995 Markham Road   Chicago, IL 60610
Toronto, ON M1B 5M8   www.ipgbook.com
toll free: 1 800 387 0117   toll free: 1 800 888 4741

Introduction

In 1914, on the eve of the outbreak of the First World War, Stephen Leacock, the multi-book author and economist – once a visitor to Montreal from Toronto, now the chair of the Department of Economics and Political Science at McGill University – published his collection of comic short stories, *Arcadian Adventures with the Idle Rich*. Set in an unnamed American city, which is only a thinly veiled Montreal, the book focuses on "the very pleasantest place imaginable," Plutoria Avenue and its Mausoleum Club.

> Just below Plutoria Avenue, however, the trees die out and the brick-and-stone of the City begins in earnest. Even from the Avenue you see the tops of the skyscraping buildings in the big commercial streets, and can hear or almost hear the roar of the elevated railway, earning dividends. And beyond that again the City sinks lower, and is choked and crowded with the tangled streets and little houses of the slums. In fact, if you were to mount to the roof of the Mausoleum Club itself on Pretoria Avenue you could almost see the slums from there. But why should you? And on the other hand, if you never went up on the roof, but only dined inside among the palm-trees, you would never know that the slums existed – which is much better.

From this perspective, Leacock sets out to deflate and destroy – with sometimes bitter irony – the pretensions of the wealthy, their materialistic drive towards more and more money, at the same time showing that materialism denies the inhabitants of the Mausoleum Club the sense of well-being which is the essence of life in society.

Leacock's portrait, centered in the homes of Westmount society, dominated later fictional depictions of anglophone Montreal, though these later presentations lacked Leacock's irony. Gwethalyn Graham's *Earth and High Heaven* (1944), for example, exposed racism among the people of Westmount, winning the Governor-General's Award for Fiction. Hugh MacLennan's *Two Solitudes* (1945), another Governor-General's Award novel, brought its characters from rural Quebec to Westmount dining rooms. Meanwhile, heralding the beginning of contemporary Quebecois fiction, Gabrielle Roy's *Bonheur d'occasion* [*The Tin Flute*] (1945) chose the slums below Westmount to map out the lives of the underprivileged French in the Saint-Henri district, winning its own Governor-General's Award.

In late 1948, Morley Callaghan, another visitor to Montreal from Toronto, who had spent some summers there too, came to know a woman at Slitkin's and Slotkin's in Montreal. "I'd seen something about her, a guilelessness that was dangerous – she, among other things, refused to see that as she socialized openly with men, and with black men, too, she aroused rage not only in white men but in black women; anyway, she became Peggy in *The Loved and the Lost*." From this point, Callaghan developed his story, which was the first to depict anglophone Montreal from Westmount downwards to the dingy apartments and Negro Clubs well below Westmount's boundaries. Two years later, he finished his novel.

As *The Loved and the Lost* opens, the focus falls on the mountain:

Joseph Carver, the published of the Montreal *Sun*, lived on the mountain. Nearly all the rich families in Montreal lived on the mountain. It was always there to make them feel secure.... But the mountain is on the island in the river; so the river is always there too, and boat whistles echo all night long aainst the mountain. From the slope where Mr. Carver lived you could look down over the church steeples and monastery towers of the old French city spreading eastward from the harbor to the gleaming river. Those who wanted things to remain as they were liked the mountain. Those who wanted a change preferred the broad flowing river. But no one could forget either of them.

Carver and "his handsome divorced daughter, Catherine," inhabit the Westmount world, an enlightened liberal enclave of business men and their families. Into this tightly controlled realm arrives James McAlpine, a lieutentant commander in the Navy in the Second World War and now an associate professor of history at the University of Toronto; he is eager to leave the academic profession in order to write an invited and uncensored column on world affairs for Carver's paper. Impressed by McAlpine's quiet self-confidence, Carver vows to do all he can to aid McAlpine in obtaining his newspaper job. And his daughter becomes romantically entangled with the would-be journalist. "She talked quickly and brightly; she reached out to make his plans her plans, and she held him silent and wondering at the glow of her generosity."

From outside Westmount appears Peggy Sanderson, the college-educated daughter of a Methodist minister who has lost his faith. At the age of twelve she had viewed a naked black boy, young Jock Johnson, and this sight proved to be her introduction to the happy companionship of the entire Johnson family. Her subsequent affection for the black race irritates the more conventional world of Westmount, and many others too.

How people react to Peggy reflects their attitude to the enigmatic mystery of life itself. The Carvers, for example, cannot ultimately forsake the security of their Westmount enclave. Although McAlpine is increasingly attracted to the beauty and charm of Peggy, he, like everyone else, is thrown off balance by her air about her– simple and light, that air of "dangerous guilelessness." And so there comes a night when he abandons her to her fate. Having seen the wintry vision of "a little old church, half Gothic and half Romanesque, but light and simple in balance" on his first walk with Peggy, he looks in vain for the same church at the end of the novel:

> he went on with his tireless search. He wandered around the neighborhood between Phillips Square and St. Patrick's. He wandered in ths strong morning sunlight. It was warm and brilliant. It melted the snow. But he couldn't find the little church.

In his realistic presentation of anglophone Montreal in its post-Second World War materialism, Callaghan fashions a haunting story. A tale of love which ends tragically, *The Loved and the Lost* is also a social portrait which encapsulates Westmount bigotry and the very same quality from beyond Westmount's borders. The novelist's duty is, as Callaghan remarked, "to catch the tempo, the stream, the way people live, think, and feel in their time."

The Loved and the Lost appeared in March 1951. In the March 24th issue of the *Globe and Mail*, William Arthur

Deacon, the literary editor, concluded that this novel, Callaghan's seventh, "must be rated Mr. Callaghan's best novel to date." It went on to win the Governor-General's Award for Fiction.

The Loved and the Lost is as timely, and as timeless, as the little church McAlpine cannot find on his own.

David Staines
September 2010

⚜ ONE ⚜

Joseph Carver, the publisher of the Montreal *Sun*, lived on the mountain. Nearly all the rich families in Montreal lived on the mountain. It was always there to make them feel secure. At night it rose against the sky like a dark protective barrier behind a shimmering curtain of lights surmounted by a gleaming cross. In the daytime, if you walked east or west along St. Catherine or Dorchester Street, it might be screened momentarily by tall buildings, but when you came to a side street there it was looming up like a great jagged brown hedge. Storms came up over the mountain, and the thunder clapped against it...

But the mountain is on the island in the river; so the river is always there, too, and boat whistles echo all night long against the mountain. From the slope where Mr. Carver lived you could look down over the church steeples and monastery towers of the old French city spreading eastward from the harbour to the gleaming river. Those who wanted things to remain as they were liked the mountain. Those who wanted a change preferred the broad flowing river. But no one could forget either of them.

Joseph Carver lived in the Château apartments near the Ritz, high above the roofs of the houses sloping down to the railroad tracks and the canal. In the grey winter days when the clouds were low on the mountain the Château with its turrets and towers and courtyards looked like a massive stone fortress. It suited Mr. Carver. He and his handsome divorced daughter,

Catherine, were as comfortable in the Château as they had been in the big house in Westmount before Mrs. Carver died. All he missed was his rose garden. He still wore a rose in his lapel every day, and roses were always on the long bleached oak table in the drawing room. In the evening, sometimes, key men from the St. James Street publishing office came to the apartment for informal conferences. Mr. Carver had a weakness for conferences.

He thought of himself as an enlightened liberal, and he was much impressed one evening late in December by an article in the latest *Atlantic Monthly* entitled, "The Independent Man." The style was lively and authoritative, the reasoning sound. It reminded him that for months he had been considering having someone do a provocative column on current events. It had been difficult to find the person with the right touch, the human personal approach to everything, and this McAlpine seemed to have it. Turning to the notes on the contributors in the front of the magazine he found that McAlpine was an associate professor of history at the University of Toronto. It surprised him, and he smiled to himself. Being a member of the Board of Governors at McGill, Mr. Carver had given up expecting too much from professors. This James McAlpine seemed to be worth a night's thought.

The next day he wrote a letter asking him if he would come to Montreal to discuss the possibility of doing an uncensored column in *The Sun* on world affairs, and he enclosed a cheque covering the cost of a return ticket to Montreal.

In the second week of January, when it was mild with no snow, James McAlpine came to the Château to have a drink with Mr. Carver. He was a tall broad-shouldered man in his early thirties. He wore a double-breasted dark blue overcoat and a black Homburg hat. He had brown eyes, black hair, and a good dignified bearing that he might have acquired in the Navy when he had been a lieutenant commander.

Something about McAlpine compelled Mr. Carver's immediate attention. It was not simply his manner, which was straightforward and poised, nor his quiet self-confidence; as soon as they shook hands McAlpine made him feel they had been waiting a long time to meet each other. Mr. Carver was both amused and impressed.

That first night Catherine, arriving home from a Junior League meeting, heard the voices in the drawing room, and she stopped to listen. She liked the stranger's low deep voice. She was a tall girl with good legs, candid blue eyes, and a handsome face with a mole on the left cheek. While she took off the beaver coat her father had given her for Christmas she continued to listen because she was twenty-seven and lonely after her divorce. A gossip columnist had written that he counted it a fine day when he happened to see Catherine walking in the sunlight on Sherbrooke Street. Yet her friends had noticed that she had the air of not quite believing in her own loveliness, of not being sure she was really wanted, and they were sometimes touched by her hesitant eagerness.

She liked the stranger's laugher; but because he sounded attractive she drew back with an instinctive shyness. This shyness came from a secret knowledge of herself she had gained in her brief marriage with Steve Lawson; it made her watch herself with everyone and hide the ardour in her nature from anyone who attracted her, fearing if she revealed it she would suffer again the bewildering ache of her husband's resentful withdrawal.

When she finally entered the drawing room, her shyness was hidden by her cultivated, cool friendliness. She had a fine walk, a slow stride as if her shoulders were suspended from a clothesline, her legs swinging effortlessly. She met McAlpine and sat down to listen.

From that night on she was there listening. Her father would be striding up and down, his grey head like a silver bullet on his big shoulders, and he wouldn't be talking directly about what was going on in the world, nor asking McAlpine for direct opinions that might interest the readers of *The Sun*.

They would argue instead about Oxford and the Sorbonne, or whether there had been any real order in the world since the fall of the Roman Empire, then switch suddenly to the Latin poets. "What about Petrarch, McAlpine? You like Petrarch?"

"I prefer Horace."

"Really? You prefer Horace?"

"It always seemed to me there was something too deliberate about Petrarch."

"Well, look here, McAlpine. What about Catullus? Couldn't we settle for Catullus?"

"Fine. I'll take Catullus," McAlpine would say, and they both would smile.

And Catherine, watching McAlpine, said, "You know, Mr. McAlpine, you don't look much like a professor to me."

"No?" he asked.

"No, but I imagine that's why you were probably a very good one."

"No," he said quietly. "I was a failure as a professor."

"Oh, but not with your students, surely."

"No," he agreed, smiling. "That part of it was fine, but I did not get along with my superiors. They didn't like my methods."

"These academic men," Mr. Carver snorted, making an emphatic gesture with his horn-rimmed glasses. "I know them, McAlpine. I have to deal with them at my own university. It's all to your credit if they didn't approve of you."

Sitting back with his long legs folded, Mr. Carver, listening closely, noticed that when McAlpine talked to Catherine his tone would change. Whether he was talking about Winston Churchill, the United Nations, or guerrilla warfare in Greece, his tone would become easy and intimate. Catherine would break in with an eager question. For months Mr. Carver hadn't seen such a quickening in Catherine, and now the pleasure in her eyes moved him.

"Yes, he's got a good mind," he admitted to Catherine when McAlpine had left. "He says some good things, too. H'm-m, what was that he said about Churchill? 'Eighteenth century syntax and nineteenth century hats.' I liked it. Provoking and amusing." Then he reflected a moment. "And if I should decide I want him he seems to be free to start at any time."

"I think you'll want him all right," Catherine said quietly. "No matter how long you take, you'll end up wanting him."

They agreed that he had a quiet faith in himself that he must have nursed for years while he waited for the kind of job he wanted. But Catherine did not say how much she liked him, or how she had begun to put her own meaning on his words, or how she had come to believe he possessed an exciting strength of character.

It was her town, at least the small part of it that was not French, and, wanting to be helpful, she had a drink with McAlpine in the Ritz bar; after that in the afternoons they had many drinks together in little bars and places where she hadn't been for months. It was a fine week for walking, very mild with still no sign of snow, and no skiing in the Laurentians, and the old *calèches* were still lined up at the curb by the Windsor Station. They always talked about the job; but in the way they walked, her arm under his, he made her feel not only that she belonged to his happiest expectations of Montreal, but that he wanted to tell of his plans and have her approval. At first she was restrained and diffident. Then he seemed to ask for her support. He could make her feel he really wanted her opinion and her sympathy. His need of her appeared to be so genuine it gradually broke down her diffidence; it became like a caress, opening her up to him and setting her free to indulge her ardent, generous concern. Walking along in step with him, her whole being was suffused with a new light happiness. Her shyness vanished. She talked quickly and brightly; she reached out to make his plans her plans, and she held him silent and wondering at the glow of her generosity.

She told him he ought to go to the clubs and be with managing editors and publishers and people who really influenced opinion. She intimated it would be unwise to hang around with his friend Chuck Foley in the Chalet Restaurant, where only the wrong sort of newspapermen went. Her father had suggested that if he and McAlpine came to an arrangement it would be necessary, later, for McAlpine to go to France, Italy, and England to see with his own eyes what was happening in these countries; and she talked about Rome and Paris as if she would be walking with him through the streets of those cities, showing him around. She talked, too, about her father's temperament and advised McAlpine on how to get along with him; if there were difficulties, she could be helpful in smoothing them out. And he would need an apartment with a good address. She might be able to find one for him if he wanted her to.

The warmth of her generous interest stirred McAlpine, and he wondered how he had evoked it, and how he had had the good luck to come on such a handsome woman when she was waiting shyly to attach herself to someone who knew how to appreciate the fullness of her ardour. They walked in the twilight, and she felt compelled to talk about herself. All she said, though, was that her own marriage had been a mistake; she felt that she hadn't been married at all. It had only lasted three months because Steve had been such an alcoholic.

"I understand," he said, knowing they had been really talking all week about the failure of her marriage, touching on it again and again when they talked about other things.

"It wasn't my fault," she insisted. "I know you'd expect me to say so. The Havelocks, though, were on my side from the beginning."

"The Havelocks?"

"My husband's uncle."

"Not Ernest Havelock?"

"No, that's another family. They're around here too. There are as many Havelocks as there are Carvers. Why? Do you know Ernest Havelock?"

"It was the children, Peter and Irma – when I was a boy."

"I heard someone say they were in Europe now. I like to think of you knowing people I might know."

"Do you?"

She nodded, and he smiled down at her.

"Well, don't get a wrong impression," he said. "I was no family friend. The name reminded me of the time when I knew them. That's all."

"You mean you lived near them?"

"Not exactly," he said. "My people had a little summer cottage at the end of the beach where the Havelocks had their big country home. A cottage stuck down among a swarm of other cottages. But you know how kids get around and meet each other. There was a pavilion, a dance hall, up on the highway, and all the kids used to go there. No," he added half to himself, as he smiled, "I don't think the Havelocks ever knew how important they were to me."

"Important in what way, Jim?"

"Oh, I don't know," he said with an easy laugh. "You know the way a name or a house looms up in a kid's mind."

"Their house impressed you?"

"I was never in it, and yet I nearly made the grade one night." He was making it an amusing story. "It was almost a start in life for me. When I was fourteen! I must have been impressed, too, or I wouldn't remember it so clearly, would I? The night I nearly made the grade I had been walking with my father and mother down the oiled road running behind the cottages, and I remember we had to step off the road because the Havelock car was passing. Peter and Irma and their cousin, Tommy Porter, from Boston, called out to me they would see me up at the pavilion. My mother – she died of cancer two years later – was impressed, I think, and so was my father. He's still quite a guy, jolly and eloquent. He used to like writing poetry. He stood there making a speech about Havelock's fine liberal interests and how he had practically known him for years since he saw him coming out of his Trust Company every day at noon time when he, himself, was coming out of the post office where he worked. I didn't like listening to him because I liked him, and I had noticed that Havelock in his big car hadn't even nodded to him."

He was silent, remembering, and Catherine waited to hear about his youth and his family. His good humour as he looked back didn't fool her, for when he spoke of his father and mother his tone changed; it was full of affection, and she was sure a wound was hidden under his calmness.

"I left my father and mother and went over to the pavilion and played the pinball machines; and a little later Irma and Peter and their cousin Tommy came, in their school blazers, and we fooled around, and I noticed a lot of big cars passing down the road to the Havelock house, and in a little while Irma said they had better be getting back to the house. They were having a party. City friends of theirs. And Tommy, their cousin, asked me if I wasn't coming and I said I wasn't invited, and he said neither was he, we were all on the beach, weren't we, and I should be a sport and stick with them, so I followed along with Tommy."

He laughed apologetically. "Isn't it ridiculous how you remember these little details?"

"No, go on," she said.

"A kid remembers, I think, because he sort of likes everything to happen right, and when it doesn't it sticks in his memory." Again he laughed softly. When he got to the Havelock gate, he said, he trailed in with the cousin. It was the first time he had been inside the big hedge, and there were the wide green lawns and the fountains and the big sprawling house. Strange kids in English flannels came toward them from the terrace, and he was shy and hung back. "I forgot to say I had a little spaniel," he said, "and I was glad he was there, dancing around. Then Mrs. Havelock came out. She was stout and had streaks of grey in her hair, and she just looked at me, and I felt awful because I had shorts on and an old sweater and my hair was rumpled. 'Who's that boy?' she asked, and her son, Peter, said idly, 'Oh, that's Jim McAlpine – he lives down at the end of the beach.' All she said was, 'Oh.' She didn't tell me I wasn't invited. It was her wooden expression that hurt me and made me move closer to Tommy Porter. When she left us I wanted to behave with dignity and let her see, if she were watching from the house, that Tommy counted on me being with him."

They picked up two croquet clubs, he said, and began to knock the ball back and forth. It was getting dark and he missed the ball and it shot past him and through the hedge, and he ran out the gate to get it. He tossed the ball over the hedge, then stood there, feeling lonely, yet glad he had got out, for now they would notice that he was not with them. Now Tommy or Peter would call out, "Oh, Jim! Where's Jim gone? Hey, Jim," and come down to the gate and look along the road for him.

He knew it might take some time before they noticed that he was missing, so he waited, with the spaniel wagging its tail and looking up at him. It began to get dark. Where there had been only the one evening star there were now many stars.

The voices on the lawn faded away toward the house, and no one called him; but they might not miss him, he thought, till they got inside. The moon rising over the lake shed its light on the roof of the Havelock house and gleamed through the thick hedge.

Lying down beside the hedge he watched the gleam of the Havelock lights. The moon rose a little higher. Then the road was all moonlight, and the little spaniel which had been lying beside him got to its feet and began to bark and circle around, then rush at the Havelock gate. The dog came frisking back at him to rub its nose in his neck and then darted at the gate again and scratched and whined. The bright moonlight was driving the dog crazy. From the house came the sound of a piano, and singing and laughing, and in chorus all the songs he knew so well.

The lights gleamed through the high hedge, and he watched them and waited, forgetting about his spaniel until he heard it scratching at the hedge beside him, thrusting its nose at the break in the hedge he had been making with his own hands. Suddenly the dog squeezed through the hedge and barked and bounded at the Havelock house.

"Come back, Tip, come back," he called. Then he stopped calling. One of the Havelock children might recognize the dog's bark and come out. "It's Jim's dog out on the road. Jim must be out there. I thought he was here," they would say. "Let's go and get him."

A door opened, a shaft of light slanted across the lawn, and his heart thumped in his throat. A servant's voice cried, "Go on, scat, do you hear, scat!" and the dog yelped and came running back to the hedge and wriggled through and into his arms. He held it hard against him, staring at the house. Then he jumped up, still holding the dog in his arms, and backed away from the tall dark hedge. He started to run down the road, and as he ran his pounding feet beat out the words, "Who's that boy? Who's that boy?" He stopped, breathing hard, his fists clenched, and stared back at the gleaming hedge, darker than the night, and whispered fiercely, "Just wait. Just wait."

He walked along with Catherine, remembering, and then he laughed again. But she was shocked that he could reveal himself so calmly and finish the story with an easy laugh. I could never tell that story about myself, she thought. No one she knew would put himself in that light – a boy outside a hedge. No touch of snobbery troubled him, for he had faith in himself; he had reached his goal; the job on *The Sun* was to be his; he could afford to smile at his beginning. He had revealed himself to her in order to draw her closer to him, just as his arm tightening on hers drew her closer; she felt she was wanted in the secret part of his life and wanted right at the beginning. She was happy and proud and quietly content. "You'll come to dinner tonight, won't you, Jim?" she asked suddenly.

"Tonight?"

"I know Daddy would like it, too."

"Of course I'll come," he said.

It was an intimate dinner made bright with easy conversation. They sat around, taking their time.

"Have lunch with me tomorrow, Jim," Mr. Carver said when McAlpine was leaving. "I'm speaking to my managing editor, Horton." And after McAlpine had gone, he said to Catherine, "You like him, don't you?"

"Yes, I like him a lot. He's interesting."

"Mind you, he hasn't got a nickel."

"But he hasn't been a businessman."

"And he's staying at the Ritz. Just a gesture. Burning his professorial bridges behind him."

"I like that, too. Don't you?"

"Oh, I don't hold it against him."

"Is there something you do hold against him?"

"Yes, there is something, Catherine."

"Oh. But I thought you were enthusiastic?"

"I am. I am. But after all, my dear, I run a newspaper. And that quality of his which you've noticed too – I mean his absolute faith in his own judgement—"

"Yes, I've noticed it."

"It isn't just faith in himself. It's an unshakable belief in what he thinks he sees."

"But that's rare and good," she insisted.

"I know it's rare. And I know it's good," he agreed. "I like it, too. But I do run a newspaper. I have to wonder if a man like that doing a column on the paper might some day embarrass me. It's simply something I have to take into consideration."

"Oh, you're trying to be so cautious," she said, laughing. "But you don't fool me. I know you're sold on him."

"I am," he admitted. "Only I want to make sure I won't be left holding a tiger by the tail."

❧ TWO ❧

The next night at eleven McAlpine was to meet Catherine at the radio station where she was making an appeal for funds for crippled children on a program sponsored by the Junior League. With time on his hands, he intended to have a drink with Chuck Foley. Though they had been separated by the war and the fact that they worked in different cities Foley was still his best friend. Years ago Foley, an advertising man, had wanted to be a poet and had written one slight volume of sentimental verse. But after he had become an account executive in a Montreal agency he had stopped writing poetry, rarely saw his old college friends, and paid his wife to keep away from him. Yet he always wanted to know what was happening to McAlpine. Before he had got his university job, McAlpine had had one bad winter when he had been broke and in debt and had gone around shivering in a light spring coat. Foley, who was doing well at the time, had been the only one who noticed that McAlpine looked thin and cold. He had pretended he needed a new coat and had bought one and had come around to McAlpine's place with his old perfectly good and expensive coat, claiming he didn't need it any more. McAlpine had always remembered that coat.

Loafing in the hotel lobby as he waited for a telephone call from Foley, McAlpine made fluent French conversation with the desk clerk. A big red-faced man wearing a Persian lamb hat came out of the elevator and called, "Why, hello, McAlpine.

Foley didn't tell me you were around. What are you doing here?" McAlpine had no recollection of him at all.

"What am I doing?" he asked, forcing his heartiness as he tried to place him. "I'm wondering why the same Foley didn't tell me you had that hat. It makes you look like a character."

"When you can afford to buy a hat like this one," the big man said, "you'll know you've landed on your feet." Glancing at McAlpine's conservative clothes he added, "Sure I'm a character, but anybody can look like Truman." With a big laugh he took McAlpine's arm, asked how he was doing with the French girls, admitted it was all right to have a splurge with them for the sake of the novelty, warned him he would learn in the end it was better to confine himself to girls like his own people; and when the switchboard operator called, "Here's your party, Mr. McAlpine – will you take it now?" he followed him to the booth, shook hands, and said, "Check on it with Foley," and departed.

"I'm to check on something with you, Chuck," McAlpine said. "I'm to get tired soon of the French girls. Is that a fact?"

"Who asked you to check with me?"

"A big guy whose name I can't remember. In a fur hat."

"Men in fur hats don't know what I think about anything," Foley said brusquely. "How are you doing with the great publisher?"

"Fine. Tell me something about the great publisher's daughter. What was her husband like?"

"Just another pleasant drunk – in the leather business."

"What was the trouble between them?"

"Search me. Maybe her husband got tired handling leather."

"Come on, Chuck."

"Maybe Miss Catherine was a dragon. Maybe the poor guy got married and woke up and wondered why. Who do you know who wants to get married? Shall we meet where we met last night? The Mount Royal?"

"At the Peel Street entrance."

"I may bring someone along with me. I'm not sure yet, but I may."

"Who?"

"A little girl in the office. I've been having a drink with her. She'll be good for us."

"I have to meet Catherine."

"It's got nothing to do with Catherine," Foley insisted. "Don't you like meeting someone fresh as a daisy? Come on. It won't do us any harm to have a drink with her. We may end up believing the dew is still on the grass. I'll be seeing you in twenty minutes. Okay, son?"

"I'll be there," McAlpine said, and he hoped the girl would not show up.

It was the way the snow had begun to fall that gave everything a lazy deceptive mildness. Looking up at the faint feathery wisps of snow, McAlpine wondered if he ought to go back and get his overshoes. He went along Sherbrooke and turned down Peel. The night was still mild, but the snow now streamed in thin lines across the lighted Mount Royal entrance. At that time the taxis had left for the station; there was no traffic jam. The doorman stood idly at the curb. Across the road from the open upstairs windows of the Samovar came the sound of gypsy music and a contralto wailing and then a little burst of applause. McAlpine, in the shelter of the hotel entrance, looking up vaguely at the open windows of the nightclub, wondered why he hadn't asked Catherine to go dancing with him.

From the nightclub across the street came a slim girl in a short-sleeved black dress who stood in the lightly falling snow and waved to two swarthy men standing a few feet away from

McAlpine. They beckoned to her and she crossed the road, leaving her footprints in the snow, and soon they were laughing and joking with her while one held her bare arm. She was very pretty, and the fact that the men had only needed to beckon to her offended McAlpine. Now she was going back, going alone into the Cadillac Restaurant, and the pair watched her. "Yeah, it's like that," one said, snickering coarsely and making a motion with his fingers. "Not bad either. Why didn't you say you wanted to?" Listening like an Arab, McAlpine grew more offended. His sense of order was disturbed. At least the two men should have crossed the road to the girl. They were mugs. A slim good-looking girl like that shouldn't have known them. It was all wrong.

McAlpine was not usually concerned with what went on on the street. Now it was different because of the way the snow was falling; maybe it was the whiteness of the street in the lights; but instead of going into the hotel lobby and buying a copy of the *Nation* and sitting down he stood there. A passing taxi left two black streaks on the snow-powdered road and stopped in front of the hotel. A French Canadian priest from Quebec City got out and with a fastidious air helped his sister, a middle-aged woman, to alight from the cab. With an elegant gesture he put a small tip in the driver's hand.

There was Foley coming up the street in his expensive camel-hair coat and brown fedora, and with him was the girl in one of those plain fawn-coloured belted trench coats. She was hatless. Her fair hair was parted in the middle and, with the snow melting on it, she looked like a child.

"Hi, Jim," Foley said. "This is Peggy Sanderson." By the way the girl smiled McAlpine knew she had heard all about him.

"How do you do?" he said as she put out her hand. The expression on Foley's face caught him off balance. Foley was an indifferent, red-headed, cynical, freckle-faced man with glasses, and Miss Sanderson wasn't even his girl; but he looked as if he had just had three quick drinks, and he obviously expected McAlpine to feel just as good as he did.

"Peggy is going to have a drink with us," he said. "But she doesn't want to go to the hotel. Let's find a place on St. Catherine. How about Dinty Moore's? Peggy?"

"Suits me," she said. On St. Catherine the women now wore galoshes and snow boots; it was snowing harder.

"Won't your head get wet?" McAlpine asked her.

"I never wear a hat," she said. She barely came up to his shoulder. She had none of Catherine's style and obviously didn't care, and probably wore the belted coat in the spring, fall, and winter. Yet he had been able to recognize her by Foley's description. Her small face had a childlike prettiness, and yet she was not baby-faced; she possessed a strange kind of stillness.

In Dinty Moore's they went back to the tables near the bar. McAlpine and Foley took off their coats, but she only opened hers. "I can't stay long," she said. "I'll just have one beer. I like beer. It's a pleasant drink for a brief encounter." As she smiled, the melted snow drops shone on her fair hair.

"You're a historian, I hear, Mr. McAlpine," she said, turning to him to make him feel at ease.

"It was my subject," he said.

"History?"

"Yes."

"I suppose it's Chuck's subject, too, and mine, too. I suppose we're all historians, aren't we?"

"What do you mean?"

"Well, we each make up our minds about what we see going on, don't we?"

"Oh, it isn't quite as simple as that, Miss Sanderson."

"No?"

"Oh, no, it's a philosophical subject, you know."

"Tell me what's going to happen to the world, Mr. McAlpine."

"When?"

"In the next few years."

"It's a large order, isn't it?"

"But haven't you got it worked out scientifically – like all the smart men?"

"Nobody can foretell what will happen," he said, "because people are involved."

"I like that," she said gravely.

"Don't let her kid you, Jim. She's a college graduate herself," Foley said. "And from your own university, too."

"Oh, I'm not kidding him, Chuck," she said.

"Of course not," McAlpine agreed. But he felt that somehow he was not being taken seriously. He wanted to explain himself to her, but of course it couldn't be done – not without some justification. He watched her put down her drink and smile at Foley, and believed he perceived a remarkable quality in her; it was not just the expression in her eyes, or her calm face, or even her relaxed stillness; everything together revealed a charming innocence that was his own remarkable discovery.

A little green book was sticking out of her pocket. Reaching over he took it, and while Foley talked to her he glanced through it and saw it was a digest of Negro writing. He was familiar with the names of some of the authors.

"Some of these Negro writers are pretty good," he said, interrupting Foley.

"Know any of them, Mr. McAlpine?"

"Some of their stories and poems. Pretty good, too."

"I think so. Don't you, Chuck?"

"Sure," he said, but his manner changed; it was just a slight stiffening. "Don't we all like them?" he asked, brushing the Negroes aside.

"No, some don't," she said casually, taking the magazine from McAlpine and standing up. "I have to go now. I really must."

"One more drink, Peggy," Foley coaxed her. "It's about eleven, and you don't have to go anywhere at this hour."

"Oh, but I do, and I don't want to be late. I said only one drink. Remember?"

"Can't you stay, Peggy?" McAlpine asked. Her mouth twitched with amusement: he was so concerned. They both coaxed her and she didn't resist with any determination, she simply went on buttoning up her coat.

"See you tomorrow, Chuck," she said.

"You'll be around, won't you?" McAlpine asked.

"Sure I will," she said. "I try to get Chuck to buy me a cup of coffee in here at four-thirty every afternoon. Well, so long." And, glancing at the clock over the bar, she hurried out.

"Now where would she be going?" McAlpine asked.

"Meeting someone, I suppose."

"A man of her own?"

"She has a guy she hangs around with, Henry Jackson. A screwball commercial artist. But I know he's out of town."

"Then who would she be meeting at this hour?"

"Now how do I know?"

"I'm only wondering," McAlpine said as Foley grinned. Yet the fact that she had gone out by herself, making it so plain she didn't want them with her, annoyed him. He had felt an urge to protect the charming innocence he had discovered, but of course he had to conceal his feelings from Foley.

"Do you get what I mean, Jim?" Foley asked. "I know she didn't say a damn thing. What does it matter? Another girl would have made a self-conscious effort to say a dozen things. Peggy doesn't have to try. I like it, Jim. She makes me feel young."

"It's not I, but you, that should have met her some time ago," McAlpine said.

"I wish I had. She came to our office – a copy writer. I remember the impression she made. Maybe you've noticed that she hasn't much style, and yet she's completely feminine. It doesn't matter what she wears. I think we're all glad to have her in the office. When she's around we smile at each other. You know what we're really like – a bunch of gimlet-eyed hucksters. I don't know. It's nice to feel young again. A woman chaser, Fred Lally, is making a play for her. We offered to bet him real money he wouldn't lay a hand on her."

"If you like her, why cheapen her that way?"

"To show up Lally."

"But it pushes her at him."

"Well, if he does any pushing, he'll get pushed in the nose."

"Are you in love with her yourself, Chuck?"

"Don't be silly. I've had enough of that stuff. I like to feel good. That's all."

The two friends had never felt so close together. Finishing their drinks, they put on their coats and went out. The thickening snow now covered the sidewalk and the road and whitened the hats and coats of pedestrians. In the doorway, McAlpine stared at an unbroken stretch of white on the road. It covered the girl's footprints, and no one could tell which way she had gone.

"It's really going to be a storm," Foley said.

"Yes, a real storm," McAlpine agreed. "Peggy had no rubbers on, did you notice? Just those thin little pumps. If she walks very far in this snow—"

Smiling a little, Foley asked, "Was I right about her, Jim?"

"An odd girl – yes, I think I know what you mean, Chuck."

"I knew you'd get it," Foley said. They remained there, sharing a simple happy recollection, not wanting to part, and the snow formed a crown on the brims of their hats.

"Oh, Lord, I'm late!" McAlpine said suddenly. "This is awful."

"You're just across the street, Jim."

"Why don't you come with me, Chuck?"

"I'm going down to the Earbenders Club."

"The Earbenders?"

"The Chalet Restaurant – down on Mountain near Dorchester," Foley said, grinning. "I do my heavy drinking there. Well, so long, Jim."

"See you tomorrow," McAlpine said; and he hurried across the street to the radio studio.

In the slow-moving elevator he blamed himself for having been distracted, and when he got to the big studio on the third floor and peeked in he saw that he was too late. The musicians were packing up their instruments. Catherine was talking with some of the musicians and three of her Junior League friends. Her coat was draped around her shoulders, and her Cossack-like beaver hat made her look taller than the others. The blonde producer with his built-up heels and bright lumberjack shirt had come out of the booth to congratulate her on her speech. Standing awkwardly by the door McAlpine thought, I'll tell her about the strange girl I met and how she fascinated Foley, and she'll be just as curious as I was. Then Catherine looked at him, and her eyes were hurt.

❧ THREE ❧

Sit down, Jim. I'll only be a minute," she called in her clear, penetrating voice. But she didn't hurry; she was deliberately keeping him waiting, and he knew it.. He sat down at a table near the door, picked up some paper lying on the table, took out his pencil, and drew until she broke away.

"I'm ashamed of myself, Catherine," he said, jumping up apologetically. "How did it go?"

"They're trying to tell me I did it with great talent and authority. What's that?" she asked, reaching for his drawing. "Who's it supposed to be? Why, it's me! It's good! Can I show it to the others?"

"No."

"Well, I'm going to keep it anyway. Write something on it."

Jim smiled and wrote, *Madame Radio.* "How's that?"

"Just what I feel like," she said, putting the drawing in her purse. Let's get out of here. That producer is the quaintest little man. Aren't radio people bewildering? In the woods too long. Sort of treed."

"You mean bushed."

"All right. I knew I had the wrong word."

Going down in the elevator, she said, "Come on, Jim, tell me what made you late."

"I was with Foley. The time passed so quickly."

Outside, the snow was now two inches deep. "Look, isn't it wonderful, Jim?" Catherine cried. "This is my time of year.

When it's like this I want to go to the mountains. I want to ski. Can you ski, Jim? It's no good if you can't ski. You didn't say where you were with Foley, Jim."

"Just across the street. We had a drink," he said.

"Just across the street," she repeated. "Was he that interesting, Jim?"

"Chuck is good company when he's in a good mood."

"I know all about Foley. You'll say I don't like him because my husband liked him. But really, Jim, why does he have to spend all his time with mugs and fighters and drunks? It's a pose. I think he's an awful fraud. I know people he went to school with. I know where he belongs and where he doesn't. Has he a grudge against his own class because he couldn't get along with his wife?"

"I don't know. I'll ask him. I know he has a pretty good feeling about people." His head down against the snow, he glanced at her handsome leather snow boots. "It's just as well you wore those boots, Catherine," he said. "A girl with light pumps would get her feet soaking wet just crossing the road, wouldn't she?"

"I suppose so. Why?"

"Oh, nothing."

"You just don't want to talk about Foley, do you?"

"I don't mind talking about Foley."

"Come on then, tell me what you talked about so long."

"I don't think it'll make you like him any better." He was irritated by her resentment of his friendship with Foley.

"I've told you, Jim, I think you waste your time hanging around with that Foley," she said. "He'll never do you any good in this town."

"Won't he?"

His tone, so quiet and withholding, startled her, and made her afraid of her own assertiveness. She felt him guarding himself against her. Oh, why did I sound like that when it's not the way I feel? she thought. They walked close together in the snow, but they knew they were opposing each other. They knew they had come to a place where he could no longer be simply a man whose company she enjoyed. They had to become aware of each other in a new way and know how much of each other they could count on. Soon she may tell me not to see Foley at all, he thought. Am I not to have my own friends? I knew I couldn't tell her about that girl. And Catherine, whose face was hidden in her turned-up fur collar, was reminded painfully of moments she had known with her husband. She couldn't bear to turn and look at Jim and feel him guarding himself, and see that expression she had seen in her husband's eyes.

"Oh, it's too beautiful a night to worry about Foley, isn't it, Jim?" she asked.

"I could walk for hours on a night like this," he said.

"It's exhilarating," she said. And then she slipped and lurched against him, he held her up, they both laughed, and the bad moment was gone and they felt free and happy with each other.

The apartment house had many entrances that were like alcoves in a cloistered stone corridor. In a shadowed alcove he said, "Shall I come in, Catherine?"

"No, not now, Jim."

"Well…"

"Well…" she said softly.

The alcove light touched one side of her expectant face, and as she moved her head from the light to the shadow the bold line of her face softened. She undid her coat; the folds fell away, the light touched her breast line, a shadow was at her waist where the belt gathered in the black dress tightly, and she waited, looking up at him. "I thought of our conversation this afternoon," she said. "It kept going through my head. It's a funny thing, Jim. Your words would keep getting mixed up with mine. I couldn't remember what you had said, or what I had said, yet it was all there. A kind of sympathy. It was nice. Yes, new and nice." Then the words trailed away.

"I know," he said. "When I was crossing the street, you were in my mind like this." He put his arms around her waist and he kissed her, but did not hold her hard against him. It was not a warm full kiss. When he released her she waited awkwardly, thinking: It was that one moment on the street. I felt it. He was resentful. It still bothers him. That's all it is. He's not like Steve. He *really wants me*. But her doubt showed in the way she lifted her head; he saw it, yet was afraid to hold her against him, afraid she would know his heart was not beating against hers, and know, too, that his mind was somewhere else, enchanted by a glimpse of something else. If he had only mentioned the girl it wouldn't be like this.

"Everything has been going so well, hasn't it?" he asked awkwardly.

"Going well, yes, Jim," she said, still waiting.

"Of course a lot will depend on the luncheon with your father tomorrow."

"It will go well, Jim."

"I'm sure it will."

"Well good night, Jim."

"Good night, Catherine."

"Phone me tomorrow," she said, and she turned away swiftly.

⤜ FOUR ⤛

The snow whirled in gay little spurts over the low skyline of the grey antique stone office buildings when McAlpine and Mr. Carver left the Canadian Club and came along St. James Street with the magnates who were returning to their offices. They walked arm in arm. They took turns guiding each other across the street. "Watch yourself now, Mr. Carver," McAlpine would say when a taxi skidded by in the snow. And a few steps later Mr. Carver would say, "Look out now, Jim. You're walking right into that drift." In between these admonitions, offered with such friendly warmth, Mr. Carver told why his managing editor, J. C. Horton, opposed having McAlpine do the column.

"You understand, Jim, I can't have a managing editor and not appear to give some weight to his opinion," he said as they ducked their heads in the same motion against the wind.

"Of course not." For the moment McAlpine could hardly conceal his anxiety, and Mr. Carver felt it. Then with sudden confidence, believing he could rely on Mr. Carver, he said, "After all, Mr. Horton ought to have some doubts about me. It's your judgment I'm counting on, Mr. Carver."

"Which is as it should be," Mr. Carver agreed. He liked having McAlpine count on him. He was accustomed to having paternal sympathy for any employee who was in trouble. Many times in the past he had gone out to visit the wife of a reporter who was a drunkard or a gambler to assure her she could count on him. An alcoholic gambler's home was never broken up. Mr.

Carver would make an arrangement with the wife and the humiliated husband that would permit *The Sun* to advance her money and take over the management of the weekly salary until the debt was paid off. But his feeling for McAlpine was different, and he wanted to be certain he could rely on him.

"Don't let what I say about J. C. trouble you too much, Jim," he said.

"I'm not going to, Mr. Carver."

"I can't brush him aside. I have to reason with him."

"I understand. What has he got against me?"

"Nothing whatever, Jim. You have to understand J. C. He's a big blunt fellow. A big-nosed, hard-headed fellow. Well, he's read your *Atlantic Monthly* article. It happens that J. C. thinks of himself as a publicist, a moulder of public opinion. Well, he sees you in that light too, Jim."

"Ah, I see."

"In a sense he's an old-style, narrow-minded businessman," Mr. Carver said, smiling indulgently.

"I think I should have a little talk with Mr. Horton."

"That's exactly what I don't want you to do, Jim. I want you to keep away from the practical men who can't see beyond their own noses. If you let Horton get you into his office, well, he'll have you there every day, and he'll have his hand in every column you write. Leave it to me," Mr. Carver added. "I'll try and push this thing through in my own way."

Pink-faced from the wind and snow, they crossed the road to *The Sun* building. It was a four-storied grey stone building of nineteenth century architecture with a large brass name plate to the left of the entrance. For fifty years *The Sun* had been published here by the Carvers. The building wasn't impressive; it didn't look much like a modern newspaper plant, but *The Sun* was as influential as any newspaper in the country. In a French city like Montreal it couldn't have a circulation as large as the French language journals, nor did it have as many readers as the *Evening Mail*, but it had better readers. Everybody who felt established in Montreal read *The Sun*. It was the only Montreal newspaper that had national influence and was widely quoted in the financial districts, the universities, and by newspapermen on other papers. It didn't pay big salaries. It had only one page of comics. The international scene was its special field; it carried the *New York Times* correspondence. Newspapermen looking for more money in other cities liked to be able to say they had worked for Carver of *The Sun*, because no one could mention *The Sun* without thinking of Carver and his liberal editorials.

Mr. Carver wanted to show Jim the new presses, and so they wandered around talking to foremen and typesetters. In that idle half-hour Jim felt himself liking Mr. Carver. He liked him for the pride and pleasure in his eyes. And Mr. Carver, responding to that sympathetic quality, insisted that if he had to he could operate the presses himself, even run the typesetting machine himself.

"And get out on the street and sell the papers?" Jim said.

"That's right, that's right," Mr. Carver beamed. His newspaper was his life. He wanted to be in the independent liberal tradition of the *Manchester Guardian* or the *New York Times*. The world was in a philosophical breakdown, he said, a morass of mass thinking; the great trick was to recognize the necessity of independence. He wondered how it was McAlpine could make him feel he had been waiting a long time to tell all this to someone. Yet he did not forget to turn and smile at a passing employee, calling him always by his first name.

When they entered the editorial offices and passed the row of reporters' desks and the big round city desk, it was like a tour of inspection with Mr. Carver smiling at each desk man and reporter. "Good afternoon," he said, and each one said, "Good afternoon, Mr. Carver," or "Good day, sir. Still snowing, sir?"

Only one very fat young reporter with brown curly hair sitting at a desk by the window did not speak. Though Mr. Carver glanced at him hopefully he only scowled. McAlpine, thinking the scowl was for him, took it to mean that he and the reporter had met somewhere and the reporter disliked him.

"I should apologize, Jim," Mr. Carver said when they were in his private office taking off their coats.

"Apologize? What for?"

"The way that fat young man, Walters, scowled at us. Surely it's a bit annoying for a visitor to see an employee of mine behaving like that, but you see, Jim, it was directed at me." He smiled, but his neck had reddened. He always blushed with his neck. "A ridiculous situation," he said, sitting down and leaning back with his hands clasped behind his head. "I suppose I'll have to do something about it. Did you know I went on a tomato diet?"

"You hadn't mentioned it."

"A damned good diet. Took off twenty-five pounds. Well," he went on with an embarrassed air that was oddly attractive, "you can see that young Walters is sluggish and overweight. I recommended my tomato diet to him. He took off two pounds, then began to pull my leg. I'd pass him and ask about his weight, and he'd give me false reports. Well, I made a mistake. I mentioned it to Horton, and what did he do but make Walters get weighed every day in the shipping room? I suppose it made him a laughingstock, because his wife phoned and I had to put an end to Horton's nonsense. Well, never mind Walters. I feel a certain responsibility about you being here in Montreal, Jim."

"It's my own choice."

"But you're having expenses while I'm pushing this thing through. What about an advance to cover them? What about a hundred and fifty? I'll look after it myself."

"No, it isn't necessary."

"Nonsense. It may be two weeks or so."

"I can wait the two weeks."

"You won't hesitate to draw on me if you're short?"

"It's a promise," Jim said, wondering if he was being stubbornly independent to prove he would never be like young Walters.

"Good," Mr. Carver said. "Now don't get the impression Horton doesn't like some of your ideas. He agrees there's a philosophy abroad destructive of all individual initiative. Take a depression. A real challenge to a man, and Horton—"

"I wasn't writing only about a man and his job," McAlpine interrupted.

"Of course not. There now. Do you see how you'd have to watch Horton?"

"The job is only one thing," McAlpine said. "Mr. Horton seems to have missed the point. What I was trying to say in my article was that a man can make adventurous choices in his own life, particularly in his difficult relationships. It might be necessary for him to say to hell with the job."

"H'm-m. Absolute independence, eh?"

"The trick would be never to knuckle under in the face of a difficult relationship. Do you see?"

"I think I do," Mr. Carver said. He meditated; their eyes met; they measured each other, and McAlpine's smile was just as inscrutable as Mr. Carver's as he asked himself if it was Horton he had to watch or this shrewd man who was so friendly. Horton was indeed the managing editor, and it was necessary to have his approval, necessary to allay his doubts. But what if Mr.

Carver knew how to use Horton to mask his own doubts? He could use him in this way every day in the office. Right now he's weighing me, he thought, weighing me as he had Horton weigh young Walters. His reflective smile began to bother Mr. Carver, who coughed.

"The challenge of difficult relationships," he repeated with a faint smile. "Why, yes. That's right, Jim. Take young Walters now. He's really challenging me every day with his sullen face, and I shy away from doing anything. H'm-m. You'd say weakness on my part, wouldn't you?" He rubbed the side of his face. Then he picked up a pencil and made a note on a memo pad.

He's only showing me I'm right about him, Jim thought. The little memo would go to Horton; the fat young man might get his dismissal notice that night. He would go out with it in his pocket, and if it were still snowing his footsteps would be lost, as Peggy's had been lost last night. But why did he remember Peggy Sanderson now that he had caught a glimpse of an unfamiliar world of humiliating bondages? And why did he feel unhappy?

"Um-m, well—" Mr. Carver cleared his throat and chuckled. "If it keeps on snowing like this it will also be an interesting challenge to the city's new snow ploughs."

"The chances are it won't be snowing by nightfall," McAlpine said vaguely.

"It's the first heavy fall," Mr. Carver said. "Everything is freezing up hard." And then he turned to McAlpine with a wistful expression. "Did you ever do any ice fishing, Jim?"

"Not since I was a boy. Why?"

"I used to like it. The hut on the ice! The stove! A good drink! How would you like to try it with me, Jim?"

"Any time you say."

"We'd be there by ourselves. We could talk and take our time and take it easy." He sounded lonely. "I'll take you at your word, Jim." He was silent a moment, then he said, "Well, I've told you what the situation is around here. I suggest you relax for a week. I suppose you'll be seeing Catherine tonight?"

"I hope so."

"I think you're good for her, Jim." And he put out his hand.

McAlpine walked out of the office and past the row of desks where the reporters sat at their typewriters, and as Walters looked up his eyes met McAlpine's and he smiled politely. It was a natural, friendly smile, but McAlpine averted his own eyes. He felt ashamed. He fled with a brusque, angry stride.

He intended to go to the hotel and write some letters. When the taxi approached the St. Catherine and Drummond corner, he found himself dreading the loneliness of the hotel room where he might only worry over the relationship between Mr. Carver and a man named J. C. Horton. "Let me out at the corner here," he called to the taxi driver. And there he was on the corner in the snow, looking along the street at the restaurant where Peggy Sanderson had said she might be at that hour.

FIVE

If he hadn't been upset by the humiliated fat boy and his suspicion that Mr. Carver was using Horton to conceal his own doubt about him, he wouldn't have been on the corner; but there he was, the snow whitening his shoulders and forming a halo on his Homburg. A recollection of Foley and himself standing on that same corner, quietly at peace after the half hour with the girl, came stealing into his mind. It was the way he should have been feeling now after lunching with Carver, he thought. All of a sudden he understood why he hadn't mentioned the girl to Catherine; he hadn't understood the emotion she had aroused in him and Foley, and he wouldn't have been able to explain it to Catherine. Yet what was the nature of the girl's repose, and how had she been able to communicate it? If it was simply her childlike suggestion of innocence there was nothing much to it – innocence would vanish quickly; but if it were something in her nature like an act of peace anyone who had been touched by it would have a vast curiosity to learn something about her life.

The power of his curiosity surprised him. Had he really found her so attractive? But he brushed the question aside, telling himself she presented only an amusing problem, an idle intellectual diversion.

A big red-faced grinning cop in white gloves and white shoulder straps directed the traffic with charming gallantry. A pretty girl was snowbound at the curb. The cop, waving to her, blew his whistle, stopped streetcars and taxis, suspended the whole flow of winter traffic, and personally conducted her across the road.

Then Peggy Sanderson came out of the restaurant. She had on the same light belted coat and was still hatless. Waiting until she had gone a little way along the street, he crossed the road and caught up to her.

"Where did you come from, Mr. McAlpine?"

"St. James Street. I'm going to work for Carver, on *The Sun*."

"Really? I thought you were a professor."

"Oh, I'll still be doing the same kind of work. Am I going your way?"

"I don't know," she said. "I'm only amusing myself. All by myself. What are you doing?"

"Nothing at all. I'm free."

"I'm walking along a few blocks. There's a leopard I want to see."

"A leopard? In a zoo?"

"No, in a department store over by Phillips Square. It's a carving. Do you want to see it?"

"Well," he said, hesitating and glancing down at her rubbers. "Hadn't we better take a taxi? You'll get your feet wet, Peggy."

"It's lovely out. I like it like this," she said. With a slow smile she regarded him steadily. "Are you sure you want to come?"

"Yes, yes. Of course, I do," he insisted, a little catch in his voice. Why the simple grave question and his own answer became so mysteriously impressive, he did not know.

"All right," she said. "Come on."

She took his hand and walked him along, unaware that he felt self-conscious. An elderly man who was passing looked back at them and smiled. But McAlpine didn't drop her hand, for almost magically that loneliness which had been mixed up with his resentment of Carver left him.

In Montreal a great many of the English were acquainted and someone he knew might see them walking hand in hand; but he didn't care. He began a conversation about their university, intending to find out all about her. It became important.

"I never tire of the snow," she said. "When I'm old I may hate the winters and want to go south, but now it's still like it was when I was a kid. Don't you remember how gleeful you were at the first snowfall?"

"No, it was ice we wanted. Ice to skate on. We didn't care about the snow."

"I didn't care about ice. I still don't," she said. "But I used to love getting up in the morning and looking at the first blanket of snow on the fields. It was a completion of something, a beginning of a great winter stillness."

"There's usually lots of snow in Montreal."

"I like Montreal," she said. "I think I've been happier here than I've ever been. It's an old city and yet it's new; and it's a seaport, and the different races get used to each other. All the church bells wake me up too early in the morning, but I'm at home here."

"You're lucky, Peggy. Some people are never at home."

"I'm lucky knowing when I am," she said.

They went into the department store and up to the fourth floor, where there was a wood carving of a leopard about three feet long in a glass case, crouching, ready to spring.

She studied the leopard, and he watched her grave face and steady eyes and wondered why it had such importance for her. The light overhead shone on her wet fair hair, and it was like standing with a child whom he had brought to the toy department.

"It looks unbelievably fierce and powerful, doesn't it?" she asked.

"It's really very good," he agreed. "Quite a suggestion of power, of lurking violence. How did you know it was here, Peggy?"

"Oh, I heard about it. Does it make you feel uncertain and watchful, too?" she asked in a whisper. "It's fascinating, isn't it?"

"In a way, yes." He was surprised by her rapt attention.

"It all depends on what it suggests," she said. But she did not turn; maybe she could not turn from her contemplation of the leopard's jungle violence; she was rapt and still, waiting for the beast to spring at her, and his hand went to her arm to pull her away just in time. She turned. "Well, if you've had enough, there's something else I intended to look at this afternoon."

"Another carving?"

"No, an old church with very good lines. Do you want to come? It's only about twenty minutes away."

"Of course I'll come," he said, indulging her.

Outside, a bluish light was on the snow, the glint of winter twilight. He didn't know where he was going and he didn't care. It was just an idle, gentle interlude, and his vast tranquillity amused him. They were crossing Phillips Square, where lights were on in all the office windows and the bluish winter light deepened and the snow slanted across the statue of King Edward VII. A flat little snow crown reposed on the king's head.

From then on McAlpine didn't notice where he was going; he went down two blocks and turned east, but he got mixed up because he was making lazy bantering conversation, sauntering along.

"Here it is," she said, and he was looking at a little old church, half Gothic and half Romanesque, but light and simple in balance. "Isn't it beautiful? I've known it was here, but I never took the time to come and look at it."

"What an odd little church!" he said.

The church hung there in the snow; it could sail away lightly like a ship in the snow. Then he turned and looked at Peggy's lifted face, on which the snowflakes glistened and melted, making her blink her eyes. He looked again at the church and then at her face. Her shoulders were white, his own arms were white, and the slanting snow whirled around them. Feeling wonderfully lighthearted he started to laugh.

"What's so funny?" she asked.

"I don't know. A leopard and a church. On the one day."

"That I should want to see both?"

"That's it."

"A leopard and a church. Don't they go together?"

"From now on they do for me," he said.

On the way back, he realized he hadn't satisfied his curiosity about her at all. Nor had he mentioned the Negro writers. He asked now, instead, about other books she had read. Her comments when she offered them were intelligent enough, but her irritating serenity made him feel he wasn't really interesting her. People had always told him he talked beautifully. Everybody said so.

"You're neither arguing with me nor agreeing with me," he said with a sigh.

"I'm listening to you, Jim."

"Not really."

"Yes, I like listening to you and, whether you realize it or not, you're walking me home. I live over on Crescent."

They had passed Peel and Stanley and were now at Drummond, and in the window of the corner grocery store were pyramids of Malaga grapes. "Just a minute," he said. Going into the store, he bought two pounds of the grapes and came out smiling. "They don't go with the snow," he admitted, "but when you get home you can eat them and look out your window."

She lived a little way up Crescent Street in a three-storied stone house in a long row on the slope up to Sherbrooke. The main door at the top of a long flight of steps looked like a centre window with an overhanging balcony, and the other entrance on the street level opened into the ground floor. Some of these old places had had the stone scraped clean. Many doctors had their metal plates at the main doors. Peggy lived in one of the shabbier buildings, and she led him to the basement under the main steps.

A plump woman of fifty in a green coat and a shapeless green hat had also turned in and was climbing the stairs to the main entrance. Snow that she kicked off the steps on her way up fell on McAlpine's hat. He shook it off and looked up. "Hello, Miss Sanderson," the woman called, leaning over the stoop. "In early, I see." She had a soft red face with lonely eyes.

"Hello, Mrs. Agnew," Peggy called through the steps.

Mrs. Agnew leaned over the rail, peering at McAlpine, the door light catching one side of her aging face. She was half Scotch, half French. Her husband, who had been dead for ten years, had left her the house, in which all the apartments were rented. She gave them a wide, friendly, understanding grin. "The snow gets in my eyes," she said, brushing her hand across her face. "Having company, eh? Lots of company, eh, Miss Sanderson? Well, it's a good thing. Lots and lots of company is always a good thing."

"Oh, you're not so lonely yourself, Mrs. Agnew," Peggy said, pulling McAlpine back into the shelter as some more snow fell from the banister. Looking up, they could see only the toes of her galoshes sticking out over the edge of the step.

"Not at my age," Mrs. Agnew said. "And it's a very sad thing, Miss Sanderson – I mean for me. I'm at the state where I get all wistful if a man just smiles at me. And why not? It may be the last time," she added with a deep chuckle. "Some day you'll understand, Miss Sanderson. Not now, with all your company, but some day – yes." And with another scrape of her foot that sent more snow tumbling down on McAlpine, she went in.

They went along a badly lighted corridor to a door at the end. "Here's where I live, and I like it, sir," she said, with a little bow. "Enter."

It was a small plain room with a window looking out on a back fence. A ridge of snow was on the fence. The room, like a monastic cell, had only a few sticks of furniture, an iron bed, a little shelf with an oil cloth curtain on which she kept some dishes, a small electric heater for light cooking, two ladder-backed chairs, and a worn thin rug on a painted floor. On the bare walls were yellow moisture stains. The whole room was bare, but not with a monastic spotless bareness; it was hardly tidy. As she picked up a magazine from the bed and put it with some books on a little side table, she looked at him out of the corner of her eye. "How do you like it?" she asked, her mouth twitching.

"It's like a jail cell," he said. He looked so shocked that she couldn't help smiling broadly. Knowing that she must earn a decent salary, he resented the room; she didn't belong there.

"Take off your coat if you want to," she said. When she had removed her own coat and rubbers she lay down on the bed, crossed her legs at the ankles, watched him with amusement as he fumbled with his scarf, and waited for him to ask himself, What in the world am I doing in this hole in the wall?

Like a doctor attending a patient, he sat down by the bed, and then he felt so awkward he got up and began to walk round the room.

"Why don't you offer me some grapes?"

"Why, of course."

"There's a plate there on the shelf."

"Nice-looking grapes," he said, putting them on the plate and passing them to her.

"All right now. Why are you here?" she asked. "What's your interest in me?"

"I don't know," he said simply.

"Please come and sit down. You bother me walking around so restlessly."

"All right." He sat down on the bed beside her. "And why have you let me come?"

"I like you," she said. "I think you're essentially kind-hearted and generous. Some people wouldn't take the time to find it out."

"And when did you find out?"

"That I liked you?"

"Yes."

"Oh, something you said last night."

"That I said? When?"

"Talking about the digest I had in my pocket."

"What did I say?"

"It was what you didn't say."

"All right. What didn't I say?"

"You didn't say, 'nigger.' You said 'Negro.'"

❧ SIX ❧

"I wasn't watching what I said."

"In that case, so much the better."

"Then – well, it's not just Negro writing?"

"Writing is supposed to be about something."

"I meant – you have some Negro friends?"

"Would it surprise you?"

"Around here? Yes," he admitted.

There weren't many Negroes in Montreal, and those who were there lived between St. Antoine and the railroad tracks, with Mountain Street the base of a triangle, and the apex cutting east across Peel. They were mainly porters and redcaps and busboys and entertainers. In their own small neighbourhood they took in one another's washing and had three nightclubs and the French liked them; but they couldn't live in the good hotels or go into the select bars and knew it. There was never any trouble.

"How have you managed to do it?" he asked.

"Have you ever been down to St. Antoine?"

"No."

"It's the Negro section, and there are some Negro nightclubs down there. And some fine people too. Ever heard of Elton Wagstaffe? He's a band leader. And a good trumpet player named Ronnie Wilson? Ever heard of him?"

"No. But I haven't had much of a chance, have I?"

"I guess not. Well, they're wonderful musicians, anyway."

"I'll go down and hear them sometime," he said.

She lay on the bed, her hands clasped behind her head, and he bent down over her and looked into her hazel eyes. Candid, gentle, and friendly, they appraised him without any embarrassment. She was relaxed, and yet he felt himself being drawn close to her. Her blonde hair and pretty face on the pillow invited his caress. She had a voluptuous, suggestive appeal which drew him down to her. He wanted to kiss her and hold her against him, and felt sure she would let him do it. He bent down to kiss her on the mouth, but when his lips came close she turned her head away slowly. It was her only gesture of resistance. He could have kissed her on the neck; instead, he tried to meet her eyes, wondering if he had been rebuffed by the denial of her mouth. While she lay there motionless he put his hand gently on her breast, cupping it, and it was small, round and firm, and then he caressed her neck, and he showed his liking for women and his ease with them in his light gentle touch. She kept her head turned. It was her only rebuke. But it became more than enough for him; it was the most effective rebuke of passive indifference he could imagine and made him wonder why he had believed she would welcome his caresses. Then their eyes met and he drew back and smiled.

"My mistake," he said.

"It's all right," she said. "No harm's done."

"None at all," he said. "But I don't want you to think—"

"Think what?"

"Nothing. Nothing. I mean I have the greatest respect for you," he said. "That's all."

"There's a sweet streak in you, Jim," she said. "Why don't you give it a chance to develop? It's all cluttered up, but it gets the best of you sometimes, doesn't it?"

Easily, like that, she restored a pleasant intimacy.

"I wish I had known you when we were both kids," he said.

"Why?"

"It would have been fun."

"I don't know as it would, Jim. You were probably a strait-laced, ambitious boy. I don't think you would have liked me. Oh, no! Of course not. Why, you wouldn't have liked me at all."

"Why wouldn't I?"

"For the same reason you disapprove of me now."

"I don't disapprove of you, Peggy."

"Oh, yes, you do. Yes, you'd have been just like my father. He didn't like my having Negro friends either."

"You mean when you were a child you had Negro friends?"

"Of course I did."

"I don't see how," he said, bewildered a little. "Where did you come from, Peggy?"

"A town in Ontario on Georgian Bay."

"A town with a lot of Negroes? I don't know any such town."

"Oh, there was just one family." She smiled to herself, remembering. "A family of six kids living in a funny three-storied roughcast house, narrow and high with a sloping roof, stuck in the middle of a field. The house got no shade in the summer-time, and it was windswept in the winter, and there were big blotches on the roughcast walls where the plaster had fallen off. It also leaned a little like the Tower of Pisa, and I used to imagine that a strong wind would blow it down. Well, my father was the Methodist minister in that town."

"Oh, I see."

"Is that supposed to make something clear?"

"No. No. Go on, Peggy."

"I can see now that my father in those days was a sincere man. But he was very eloquent, and you could tell even then that he was going to get along. This Negro family belonged to his church. I used to see a lot of the kids. You see, their mother did our washing. My own mother had died. I never really knew her. One Negro kid and then another would come to the house, and in a way I grew up being used to them. My father never said anything about them being coloured. Since I was the minister's daughter, nobody ever said anything to me either. I think now I was always impressed that those children had such a happy-go-lucky time even though they were very poor. I suppose even their poverty became attractive."

"Maybe you were a lonely kid," he said.

"Well, my father was pretty busy. But we had a house-keeper. Mrs. Mason."

"And she had to raise you?"

"The devil she did. I couldn't stand her pious face."

"So you kept to yourself a lot?"

"I suppose it was lonely in the house. But I was happy."

"Lonely or not, I think you would be happy."

"It's true. I always remember something that happened when I was about twelve. One day I went berry-picking all by myself. I walked down the dusty road that followed the curve of the bay and then I cut into the bush and picked raspberries until the pail was full. I came out to the edge of the woods and sat down to rest and watch the whitecaps on the water. I was about a mile beyond the outskirts of town. Then I saw some-one a little way out in the water swimming. It was the Negro boy Jock, who was about thirteen. I don't know where he picked up that Scotch name. Before I could call to him he came walking in. He didn't see me sitting there, and maybe he was tired – I don't know; but he lay down on the sand in the sun and stretched out on his back, and he had no clothes on, Jim. I was scared. I turned to dart back into the bushes before he could see me. If he saw me I thought I'd die of shame, and

I did turn back and lie down on the sand, hiding behind a big rotten stump. I watched him, and my own feeling puzzled me. I had never seen a naked boy. The strange feeling creeping over me so slowly was like a sharp stab; it hurt me. I wanted to cry. I had never seen anything so beautiful as that boy's brown body lying there in the sunlight. His hands were behind his head and the sun glistened on his wet shoulders and legs. I was aware for the first time that beauty could be painful in a strange way…

"Well, I waited there, and Jock, having rested, got up and pulled on his worn blue overalls and his faded blue sweater with the short sleeves and a big floppy straw hat with the brim down. He started off along the beach in his bare feet. Jock was always in his bare feet. I was too shy to hurry after him. I was afraid he would know I had been watching him. So I let him get a good distance away. I wanted him to think I was coming out of the woods. With my berry pail I began to follow him, keeping well back for about five minutes. Then I yelled, 'Jock!' and he waited for me. He took my heavy pail of berries and we began to walk home together.

"It was like walking along the road with my own brother except that he seemed more wonderful and more important because I had the secret knowledge that he was beautiful. We walked along that dusty gravel road, and he wasn't used to carrying the pail and it broke his stride a little. Jock was usually so sure-footed he could walk anywhere in his bare feet, but he stubbed his big toe on a sharp jutting stone. The nail began to bleed. He had no handkerchief, so we sat down in the ditch and I bandaged up his funny big toe with my handkerchief. From then on we carried the pail between us the mile to our house. Then he asked me to come over to his house and have some fun. It was his little sister Sophie's birthday.

"I had never been to a party where I really had fun. In that town I got invited to all the nice little parties because I was the minister's daughter, but I never really had fun. In that tumble-down old roughcast house there was no important furniture and nothing valuable that could be damaged, and we just chased one another around the house screaming happily, and we sang, and Mrs. Johnson, a huge woman doing her washing, would call out to us, 'Take it easy and don't hurt yourself.'

"We had an orchestra; not that there were any instruments, but each kid could imitate some instrument with his voice and his hands. I was the only one who couldn't do anything. I felt ashamed. They were trying to show me how to have fun and were sorry for me, and I forgot about the time. It was almost dark when I got home, and my father asked me where I had been. 'Over at the Johnsons' place,' I said. 'The Johnsons' place,' he said, looking startled. I remember the way he put down his evening paper and pondered. My father had tufts of hair over his ears, but the top of his head was bald. He had a firm nose, and sensible eyes. 'The Johnsons' place,' he repeated, and then apparently he solved some little problem because that's all he said. Later that evening I heard him talking to our housekeeper. 'They're God's children just like you and me, Mrs. Mason,' he said in that tone that always impressed me.

"All that year I went to parties at the Johnson house, and I think I was happier than I had ever been in my life. That boy, Jock, who was my own age, or his older brother, or the little ones couldn't have been nicer to me. When I was thirteen I wanted a birthday party of my own. Oh, I wanted to have such a fine party. My father was willing to indulge me. One night he took out his fountain pen, got a sheet of paper, sat down at his desk and put on his horn-rimmed glasses. 'Now whom do you want to invite?' he asked me. 'The Johnsons,' I said. 'The

Johnsons? Oh, dear, Peggy, no!' And he looked really pained. 'Yes, the Johnsons, all of them, even the little ones,' I insisted. 'If the Johnsons can't come I don't want to have anybody.'

"He tried to reason with me; he told me that at a party the guests should all be friends, and the Johnsons would not feel at ease and happy among the other children and, of course, one should never do anything to make people feel uncomfortable. I kept shaking my head stubbornly as he walked up and down. I think I made him feel angry and ashamed. I think he felt guilty, too. He grabbed me by the shoulders and shook me and said loudly that all the factors had to be considered; his usefulness to his flock as a whole had to be considered. He tried to shake it into me. It didn't mean anything.

"Well, the little white girls and boys were invited to my party, and I sat in the living room holding my hands tight together, hating their clean white shiny faces and loving the Johnsons all the more. I hardly spoke to any of them. I remember I went out to the kitchen and took a napkin and filled it with sandwiches. I cut the cake in half and wrapped it up in another napkin, and I fled. In my nice new blue birthday dress I fled along the road for three blocks to that bare field where the roughcast house stood, bursting into the Johnsons' place and yelling it was my birthday. They all grabbed me and slapped me thirteen times. They took the food, and we sat down on the floor and I was happy.

"It was getting dark when old Mrs. Mason came to the Johnsons' house, and I hated her. I hated the toss of her head, the tilt of her nose, the disgust in her eyes, the way she grabbed me by the hand in front of the Johnson kids, who looked frightened. Mrs. Mason marched me along the road. I remember we never spoke to each other. I remember the angry, outraged scowl on her face as we hurried along the road in the dusk.

"All the children had gone home. My father's respectability was offended. 'I'm sorry about the Johnsons, Peggy. It's a very complicated thing and hard to explain,' he said. 'But I don't want you to go to their house any more. No more parties with the Johnsons, or I'll whip you. Understand?'

"'No more parties, even at their place?' I asked.

"'You're thirteen years old now, Peggy. You're a little lady now, not a child. I know you'll remember to be a little lady now, darling. Won't you?'

"'I don't want to be a little lady,' I said.

"I cried that night. I hated myself for growing older. I knew that the Johnsons, the coloured Johnsons, all the Johnsons of the world, were never to be among the invited guests wherever I went."

She smiled sadly, not noticing how intently McAlpine had listened, not noticing the light in his eyes. "No matter how long I live," she said, "I think I'll always remember the way that old roughcast house leaned against the sky at night."

"Of course you will," McAlpine said, and he had a strange desire. He wanted to make her laugh like a happy child, for so far he had only seen her smile. He wanted to hear her laughter, to see her eyes full of mirth. He wanted to be witty and gay and amuse her. He began to talk with enthusiasm about his colleagues at the university; he made gestures, acting out the roles, and thought he was being very funny, and she did smile broadly once or twice. It grew dark outside. Doors opened and closed. There was a smell of cooking and the sound of feet on the stairs.

But gradually she became completely indifferent; she kept glancing at the cheap alarm clock on the shelf. Finally he could no longer hear his own words, he could hear nothing but the ticking of the noisy, tinny alarm clock telling him she wanted him to go.

"I've got someone calling for me, Jim," she said at last. "There's no point in you being here."

"No, I guess not." But he sat there.

"I have to wash up a little," she said, and she frowned.

"Well, all right," he said, sighing. "I'll go." But even at the door he talked on monotonously. He wanted to defend the room.

It was six o'clock and dark out and still snowing. He walked reluctantly down the street, feeling disturbed by what she had told him. Yet she had only tried to show him why she had certain sympathies. Her own life could be blameless. But was there another side to her nature suggested by her actions? Blamelessness could be carried too far – it could have dreadful consequences. When he had tried to kiss her, she had been blameless; she had merely turned her head away. But it could have been taken as a coy gesture. It could have provoked him to grab her and kiss her and go ahead. Her passive rejection had been a powerful rebuke to him, but would it stop another man? And if it didn't would she lie there unresisting?

In the drugstore at the corner of Peel and St. Catherine he called Foley, who unfortunately was having dinner with an executive from the New York head office and going on with him to the hockey game but said he would see McAlpine around midnight at the Chalet. When he came out of the drugstore it was snowing harder and getting colder.

ᓷ SEVEN ᓷ

At midnight McAlpine came down Mountain Street, his chin buried in his coat collar, and turned in at the Chalet Restaurant. A big man standing outside the door blocked his way – a big baldheaded man in a white shirt with the sleeves rolled up who was smoking a cigar as if it were a hot summer evening. His arms folded, he appraised McAlpine carefully.

"Excuse me," McAlpine said, expecting him to move and step aside.

"Think nothing of it," the big man whispered without moving at all. "Hot, ain't it?"

"I hadn't noticed it," McAlpine said, turning his face away from the icy wind.

"Maybe you don't feel the heat. Me, I have to cool off." The man hadn't raised his voice above the whisper, and as he smiled benevolently, flicking his cigar ash at McAlpine's feet, the hard snow bounced off his hairy arms and he seemed to enjoy some strange sense of power. "Thinking of going in?" he asked. "I'm Wolgast. Me and Doyle own the joint."

"Oh. Well, my name's McAlpine. Is a friend of mine, Foley, in there?"

"You really a friend of Foley's?"

"I was supposed to meet him here."

"Why didn't you say so?" Wolgast asked in a jovial whisper. "I was trying to make up my mind if you were a jerk."

"A jerk?"

"We don't go for jerks around here," Wolgast whispered. "Anybody but jerks in the bar. In the restaurant it's all right. Jerks can eat and drink their heads off as long as they pay the shot. Get what I mean?" he asked with the indulgent air of a man who was so securely established in his own city he could accept or reject anyone who came to his place for a drink.

"Come on, I'll take you in," he said.

He led McAlpine through the dimly lit restaurant to the small checkroom near the toilet, then back to the little bar at the left of the entrance which looked like a smoke-filled washroom. He took him into the babble of coughing and laughter. Blinking, McAlpine looked around for Foley. On the walls were pictures of fighters and mocking caricatures of distinguished Montreal citizens. It was not much of a bar. It had five shabby red leather stools and three chromium tables along the wall and one bigger table at the window alcove, but it obviously wasn't a poor man's bar, for the clients at the tables were all well dressed.

"There's Foley," Wolgast whispered.

"Where?"

"Behind the bar, helping Doyle. He likes to play bartender. Foley's the only guy I'd trust behind the stick. Hey, Chuck, a friend of yours," he called.

"Hi Jim," Foley called, mixing a drink. "I'm with you in a minute. Got my job to do." McAlpine grinned and wanted to fit in, but he felt ill at ease. "Pay no attention to Doyle," Foley said, indicating the swarthy lean man with the shiny black hair and small sharp eyes, who was leaning disconsolately on the cash register. "He's sore tonight. An awful hangover. Last night he went on a spree and treated us all and made Wolgast do all the work. Now Wolgast is on a spree and Doyle has to wait on him. You'd never know it, but he's drunk as an owl."

"Hey bartender," Wolgast said to Doyle. "Wake up and meet a friend of Foley's. McAlpine's the name. Give him a drink on me." To McAlpine he said, "Call him Derle and he'll feel at home. An Irish thrush from Brooklyn."

"And him! He's a Jewish lush from Poland," Doyle said sourly. After reflecting a moment he added belligerently, "Who says I'm not an Irishman?"

"Okay, who isn't an Irishman?" Wolgast said, winking.

"McAlpine, though, is a historian," Foley said.

"A historian. What's a historian? I'm a heeb myself," Wolgast said, shrugging. "Introduce the historian, Chuck." Wolgast carefully paid Doyle for McAlpine's drink, and Doyle punched the cash register with an angry disdain. "That fresh air outside is wonderful," Wolgast said, and he went out.

Coming from behind the bar to the alcove table, Foley introduced McAlpine to his friends; he was happy being among his own people, and being able to invite McAlpine to sit down with them.

Their faces shone with sweat, and they all broke into unpredictable bursts of laughter. They took turns laughing at one another. A fat blonde stockbroker named Arthur Nixon, who looked like a pink and white elephant, was trying to tell a story to an ex-fighter named Dave Green, now a successful tailor who read Spinoza. But Green, pushing the stockbroker's hand off his shoulder, was trying to argue with Claude Gagnon, the dapper French Canadian cartoonist with the fancy striped shirt, who couldn't be bothered with him because he himself had found a listener in the big grey man, a brooding Buddha. The grey man, who listened because no one any longer listened to him, was Walter Malone, an editorial writer whose life had been ruined by the war; it had compelled him to leave Paris where he had been understood and happy.

"Where did Wolgast get the whisper?" McAlpine asked the stockbroker.

"Claims he was gassed in the First World War," the stockbroker said. "Derle, on the other hand, insists Wolgast never saw the war. Just whispers like that so people will have to listen attentively. So you're a historian, eh, McAlpine?"

"It's a fact. Why?"

"How would you like to listen to me?" he asked with a shy diffidence.

"Why, of course. Go ahead."

"Good God," the stockbroker shouted happily. "At last a man who'll listen to me!"

"Not yet," Gagnon the cartoonist shouted, grabbing at McAlpine's arm. "I've a question to ask the professor. It's this. What has history to do with you and me?"

"Pay no attention to Gagnon," the stockbroker pleaded. "He'll talk all night. Look, this happened when I was in Chicago—"

"I want my little share of history," Gagnon insisted. "I'm not getting it."

"And you won't, Gagnon, no one can agree on your story," Malone explained wearily.

"The great Malone in exile trying to quote Napoleon. With Malone it's always Napoleon."

"Pay no attention to him," Malone said. "Why should anyone write his wretched little history?"

"You haven't answered my question, McAlpine."

"It's complicated. We'd do better if we had another drink," McAlpine said good-naturedly. They were kidding him about his own subject, and he liked it and ordered a round of drinks. The grinning, approving faces came closer. Doyle, his face now right at his shoulder, was derisive and happy, his headache gone.

The ashes of his cigar wavered over McAlpine's glass, and over his shoulder, and then fell heavily on his coat sleeve. "I'll give you some real history, professor," Doyle said, his impudent face full of mockery. "This is what happens after a war. A couple of hours ago a guy comes in here looking for trouble. A guy with a wooden leg, a war veteran, see? And he didn't like the table I gave him and he wanted to show off to his lady friends. 'Sit down and relax,' I said. Well, what did he do? He thumped his wooden leg at me. I stiffened my own leg like this, see, and I thumped it on the floor like this, clump, clump. 'Don't pull that wooden leg on me,' I said."

Wolgast, who had returned to the room, smiled at them blissfully, and as the smile grew wider he began to weave; then he slowly collapsed into the arms of McAlpine, who had jumped up in time to grab him. "Thanks, thanks, dear friend," he whispered. "I've wondered what professors did for a living. You're a very nice man." Beaming like a baby he patted McAlpine's cheek and tried to kiss him, and then sighed and closed his eyes.

"I should have a partner who's a lush," Doyle said rather bitterly.

"Here, Jim. Put him down on the chair," Foley said tenderly. "Around here anything goes. Even the owners, one by one. You'll always have a home here, Jim. How do you like the joint?"

"Why didn't I bring Mr. Carver along?" McAlpine answered with an ironic grin. "What do you think, Mr. Foley?"

"An idea," Foley said, snickering. "Do it next time, kid. Humanity on its last legs, and Carver here with his dignity down. Come on, my bladder's bothering me."

Only when they got to the washroom were they beyond the droning voices of the sweating, tireless storytellers.

"It goes on like that all night," Foley said happily as he led the way to the small toilet near the coat check room. "I know they're all lunkheads. I don't ask why I'm happy."

"Me neither unless the ashes from Doyle's cigar are dropping in my eyes."

"I must speak to Derle about that cigar," Foley said and if he had owned a share in the place he couldn't have been more concerned. "He should watch that cigar."

"I think he should. How about leaving now, Chuck?"

"Where else is there to go in this town?"

"Down to St. Antoine with me."

"Those nigger nightclubs?" Foley combed his red hair. "What is this?"

"I ran into Peggy Sanderson on the street," McAlpine said as they came out of the narrow washroom. "I think you missed something, Chuck. Peggy isn't interested only in Negro writers and musicians. She has Negro friends. I think she likes being with Negroes."

"You're kidding."

"It's a fact, Chuck. I talked to her."

"I see," Foley said slowly.

He was a shrewd, good-natured, companionable man who enjoyed the intimate confidences of most women, and he knew gamblers, gangsters, police officials, burlesque dancers, and important businessmen in Montreal; they all spoke of him as a friend with a wonderful quality; nothing he ever heard about anybody surprised him; nothing a friend ever did aroused any deep prejudice in him, but now, watching him, McAlpine knew he must have heard gossip about Peggy and have refused to face it, have wanted to believe she was only interested in Negro culture. Now he realized he might have got her wrong, and he was sore.

"Come on along with me, Chuck."

"Not down there," Foley said irritably. "That stuff belongs to my salad days in the early thirties. Now it's for high-school boys and débutantes. Come on back to the bar and have a drink."

"Another half-hour in there and I'll go crazy," McAlpine said, fumbling in his pocket for his hat check.

"Jim, just a minute. Aren't you kidding me about Peggy?" Foley asked.

"I'm sure she'll be there. Come on and see for yourself."

"No – no. If you want to go down there why don't you phone Milton Rogers?"

"Who's he?"

"The photographer. Don't you remember? We used to drink with him."

"I remember. But it's too late to phone anybody. I'll go alone."

"Here, give me that check." Foley handed it to the plump girl behind the counter, who was so devoted to him that she often saw he got a better pair of galoshes than the ones he had checked with her. "Give him his coat, Annie," he said, putting fifty cents in her hand. Taking McAlpine's coat from the girl, he helped him on with it. This gesture made McAlpine feel all the more apologetic.

"So long, Chuck," he said.

"So long," Foley said unhappily.

It had turned colder; the powdered snow blew up his pant legs. People passing by had their heads down and their chins buried deep in their collars. When he had crossed Dorchester, going on down Mountain Street toward the dark railway underpass, he stopped apprehensively. Lights gleamed in the black blotch of the underpass. Snow flew across the inky entrance.

And high above the railroad tracks one tall brick chimney rose against the night sky. In the underpass, on the sheltered cobblestones, his footfalls were heavy. The lighted corner was just below – the corner of St. Antoine – a glare of neon signs shining pinkly on the snow.

Negroes stood in front of the Café St. Antoine; others huddled together against the cold in the shelter of the entrance to the corner grocery store. A taxi skidded to a stop at the café entrance; three white men and a stout woman got out, and McAlpine started to follow them into the café; but he drew back; he was alone and a stranger, and he told himself he wanted to look around the neighbourhood before going in.

He wandered east toward the station, he looked into taverns, and felt conspicuous when Negroes stared at him. He peered into windows of little grocery stores, delicatessens, a pool parlour and a cleaning and pressing establishment. It had stopped snowing. The clouds overhead were breaking up. Behind the tower of the Windsor Station and the lighted tower of the Sun Life Building the moon was trying to shine through, but it was only a pale flicker. The gaps in the clouds closed again. Turning back, he looked uneasily at the nightclub entrance and went down the slope toward the tracks. In the lighted window of the room over the other nightclub across the street he could see a Negro woman with a baby in her arms walking up and down. She began to dance around the room holding the baby, dancing to the music coming from the floor below.

At the foot of the street was a little square with a row of old brick houses, and this square was all white with snow. McAlpine peered into some of the lighted windows. Music came from a ground-floor open window, the music of a cello and a piano, and he could see three figures, one a Negro at a piano, another, who looked like a French Canadian, at the cello, and the third figure, the face hidden, was bending over the piano. The piano and the cello achieved an hypnotic effect in primitive counterpoint, repeating a simple theme over and over with curious discords; but it was the posture, the attitudes of the musicians as they played their solitary theme that held him spellbound: the cello twanged, the piano repeated the minor chords with a little variation, the musicians were held in their strange rapture, and there was nothing in the world for them but the lonely little theme and that one room in the cold night and their own intensity. The shunting of engines in the station yard and the hum of the city and the grey shabby neighbourhood could never break the magic of their private, peculiar, and isolated rapture. Then they smiled at one another, their hands reached out for drinks, and the figure on the piano stool swung around.

The bass twanging of the cello followed him on down to the bridge over the tracks. From there he could look around the whole neighbourhood. Below the bridge was the St. Henri quarter along the canal, a small industrial city with wretched houses along the tracks, houses so old that some of them had earthen floors, and in summertime barefoot children, running into the houses, came out with muddied feet.

While he was surveying the shabby neighbourhood a train came toward the bridge, its bell clanging; the smoke billowed out under the bridge and shot up a white cloud in the cold darkness, and the cloud, streaked with the reflection of fire from the engine, whirled around McAlpine while the lighted coaches went swinging away from him.

He climbed the hill again. Now he would go into the nightclub, he thought. As he watched for another taxi to stop in front of the café, he found himself staring up at the mountain's dark shadow. Everything he really wanted was up there on the mountain among those who had prestige, power, and influence. The shabby street was cut off short, the way blocked by the enormous mountain barrier studded with gleaming lights.

Back at the café entrance, he stopped: like a man in a spell he saw himself going in and climbing the stairs to the tawdry café and looking for her among the noisy, half-drunken patrons, the blacks and the whites, the few loose-witted, cheap white girls, then finding her on the dance floor swaying in the arms of a whispering Negro who held her tight against him; another white girl who was a soft touch, hopped up by the music.

He turned away from the café entrance, not admitting he was afraid of what he might find in there; with a deliberate effort, using his head, he recognized rationally it was a mistake to feel so involved with her that he had to climb the stairs and suffer the embarrassment of encountering her with her friends; with an effort he broke the spell and went on home.

❧ EIGHT ❧

In the morning the whole city had a glistening winter-white brilliance, a city of barouches with jingling snowbells and fur-capped drivers wrapped in old buffalo robes. Men in coonskin coats swaggered opulently along the downtown streets, and girls on St. Catherine wore white rubber boots. It was milder, and the big wet snowflakes clung to the walls of the buildings and melted and glittered and shone.

It was a fine morning, and McAlpine couldn't take the time to dwell on his failure to climb the stairs of the café down on St. Antoine. He ordered some toast and coffee from room service and asked that *The Sun* be sent up with it. While he ate he studied the editorial page. He could see his column on the page – the eighth column. And the page badly needed a stimulating, controversial column. As it was, the whole paper had a rather dry Parnassian tone except for the sporting page, which was lively and well edited. Horton might succeed in blocking him, but only temporarily; he would get the job in spite of the delay, he told himself, and when Mr. Carver telephoned and said Horton was coming around he knew he was right.

A few hours later he had lunch with Catherine at the Café Martin; and she talked about his doing the column from Paris; she built him up and drew him out and led him far away from that Negro café. Then she took him on a shopping trip, and all the delightful signs of their happy intimacy together engrossed him. First they went to a jewellery store where she was having an antique brooch of her grandmother's reset; and as she explained to the clerk what she wanted done she kept turning to McAlpine for approval, until she started to laugh.

"What's the matter?" he asked. But she only shook her head, smiling and looking pleased, and wouldn't tell. And in the department store, buying a pair of gloves after asking if he liked them, she saw that he was now smiling to himself.

"Why the smile, Jim?" she asked. But it was his turn to refuse to explain. And then in the milliner's, where she was paying a bill for two hats, they both turned at the same time and started to laugh. Progress, progress! Aren't we getting along well! they said with their eyes.

It all contributed to his confidence. This confidence in himself grew when he went to dinner with her to the Drapers' big stone house in Westmount. It was boring for both of them. The man talked about nothing but his chain of cafeterias. McAlpine knew Catherine was imploring him to leave and go to some place where they could be alone. It made him feel completely sure of himself; yet only last night, he recalled, he had lacked the confidence to climb the stairs of the Negro café.

When he had taken Catherine home and he was back at the Ritz, he told himself it was still early and he wanted company, and easily, like that, he went out and got a taxi on Sherbrooke and drove down to St. Antoine.

Going into the café now wasn't the slightest bit embarrassing.

The foyer was done in pink, and a wide door opened into a crowded tavern. The ticket booth was there by the stairs which led up to the nightclub. Two well dressed white men were ahead of him; he got a ticket and followed them up the narrow stairs. At the top, a hard-faced headwaiter, a mulatto, asked him to show his ticket, then pointed to one of the little tables with the metallic chairs around the small dance floor. A six-piece Negro band was playing. McAlpine declined the table. At the rear of the club was a bar, all nickel and pink leather, and he knew he would not be conspicuous there. When the coloured bartender had given him a rye and water he began to look around.

Among all the Negroes there were a few white people; the white girls were mainly dowdy gum chewers, but there were a few well dressed dreamy-eyed débutantes. Nobody was really drunk. Nobody was as hilarious as Foley's friends had been at the Earbenders Club.

There she was by herself at a little table in the far corner. It was so splendidly right that she should be there by herself, dressed with the disarming simplicity that made her so noticeable. Her hair, still parted in the middle, was done in a little braid at the back; she wore a plain blue skirt and a white blouse. She looked more than ever like a composed schoolgirl.

A Negro boy, passing, stopped, made a joke with her, started on, then turned and had a serious conversation. He looked happy and went on his way. A pretty mulatto in a white evening dress, coming back from the ladies' room, heard Peggy call to her. She hurried over, opened her purse, and took out some snapshots. They held them up to the light by turns, nodding seriously, and came to an important respectful agreement about the pictures. The girl became so absorbed in an explanation of one of them that she started to sit down, forgetting her friends at her own table. They called out to her. Laughing, she patted Peggy on the shoulder and left.

The band stopped playing and the dancers began to drift off the floor. McAlpine waited to see who in the band would join Peggy. But a little old guy, brown and dapper, who ought to have been home in bed, came out of nowhere and shook hands with her elaborately. She must have made a joke, for he made a comical face and held his head with both hands; grinning to himself, he turned away and limped toward the stairs. He felt good; he felt spry and gay. At the stairs he turned and looked back at the band leader, Elton Wagstaffe, and clapped his hands for attention, and Wagstaffe smiled broadly. It was like watching people who were sure of one another visiting in their own neighbourhood.

Wagstaffe was very black and had a high forehead: he was heavily handsome. When he was crossing the dance floor he did an odd thing. He saw Peggy smile at him, and he averted his eyes. He hesitated, dubious and embarrassed, and came over to her, as he had clearly wanted to do so before the doubt had entered his mind. He sat down and relaxed and made idle conversation. It was plain he knew in his heart that he and Peggy and the busboy and the girl in the white dress and the little old guy all belonged to the same gang. They were joined by the trumpet player, Wilson. He was well built, about five feet ten, with good even features, but he did not look very powerful because he was so well proportioned; he was neither fat nor slim. His skin was coffee-coloured, contrasting well with his light brown double-breasted suit. On his left wrist was a watch with a gold band.

Neither man tried to get Peggy's attention; both were quiet and at ease. Wilson turned to a Negro who was passing, at the same time putting his hand on Peggy's, and the light, gentle, friendly touch said that the smile and greeting he offered to that friend did not separate them even momentarily. It occurred to McAlpine that neither Wagstaffe nor Wilson, so at ease with Peggy, could have gained that quiet, possessive intimacy by knowing her only in this café. If she were so friendly with them, wouldn't she let them come to her room? And they, of course, would be charmed by her unspoiled freshness and want to possess it as he, himself, had wanted to possess it when he tried to kiss her. He fumbled for his cigarettes and waited nervously until the band had begun to assemble on the platform. Wagstaffe got up; Wilson, the trumpet player, patted Peggy's hand. They left her. McAlpine approached her table.

"Hello, Peggy," he said, feeling like an intruder.

"Oh, hello." She was annoyed, but he looked so sheepish that she couldn't help laughing.

"What brought you down here, professor?"

"Well, since you had mentioned the place…"

"Oh," she said, only half believing him. She was puzzled by his shyness and the fact that he was so plainly out of place.

"Seems to me you're following me around. What's the idea?"

"Why shouldn't I come here?"

"Because you don't belong here. And you don't belong in my life," she said impatiently. "I don't like being followed around." But the way he moistened his lips, and his silent, awkward, patient stubbornness, began to bother her. "You're a funny guy. I doubt if anything that ever happened in your life, Jim, justifies your being such a funny guy. Why don't you go home?"

"I thought I might walk home with you."

"I'm not leaving yet."

"Can I buy you a drink?"

"Go ahead," she said, shrugging.

It struck McAlpine, then, that the members of the band, handling their instruments, were watching him and Peggy. Every one of them was watching. Did they have to make up their minds about him and the girl before they could play? And were they reaching out to hold Peggy in the pattern of the place? If he made one little move to take her away would there be a sudden panic among them?

His foolish thoughts made him smile, and he said, "I saw you talking to the band leader and the trumpet player. I wanted to come over and speak to them. Why don't you call them over, next intermission? I'd like to meet them."

"Well, you're not going to," she said sharply.

"Why not? I've no prejudices, you know that. Maybe we'd like each other. How about it?"

"You're not going to, I said."

"Why?"

"Why? Because I know what you're up to. I can feel it in my bones. I can feel you pulling at my coattails, yanking at me. I hate people pulling at my coattails. For heaven's sake, why do you have to come down here like an old woman?"

"But, Peggy—"

"Oh, you and your hurt silly eyes! You know I'm right. Go away."

"Peggy," he said gently. "Maybe you know how I feel better than I know myself. I'm out of my depth. I came down here because I hoped to see you. I'd like to know your friends. It's a way of knowing you."

"Why do you want to know me?"

"I don't know."

"Oh, don't sound so mysterious."

"And Wilson and Wagstaffe looked like friendly guys. Come on, Peggy. Anyway, tell me about them."

"I think they're the best in their line in the country," she said mollified by his humble tone. "Elton's from New York. Ronnie is from Memphis. They're old friends of mine. Or at least they seem like old friends."

"It looked like that. Whom did you know first? Wilson?"

"No. Wagstaffe."

"How did you meet him?"

"I came down here the first time with Milton Rogers. He's a friend of Foley's – a photographer. The next time, I came down here alone. It was a summer night, and I liked being here. I stayed late, and when I was outside and going up the street there was Mr. Wagstaffe walking beside me. He said he had seen me here. Well, we walked up the street together. When we got to Dorchester he said he felt like going bowling and would I come along."

Now she was smiling, and McAlpine nodded, encouraging her; he could see her standing on Dorchester Street with the friendly Negro who had walked up the street with her; he could see her expression when Wagstaffe asked her to bowl with him. She would have known that the Negro was waiting to have his companionship rejected simply because he was a Negro. It would have been an important moment for her, and of course she would have smiled and gone with him.

"So we went bowling," she said, her face happy. "I bowl pretty well," she added. "After we bowled he walked me home, and we sat in my place talking for an hour or so. I think there was more gentleness in him than I had ever felt in anyone, and I remember wondering how it was that walking up a street and bowling for half an hour could bring out such wonderful gentleness in a man. It was wonderful."

"Such moments are always wonderful," he agreed.

"Yes, aren't they?" Her eyes were a little sad.

McAlpine couldn't bear to look at her. He sat with his elbows on the table, his hands folded and his head down, too moved to speak. He told himself that the hour or so she had spent with Wagstaffe in her room had been friendly and innocent and not a sensually corrupt first stirring of a novel lust. It was possible she had touched the band leader with her simplicity and candour as she had touched Foley and him too. He wanted to believe completely in her own pure feeling. This faith in her was the illumination he had been seeking since the first time he had met her; it offered him a glimpse of the way she wanted to live, of the kind of relationship she wanted to have with all people, no matter what kind of a sacrifice might be required of her.

But it couldn't persuade him that Wagstaffe, or Wilson, or their colleagues, would be content to accept only her gentle friendliness, asking nothing more of her. The utter impossibility of her attitude, its wilfulness, its lack of prudence, frightened him; but he knew that if he protested she would assume he was speaking out of the dull confinement of his own orderly university experience.

"Well, that's all there is to it," she said lightly. "So now you can run along."

"I beg your pardon?"

"I said now you can go home, Jim."

"But I still want to talk to you."

"Some other time then."

"But where?"

"Well, I usually have breakfast in Honey Dew on Dominion Square at half past eight every morning," she said dryly, for she couldn't imagine him appearing at that hour to have breakfast with her.

"I'll see you then, Peggy." He got up.

"So long, Jim. Thanks for the drink."

"So long," he said.

On the way out he glanced at the band leader and the trumpet player. Wilson was eyeing him as he lifted his trumpet, his head swaying, the light catching the whites of his eyes and his pink knuckles. He looked like a sophisticated Negro who had worked in many cities and had known many white women who came to Negro cafés. McAlpine was sure that Peggy would bring out more than gentleness in him. That confident Negro would not be put off by the mere turning away of her head as he himself had been; not if his hand were on her breast. McAlpine detested him.

Outside, it had begun to snow again, a reluctant continuation of the big fall, but without much wind, a thickening of the white blanket over the city. McAlpine stood at the doorway, hating to go; he felt a compulsion to wait, a bewildering sense of urgency that he should wait and not leave her alone in there. Finally he trudged up the street and through the subway underpass to Dorchester glowing with pink neon signs. At the corner he stood watching the snow ploughs. Two little ploughs like tanks scooted along the sidewalk, scraping it clean and pushing the snow to the side of the road where a big truck with a suction pipe sucked it in. The tanks darted around, the wind blew, and it was like watching an important military operation. Soon his shoulders were covered with snow. Then one of the tanks came charging at him and he had to jump out of the way, and the happy guy at the wheel shouted, "Go on home!" But he stood there, for the enchanting, peaceful pure whiteness of the snowbound city strengthened his faith in Peggy. And he didn't even look up at that black barrier of the mountain. In the snowstorm he could hardly see it. He didn't want to see it.

❧ NINE ❧

He had counted on sleeping late, but he awoke at seven as usual, with a violent headache. An icy wind from the window he had left open eighteen inches was billowing the curtains and freezing the room. Jumping out of bed, he slammed down the window and, trembling with the cold, crawled into bed and pulled the covers around his neck and waited for the warm bed and the sound of the piping radiator to take the chill out of his bones. Why did I give Peggy the impression I liked the winters? he asked himself. To hell with zero weather! I like the summer.

But not beaches and summer cottages. When he had talked to Catherine about his family summer cottage and his boyhood he ought to have gone on and told her how he had found himself staying away from that Havelock beach. At sixteen he had refused to go any more to the summer cottage. He had withdrawn from that beach forever and had taken odd jobs instead, learning to like the sweltering heat of the city. In those hot months he also learned how to be alone. Catherine might not be able to understand it, but Peggy would agree it was important to be able to enjoy being alone. In the summer, with no one around whom he had to please or impress, he had found a happy summer loneliness which might puzzle Catherine, but which Peggy would understand. Yes, if Peggy could have been there with him in his apartment by the university! How easy it was to imagine her there, watching him as he got up late and went idly to the window to see if the day would be a scorcher, watching him as he went to the door to get the newspaper and waiting while he got his own breakfast and read the paper. She would walk with him in the sun's glare when the heat from the hot pavement singed his ankles, and she would look so cool in her light summer dress that the corner barber, his friend, standing in front of his shop, would call out, "Jees, don't she feel this heat at all?" And late at night when the apartment had cooled off and he stood by the open window getting ready to do some work, she would stand behind him listening to the night noises, and then the whole crowded restless city life would reach into the room to remind them they were together and no longer alone…

But the rattle of the icy snow against the windowpane broke his reverie. It was winter. It was Montreal. And he was alone. He got out of bed and went to the window. The street below looked bleak. The temperature had dropped below zero. He could hear the squeaking of boots on the hard snow as pedestrians hurried along Sherbrooke, their heads down against the heavy wind. On such a morning a girl wearing only light rubbers and uncovered ankles could catch pneumonia. Even the poorest girl ought to have warm fleece-lined snow boots, he told himself.

Going out for breakfast, he turned down toward Dominion Square and the Honey Dew Restaurant; after all, it would be just as convenient to have his breakfast there as any other place. His ears began to sting. He had to grab at his hat before it blew off. It was unbearably cold.

The tidy little restaurant at that hour was almost deserted. At the table near the door was the old woman who was always there, an old woman with a benevolent motherly face who sat for hours in the morning and hours in the afternoon without even buying a cup of coffee. McAlpine could have described Peggy and asked if she had come in, but he had made the mistake once before of saying good morning to this woman. If you even looked at her, you were trapped, listening to the story of her kindly life. Her overflowing, possessive motherliness was oppressive. So he got his orange juice, cereal, bacon, and eggs, and listened to the soft, subdued, piped-in music. But it was hard to avoid the eyes of the motherly crone as he watched the door. And the longer he waited the more he thought about those snow boots, and the more he worried.

A thin Englishwoman in a brown coat accompanied by two beautiful children, a seven-year-old boy and a five-year-old girl, both neatly dressed, came in; the mother, having seated the children near McAlpine, went up to the counter to place her order. These two English children had had an early appointment with the doctor. The little boy had in his hand one of the sticks a doctor uses to push down your tongue while he examines your throat. "Now open your mouth, that's a good girl," he said gravely to his solemn sister. When she had opened her mouth and he had pressed down her tongue, he shook his head lugubriously. "You have a black mark on a tonsil way back there, Susie," he said in his best doctor's tone. "But not really?" Susie said. "Oh, yes, Susie, a *big* black mark!" he insisted. He was such a good little doctor that his sister was no longer certain they were only playing. Turning to McAlpine she asked anxiously, "But not really?" "Oh, no, Susie, not really," McAlpine said gently.

He had been asking himself why he should not go along to St. Catherine to Ogilvy's, buy a pair of snow boots, and leave them at Peggy's apartment. Now the motherly old woman smiled approvingly. "Everything is so real to a child, isn't it?" she called. "I'm glad to see they're well bundled up. Bitter weather, isn't it?"

But snow boots would cost ten or eleven dollars, and he owed his bill at the Ritz; he was running short of money. The fact that he couldn't actually afford to buy the snow boots irritated him. To have to hesitate over such a trifling expenditure was intolerable. He folded his scarf around his neck, left the restaurant, and hurried up Peel and along St. Catherine to the department store with a fine brisk exuberant stride.

In the shoe department, when the salesgirl asked him what size he wanted, he blushed and laughed, and the girl laughed. He inspected her foot. It was a nice little foot, too. He compared it in his mind with Peggy's. He paid twelve dollars for the brown leather snow shoes and went out whistling on his way to Crescent Street.

No one answered his knock on the basement door, and at the main entrance he had to ring three times before Mrs. Agnew, fumbling with the cords of her faded blue dressing gown, came to the door, her grey-streaked blonde hair falling over her eyes. "Yes, of course, you're one of Miss Sanderson's friends," she said, and made him think Peggy had a regiment of assorted friends coming to the house. "I was sound asleep," she explained, like an old friend. "Why don't you step in out of the cold? I have a little congestion on the chest, you understand."

"If you would just take this parcel for Miss Sanderson," he said, stepping into the hall.

"Of course I will. Here, let me close the door. I get more colds standing at this door. I'm glad you called. I look a fright, I know. But last night— Well, I'm not used to it, you see. It was my cousin from St. Agathe. Mind you, after not seeing him for six months," she added with a grateful smile. "La, what a man! And I'm not even sure he is my cousin. You understand? What an energetic baldheaded little man he is, and he must be all of sixty! I knew what he was like that evening last summer when he took me out to the Belmont amusement park and we rode all night in those little automobiles that keep crashing and everybody laughing. All night in those toy autos with my grinning little baldheaded man. Such fun it was! And to have him show up last night! It was something, I tell you. A parcel? Certainly, I'll put it in her room. Who'll I say left it?"

"Oh, just say a stranger," he said, opening the door and starting down the steps.

"No, wait," she called. "You're not a stranger."

"Yes, I am."

"But not really," she called out. "Not really."

"Oh, yes," he called back, waving and laughing.

The wind felt good on his cheeks. The air was dry and bracing. It was an exhilarating day; and he could hear the pretty little English child as she turned to him asking anxiously, "But not really?" And he could not get the phrase out of his head. It was as if all the people who had ever had any authority in his life had been watching him buy snow boots for a white girl who liked Negroes, and knowing they had been watching him, he enjoyed it immensely. His father in consternation said, "Oh, but not really!" Old Higgins, incredulous that he could have been mistaken about him, murmured, "But not really!" And the officers in the ship's wardroom, particularly Captain Welsh, with his decorations, grew red-faced and gasped, "Oh, not really!" "Oh, no, not really!" said the president of his university, looking alarmed. "My God, no, not really!" cried Mr. Carver.

"Oh, yes," McAlpine said aloud, chuckling with satisfaction, "really!"

≈ TEN ≈

He was having lunch with Foley in the La Salle but was early, so he got a copy of *The Sun* at the newsstand and, sitting in the lobby, opened it like a newspaperman, who always reads his own paper first. He had turned to the editorial page, which was to carry his column, when he saw Foley come in.

Foley now was not the man he had been in the Earbenders Club. He was as solemn and brisk as a broker. They went downstairs to the bar and to one of the tables with the red and white chequered tablecloths. Foley wouldn't take a drink; he never drank during working hours. McAlpine had a beer and the cold salmon plate, and Foley had a mushroom omelette. Foley was not in good humour.

"Well, has *The Sun* come through yet, Jim?" he said. "Or is beautiful Joe still keeping you dangling?"

"It's going all right," McAlpine said, and he told about the luncheon with Carver and about Horton putting the fat reporter, Walters, on the scales.

"Now, isn't that a lovely story!" Foley said sardonically.

"A pretty sadistic story, I'd say."

"And you think it's Horton who's sadistic?"

"I'm not that dumb. It's not just Horton."

"As long as you see it," Foley said. "All the newspapermen are wise to Carver. You see, Jim," he grinned, "there always has to be a senior mind."

"A senior mind, yes."

"And does the junior mind ever get out of line?"

"And Horton is only the junior mind, of course."

"Fine. So if junior seems to be the one who is against giving you the job—"

"Oh, I'll have the job all right," McAlpine said quietly.

"Just like that?"

"Just like that. Everything you say about Carver is true, but there's another side to him, Chuck."

"I know all about Beautiful Joe," Foley said irritably. "I've known people who worked for him. He'll get hold of you by the short hair. He has hold of all his employees by the short hair, and some poor dopes think it's a noble grip; but he reaches right into their lives till he owns them. Hell, his office is a family plantation, and he's the kindly old master, and Horton is Simon Legree. Oh, well, to hell with Carver! He's your problem. However, Jim," he added frowning, "you're not wrong about everything."

"No? What am I right about?"

"You were right about Peggy Sanderson. I can't understand it, but you're right. I seem to have been the only one in town who wasn't wise to her. Those guys around the Earbenders know her. The trouble is," he went on, making an apology to himself, "I don't pay much attention to any woman who comes to work in our office. But your little Peggy has had three or four jobs in the last six months, and I find out that in the last place they all got wise to her."

"Wise to what, Chuck?"

"Why, about the dinges."

"The what?"

"The black boys. You were right. She goes for them, Jim," Foley said sourly.

"I didn't say she went for black boys, Chuck."

"Didn't you? Well, it seems that she does, and now at our place too she's out on her ear. They've just fired her." Foley's abrupt cynical laugh really showed how disappointed he was. "She'll probably tell you it's race prejudice, Jim. Well, it isn't really that at all," he said flatly. "The girl can't concentrate anymore. That's the dreamy look in her eyes that got me. It's what you noticed in her, too, see? Well, she can't concentrate because she's all hopped up with the dinges making passes at her and probably laying her, too."

"Now wait a minute, Chuck. You have your own eyes, your own judgment. Why not see things in your own way," McAlpine pleaded, wanting to save something valuable in Foley's own life. "You've got it all terribly wrong. That girl isn't throwing herself at Negroes. She's not lying around waiting for them to make love to her, I know it for a fact." His voice became patient and gentle; he told the story of Peggy's childhood friendship with the Johnson family.

"So that's her explanation?" Foley asked, after pondering a little.

"It wasn't offered as an explanation, Chuck."

"But you believed it."

"Yes. Don't you?"

"I think she's lying."

"But why?"

"To put herself in a sympathetic light, of course."

"That wasn't your own first judgment of her, Chuck. You're her friend. You're important to her. I know you are." In her name McAlpine was trying to hold on to his friendship.

"All right," Foley said impatiently. "I know what I said. Don't rub it in, Jim."

"How do you know you weren't right? Explain that to me, Chuck."

"How should I know how to explain it?" Foley asked. "There's something about that girl that's a big lie. Women like her love the lie that's in the first impression they make. It wins them tenderness and approval and sympathy and forgiveness. And they'll lie and cheat to preserve the initial advantage they win for themselves. They're capable of anything, and there'll always be someone around like you, Jim, to believe in them and plead that they're being misunderstood when they fly off at crazy and unpredictable angles – blue jays—"

"She's a blue jay?"

"Sure she is."

"But look here, Chuck," McAlpine protested. "You could call a saint a blue jay."

"A saint— My God, wait a minute, Jim!" Foley's whole tone changed. "Just what do you get out of this girl?"

"What do I get?"

"Yes, what does she do to you?"

"I don't know," McAlpine said, growing embarrassed. "It's – well, I don't know. It's just a glimpse of something."

"Go on. A glimpse of what?"

"I'm not sure. I really don't know." Picking up a fork, he began to make a little pattern on the tablecloth, then looked up apologetically. "Yes, just a glimpse, I suppose," he said.

"A glimpse you ever had before?"

"I'm not sure. I was wondering about it last night."

"Another girl?"

"Oh, no! It's more like the way you feel when you suddenly come on something unexpected that's just right." He hesitated, trying to get it straight. "I remember we were in some hotel in Paris on the right bank, after the invasion," he said. "It was raining. We ought to have all felt happy and victorious because we had talked about getting to Paris and the wonderful spree we would have, but there we were in the hotel room, dog-tired and inert, with the whole city dark and dead in the rain. I think we felt that we ought to celebrate. Really we wanted to sleep. We talked of going somewhere and seeing something. The rain put us off. We talked about girls. An English officer – a blonde chap, I forget his name – took me by the arm and suggested we go out for an hour. One hour, as a gesture to the freeing of the City of Light, and then sleep.

"The Englishman had never been in Paris before, but he took me by the arm and we went out into the rain. We could not see anything. We sloshed along. We talked of going back to the hotel. Finally he spoke to a gendarme, and then all he said to me was, 'Come on.' I don't quite know where we went. Some place near the Bastille.

"I remember we plunged into some doorway, then along a dark alley. Then a door opened and we stepped into bright lights. Well, it was a little amphitheatre with the benches filled with people, and there was a tanbark surface and an encircling fence painted white, and down there in the toy arena were a couple of clowns in their pirouette costumes dancing around; a girl in a silver dress was riding a white horse; someone was leading an elephant across the arena. All this going on down there under a brilliant white light! Everything was so white and clean and fantastically surprising and so wonderfully innocent and happy. Maybe it looked like that because we had come in out of the darkness and the rain. We had come in out of the war. And the bright little circus was absolutely remote from the war. I was so surprised I gaped and blinked. It was beautiful. I felt so peacefully elated. Well—"

He broke off, seeing the incredulous expression on Foley's face. "I don't know. Maybe I mean I seem to see Peggy somewhere in there – in that—"

"That oasis of happiness," Foley said dryly.

"That's right," McAlpine said.

"But you didn't go back to that little circus."

"No, and I don't think I could now."

"But you've gone back to Peggy."

"Just a couple of times."

"You shouldn't have gone back; but, since you have, don't do it again, or you'll look too closely."

"But, as you say," McAlpine smiled, "now that I have gone back—"

"What's the use?" Foley shook his head. "The tip-off on you, Jim, in those drawings you do. You're a bit of an artist."

"So what?"

"You see something in the kid you think no one else sees. If you could paint it, it would be done and you could forget it. But you want to grab it for yourself. Doesn't that bring us back where we started?"

"Where's that?"

"The Carvers. Remember? Well, there may be a reason Carver keeps you dangling."

"Go on."

"Catherine."

"Catherine? Oh, now, look here, Chuck!" McAlpine started to laugh. "If you're implying my feeling for Catherine has changed because of what I've been saying about this girl, well, it's absurd." Obviously believing every word, he said, "Catherine is my kind of people, Chuck. A fine girl. I'm at home with her. We share the same interests, the same understanding, the same kind of taste and manners. I don't know whether I love her or whether she could get to love me. It might work out that way, yes. If it did, well, fine. But this girl, Peggy. Well," he frowned, "she presents a problem, a problem in understanding. Even more so now because of what you've told me. I'm going to try and tell Catherine about her. She'll be as interested as I am. I think she'll understand her better than you do. And she'll understand my curiosity about her. I have a lot of curiosity, you know."

"And Catherine may have, too," Foley said, ironically. He felt sorry for McAlpine. His concern was touching. He was an extraordinary man. He never protested his friendship. In his redheaded bespectacled quiet way he could sit with a friend and console him simply by being with him. Foley had no interest in politics and so social ambitions; he believed only in the quiet dignity of his friendships, and no man with him ever felt alone. Worrying now about McAlpine, he said with a deprecating smile, "I thought you came to town to ride high. Don't you think you'd better get on your horse, Jim?"

"But I haven't got off."

"Jim, I'll tell you something. You certainly have the will to be ambitious."

"Go on, Chuck."

"But the will isn't enough."

"No?"

"No. You have the will, but I doubt if you have the temperament. An ambitious man can't have a set of feelings at odds with his will to advance on the target. Pin that in your hat, Jim. You can have it for nothing."

≈ ELEVEN ≈

The little balance of interests which McAlpine had achieved in his own mind helped him to believe that he was busy. He didn't notice himself pacing up and down in his room. He began to make some minor mistakes. He forgot to send out his laundry at the right hour. Having rung for the valet, he was told that he might get it done if he left it at the desk. He bundled it up in a laundry bag and took it down to the front desk and handed it to the clerk.

"What's this?" the clerk asked.

"My laundry."

"Really, Mr. McAlpine," the clerk said with a shocked air. "Not here. We don't take laundry here. I believe you want the porter's desk."

"Of course, of course," McAlpine apologized, his ears reddening. It had been his first violation of the Ritz diplomatic protocol which he had always observed so carefully.

Nor did he notice how he justified his absorbing interest in Peggy by telling himself he counted on Catherine's sharing this interest. She had telephoned, wanting him to have lunch with her and her father at their apartment: they were contemplating the purchase of an authentic Renoir, she said. He made up his mind, hurrying over to the Château, to ask Catherine to walk down Crescent Street after lunch and meet Peggy.

It was a reassuring luncheon. Mr. Carver told them that he was jogging Horton and soon would get some action. After lunch they went into the drawing room, where Jacques, the plump little French Canadian who was Mr. Carver's man, had adjusted the Renoir on the chesterfield at the right angle to catch the light from the window. They contemplated the painting learnedly. It was a study of a girl at a piano. They drew back a little, they moved closer, they cupped their chins in their hands and nodded.

"Tilt it forward a little, Jacques," Mr. Carver said irritably. "Isn't that a better light, Jim? No this way, a little more this way, Jacques."

All morning Jacques had been lifting the picture back and forth for Catherine and her friends, and now he looked tired and unhappy. Sad-eyed, he stood there tilting the picture wearily while Catherine, Jim, and Mr. Carver had a splendid discussion about Renoir's different periods. McAlpine was good at these discussions. He had a flair for conversations about paintings, wines, and cheeses.

"Jacques, could you hold the picture over there on the wall?" Catherine asked.

"Of course, madame."

"You'll never guess who the dealer got this Renoir from," Carver said.

"The Coulters had a Renoir," Catherine said. "I remember Alma saying they had a Renoir."

"Not Coulter. He doesn't need any money. It was young Sloane. You must have known young Sloane, Jim."

"Yes, of course. Economics Department, McGill."

"Jacques, let it tilt a little from the top. There! That's the boy," Mr. Carver said. The picture moved up and down slowly. "The colours blend beautifully with our walls, don't they, Catherine? Yes, young Sloane had to get rid of some of his father's treasures. Serves him right, too. These young radicals are good for everything but making a little money of their own." He moved back to appraise the window lighting. "A little more to the left, Jacques," he said, motioning. "Ah, that's better. Yes, Sloane's father had the most remarkable funeral in the history of Montreal, and along comes that son of his with blueprints for controlling everybody, sabotaging everything liberal his father stood for. Now he has to sell the family Renoir."

"Just the same, I like Bob Sloane," Catherine said as Jacques, furtively resting his arms, let the picture sink down on the wall.

"Humph! That young man is always out of line. A painter, though, has a great advantage," her father added, smiling. "He can always put people and things in the right place in the pattern."

"At heart I must be a painter," Catherine said with a helpless, good-natured shrug. Her suit coat was open, she stood with one hand on her hip, tall and erect with an easy tailored elegance; she had a glowing freshness and suggestion of charming candour, for she was at ease in her own home and, for the moment, at ease with McAlpine. She laughed and looked lovely and said, "You know what I'm like! If I'm in somebody's house and I see a rug on the floor at the wrong angle I have to straighten it, and if I see a picture on a wall a little askew there I am straightening it, too. I suppose I feel the same way about people. I'm fond of Bob Sloane. I'd like to shake him or do something about him. Jim, I suppose, thinks I should try painting instead. Eh, Jim?"

"If you're fond of the guy go to it," he said. But he felt uncomfortable that she could acknowledge with such innocent good will the flaw in her nature that made her want to tamper with other people's lives. He had been trying to believe he intended to tell her about Peggy; now he had found an excuse for a secret withdrawal: if he mentioned Peggy, she would see her simply as a picture on a wall that had to be straightened; she would want to straighten him out, too, in his attitude toward the girl. By rejecting and pitying Catherine's possessiveness he could believe he was free from the same trait himself.

"All right, Jacques, that's fine," Mr. Carver said. "Put the picture on the sofa for the time being." And Jacques, his arms aching, left quickly.

"I'll drive you anywhere you're going, Jim," Mr. Carver said affably.

"I'm only going back to the hotel. Doing anything now, Catherine?"

"I have a couple of girl friends calling for me in ten minutes," she said.

"That's my hard luck. I sort of counted on you coming out with me." McAlpine's tone was as disappointed as if he had really believed in the beginning that he intended to ask her to walk down Crescent with him and meet Peggy.

The snow was packed down into footpaths, and there was still no break in the leaden sky. Everything was still frozen hard. If Peggy were not working now, he thought she would be at home at this hour.

In the basement vestibule were three bells for the three apartments, each bell having a name under it, and the name Peggy Sanderson had been smudged by so many fingers it was almost indecipherable. He rang and went along with narrow hall to her room. He rapped and waited, then tried the door. It was open. "Peggy," he called, wondering uneasily if the door was always open.

Then he heard footsteps in the hall, shuffling uneven footsteps. A small unshaven man in a ridiculously long brown overcoat and a peak cap came toward him. He was at least sixty and he had a battered face and staring, stupid eyes. "What's the matter, ain't she in?" he asked, with a bad stutter.

"No, Miss Sanderson doesn't seem to be in," McAlpine said coldly.

"Jeez, ain't that too bad!" The little old man, crestfallen, blinked his eyes. From an apartment upstairs a male voice began to sing, "Loch Lomond... the bonny bonny baaaanks of Loch Lomond."

"Huh, listen to that bozo," the man in the long overcoat jeered. "A guy with a voice like that. Say, I'm Cowboy Lehman. Everybody knows me," he boasted. He was a well known moocher who ran little messages for everybody. And when McAlpine didn't recognize his name he looked incredulous. "Look at these," he said. "I brought her some swell Sunday editions." He drew from under his coat a parcel of newspapers he had picked up in some lunchroom, and tossed them at her bed. With a sigh and a woebegone shrug he said sorrowfully, "Jeez, I wish she was here, mister."

"Oh, I see, I see," McAlpine said awkwardly. He reached in his pocket for a fifty-cent piece. "Here. Miss Sanderson would want to give you something, I'm sure."

"Sure she would," the moocher grinned. "Well, I'm on my way. She'll be around. Just tell her the Cowboy dropped in." And he shuffled out.

Everybody, simply everybody knows her, McAlpine thought as he walked out himself. Good God, who does wander in through that open door? On the street he looked up and down hopefully, waited a few moments with his hands in his pockets and then began to walk briskly down to the corner and east along St. Catherine. He had a plan. He hurried to carry it out. Passing the newsstand at Peel where the petty gamblers stood offering amiable insults to the girls, he whistled lightheartedly. He was anticipating a quiet solitary satisfaction.

And with the good feeling came the ready thought: I know how to place her. Right in Montreal at McGill was stringy old baldheaded Fielding with his marbles-in-the-mouth accent, who had been at University College in Peggy's time and would have had her in his English classes and would know all about her. But he didn't stop to phone Fielding. Instead he quickened his pace, looking up at the sky. The clouds were exhausted; the city had its thick winter blanket on. At Phillips Square he glanced at the statue of King Edward VII and smiled; he and the King were old friends. The King looked very cold.

Cutting across the square, he tried to keep track of the distance he travelled south, making sure it was only a few blocks; then he turned east, and came to a church. But it was the big stone church, St. Patrick's. It was where the little old church ought to have been.

He approached a short, Napoleonic French Canadian. "I'm looking for a quaint little church around here," he explained. "Not like this one. Very simple. A touch of Gothic, a touch of Romanesque."

"Ah, yes," said the French Canadian. "Let's see now. There is a little old church along St. Catherine."

"No, it's not on St. Catherine."

"Wait then. The Bonsecours Church – the Mariners' Church with carvings. Everybody wants to see it. Take a taxi."

"No, this one is right around here."

"Ah, I have it. East along St. Catherine. Part of a convent – with a wax figure of little Thérèse of Lisieux in her coffin. Positively surrealistic."

"Thank you," McAlpine said, giving up, and they bowed to each other. He wandered around the neighbourhood, seeking corners and buildings he might remember. But he had missed the church and it bothered him. He had missed also the solitary satisfaction he had sought. And maybe it meant he would miss Peggy, too. If she had gone – with that door open to everybody – and if he couldn't find *her* either…

Profoundly disturbed, he hurried up to St. Catherine and took a taxi to the Crescent Street room. Without knocking, he opened the door. She was there by the stove. His relief and his thumping heart made it hard for him to speak. She was there, really there: and he was so glad he didn't notice she was wearing a suit of overalls such as women used to wear in munition plants during the war. It was only when she turned and looked at him that he became aware of her outfit and showed his astonishment.

❧ TWELVE ❧

"Oh, it's you," she said, and laughed.

"What's so funny?" he asked.

"You looked so stunned."

"Well, seeing you in that get-up—"

"Is that all?"

"I thought I had missed you."

"Why?"

"And maybe the fact, too, that you weren't at all surprised by my walking in on you."

"All kinds of people walk in on me," she said. "Now that you're here, sit down." When she had taken his coat she said, "Thanks for those snow boots, Jim. I've tried them on, and they fit beautifully."

"How did you know they were from me?"

"Who else would do anything like that? Come on, sit down. Haven't you ever seen a working girl before?"

"Sure, but you're no mechanic. What are you up to?"

"In a few minutes I'm going to work."

"In that outfit? Where?"

"A shoe polish and lighter fluid factory. I'm on the shift from four till midnight."

"Oh, my God!" He threw up his hands.

"You're comical. What does it matter where I work? I'm broke. I need money. And I'm tired of advertising agencies and so on."

He almost said, And maybe you can't get another job, maybe it's true you have special tastes, maybe people around town are starting to treat you as an outcast; but he checked himself, fearing she might think that he, too, was withdrawing from her. "Just the same, you make quite a picture in that outfit," he said. "Have you any paper?" On the bureau was some letter paper; he took a piece and sat down at the table.

"What are you going to do?" she asked.

"Just sit there. I'm going to draw you."

"Really. Are you any good?"

"If you don't like it you don't have to buy it," he said, smiling. "How about helping me with a little background? What do you do in the factory?"

"I'm a crimper."

"A crimper. What in hell's a crimper?"

"I crimp the cans that have been filled with fluid."

"And where's the factory?"

"It's a rickety old place down in St. Henri by the canal. And how that place stinks of the cheap perfume they put in the fluid!" she said, laughing. She began to talk gaily. At last she had found a place where she was sure she could be happy. The first day in the factory, she thought she would never get used to the crimping machine – it had a strange mechanical power over her, the cans coming relentlessly toward her on the belt and her snatching at them and her foot pounding rhythmically on the heavy machine; but on the second day she was used to it and could look around at the others, and was reminded of her first days at school, when the faces of the other children looked rough and lopsided.

It was all noise and cursing and laughter with the girls being scolded by Mrs. Maguire, who had charge of them, and Mrs. Maguire being scolded by old Papa Francoeur, the foreman.

"At first I don't think they welcomed me," she said. "I guess I didn't look right. But when people are poor they have to accept each other sooner or later, don't they?" They let her eat with them at noon time. They all ate in the factory, sitting in a little circle presided over by old Papa Francoeur with his beard, a lusty old French Canadian who had pinched her behind. It was his privilege to pinch all the girls.

"I see," Jim said unhappily, without looking up from his drawing.

"No, you don't. You just don't know Papa Francoeur," she said calmly. The first day at lunch no one had spoken to her; but next day Mrs. Maguire offered her a cup of tea and said she might turn out to be the best crimper they had had all year, and the French girls, who had pretended they spoke no English, thawed a little. "And you know what Mrs. Maguire said? She said, 'You're a Catholic, aren't you?' And when I asked her what made her so sure she said, 'I can tell by your eyes,' and I laughed and the other girls winked at me. They knew I wasn't. I think they were convinced I liked them, and before long they were telling me about themselves. It's a good thing to have someone around you can explain yourself to... You know, Jim, each one of those girls has a secret ambition that tells a lot about them."

With Mrs. Maguire it was a desperate hope that soon she would have enough money to take a trip to Niagara Falls, because she and her husband had never had a honeymoon and when they had first got married they had planned such a trip. And with Yvette Ledoux, well, there was an unhappy girl! She was always planning to take a job in another factory. The factory ahead where some other girl worked always looked beautiful, but she couldn't move on because her husband, whom she didn't love, had T.B. and wouldn't live and wouldn't die and she had to support him. But on the other hand Hélène Martin liked the factory; she liked it because it was a battleground where she could fight all day long with the other girls. And another kid, too, Michèle Savard, liked it because she was earning and saving and soon would be able to walk out of her crowded family and have her own cheap room in the St. Henri quarter.

But her happy eloquence, as she revealed how fully she must have made herself available to the factory workers, bothered McAlpine. He had a hard time concentrating on his drawing. "Wait a minute, Peggy," he said. "Are you sure it's safe for you down there?"

"Safe? What do you mean?"

"Well, coming home at such late hours."

It was true that loafers hung around the railroad yards, she admitted, and on her first trip home a man in a peak cap and a short jacket, a man with a wooden leg, had followed her over the bridge, whistling at her and trying to catch up to her with his stiff rolling gait. But since that night she had had company. A young shipper, an eighteen-year-old kid with red hair named Willie Foy, wanted to walk her home because he had picked her out to be his girl, but he had to yield the right to old Papa Francoeur, who was sixty and had heart trouble – and what a droll character old Papa was with his gleeful talk about her shape! On the hill he gasped for breath; he had lots of lust but was afraid of a heart attack; his legs were always swollen from climbing the factory stairs, but he was in debt and couldn't retire, and the only place he retired from, she said, her eyes bright with amusement, was the door to her house. There he was full of apologies, wanting her to understand he was still a robust lover but was simply all tired out.

"Very amusing," McAlpine muttered, thinking, she makes herself available to these people and lets them think they can do things with her... Filled with jealous resentment, he pushed the drawing away from him and blurted out, "You can't stay in that stinking factory, Peggy."

"Yes, I can, Jim," she said evenly. "You see, I want to stay there."

"But you've got education, training, refinement. It's all wrong."

"Not to me, Jim. I like these people. To you it's like riding third class. Well, I find that more interesting usually than riding first class. That's all. How about the drawing? How did it turn out?"

He watched while she picked up the drawing and studied it closely, then went to the mirror and looked at herself. "You're pretty good, Jim," she admitted. "It's me all right. Me in overalls."

"Here. Give it to me. You need to be named, since we know at last what you are," he said ironically, and he wrote under the drawing, "Peggy, the Crimper."

"I like that, too," she laughed. "Give it to me and I'll pin it over my bureau." She fixed the drawing on the wall and saluted it. Now the smell of coffee filled the room, and she got two cups from the shelf.

"Peggy," he began, sitting down on the bed, "aren't you being a little pigheaded?"

"I knew it – I knew it," she said with a sigh. "That's why I told you the other night to stop pulling at my coattails, professor. Now, let go."

"For one thing, I know why you've lost your job."

"Oh, so Foley told you," she said sharply.

"He said you didn't have your mind on your work, Peggy."

"What a silly story!" She thrust her chin out. "I know why they let me go, Jim. I was waiting for it. The root of the whole thing is right there. Do you take your coffee black, like I do?"

"All right, Peggy. No sugar."

"Oh, that patient tone of yours, Jim! If you'd only stop being so mild and injured. If you'd stop making me feel I'm abusing you!" She sat down with her cup of coffee. "I don't want to abuse you, Jim. It's just that – well, you're so damned orthodox. And yet, I don't know." She frowned, her head on one side as she regarded him. "I suppose that's not being fair to you."

"Are you sure it isn't?" he asked encouragingly.

"Since I know what you will say won't impress me, why do I like the way you say it?" she asked.

"I don't know."

"Look. Don't you know anybody else in this town?"

"Dozens of people. I know the Carvers—"

"Ah, yes, daughter Catherine. She'd be just right for you, Jim."

"Oh, so you can be malicious! Good. Well, I also know Angela Murdock. In fact we're going to her Sunday night party."

"Angela Murdock. Well, well, well," she said merrily. "Of course you'd be at Angela's, surrounded by the city's men of good will. You see, I've met Mrs. Murdock myself, Jim. Oh, that woman with her beautiful civilized comfortable tolerance!"

"I have respect for Angela Murdock," he said. "I don't agree with you at all."

"Don't you?" she asked. He had reddened and jerked his head back in a magisterial rebuke, and he looked so solemn that she began to giggle; she burst out laughing. It was the first time he had ever heard her laugh out loud. Her face puckered up, her eyes danced, her breasts shook in the kind of laughter he had been wanting to hear from her; it was so gay and free and infectious that it didn't matter that she was laughing at him or at Mrs. Murdock. "Oh, Lord, I'm getting a stitch in my side!" she said. Then he started to laugh. She bent over and then straightened up, holding her side. But when her grabbed her lightheartedly and swung her around, shaking her and gasping, "This childish!" she started to double up again, and he didn't want it to end.

"Well, to think I could get such a laugh out of Angela Murdock!" she said when she got her breath at last.

"I love hearing you laugh," he said. "But how can you when you've lost your job – when you're stuck down in some stinking factory? How can you be so happy?"

"Well," she began, frowning and reflecting. "maybe it's a feeling in myself these days I've learned to trust."

"What kind of feeling, Peggy?"

"I think it's my whirling-away feeling."

"Whirling away?"

"Yes. And it's always led me in the right direction."

"Since when? I mean starting from where?"

"You mean the first time I was sure of it?"

"Yes."

"When I first left home."

"Does that mean that you had a quarrel with your father?"

"Not exactly," she said, slowly. "We didn't quarrel. We sort of – well, reached an understanding."

"An understanding about what?"

"A lot happened to my father after those small-town days. I suppose he learned how to get along with important people; and you have to do it if you're going to be an important preacher. Anyway, he was called from one church to another, and now he's pretty highly regarded in Hamilton. Influential people go to his church. A broker named Joe Eldrich, who was the chairman of the city hospital board, a broker, you know, made some investments for him." With a shrug she added, "How did you think I got to college?"

"But this understanding…"

"Do you remember the Johnson family?"

"And the old house. Sure."

"Well, one summer, after my third year at college, I was home and one of the Johnson girls, Sophie, wrote to my father. She had come to the city wanting to train to be a nurse. She wanted my father to help her get into the hospital. It seems there had recently been some scandal about admitting Negroes for nursing training. At the time I didn't realize that the letter might have embarrassed my father, I was so pleased to hear that one of the Johnson kids had got some education. So I wrote Sophie that night, and a couple of days later I met her in a restaurant, and in no time we were good friends again. She was a smart, clean, straightforward girl. She told me that Jock — remember Jock? — was playing semipro baseball in Cleveland. Well, Sophie had sized up the local situation. She knew that if she didn't have some pull she wouldn't get into the hospital. Don't think I was naïve about it: I wasn't. I knew what I was up against. But with Sophie there smiling at me with such confidence and pride in our friendship I marched her right down to Mr. Eldrich's office — you know, the broker, the chairman of the hospital board. He was shocked, I suppose, when I said I was counting on him. He concealed his feelings awfully well though. Making my point clearer, I told him I was taking Sophie home to dinner.

"And I did, too, and my father was even more disarming than Mr. Eldrich. He wondered why a smart girl like Sophie would want to bother with anything as tedious as nursing, but he was sympathetic, and then he retired to his study — to meditate, I suppose; and soon he had a caller. Mr. Eldrich joined my father in the study, and Sophie and I waited; and I remember the way she kept watching me. When Mr. Eldrich left, my father called me into the study. The poor man had evidently had a rough time. He said, 'If only Sophie were a light mulatto – if only she weren't coal-black!' and then he talked about the little compromises that had to be made for the sake of harmony in the flock.

"Sophie was waiting for me, and I said, 'You're just too black, Sophie.' It was a cruel thing to say; but I felt cruel, and I was sure it was the way Sophie wanted me to feel. I remember how she looked at me before she hurried away. I watched her running away down the street.

"I went out and walked around myself," she said. There was a curious hardness in her voice, and sometimes she glanced at McAlpine, wondering why she felt compelled to tell these things. "It was raining, and I stayed out and caught a chill, and I got a fever that lasted three days; and when my head cleared my father was sitting beside the bed. Sitting with his eyes closed and he head bowed. 'Were you praying for me?' I asked, not meaning to hurt him, but because I thought I saw his lips moving. 'Why did you say that?' he said, and he looked haggard and miserable, and he started to cry. It's awful to see your own father cry. I felt so sorry for him. For some reason I remembered how he used to fumble with his watch chain. I wanted to comfort him. 'I can't pray,' he said. And then he choked a little and said, 'I haven't believed in God for years.'

"He knew what he was and knew how he had been corrupted and – well, we shared the understanding. I knew I could only make him more unhappy by staying at home and reminding him of things. Then it happened; while I was hating his respectable world for what it had done to him, I felt this lightness of spirit; I felt myself whirling away from things he had wanted, whirling in an entirely different direction. I left him. It was right. I've always trusted that feeling, and I've got it now that I'm down in that factory. Do you see what I mean, Jim?"

"The Johnsons," he said softly, as if he hadn't heard her question. "That tumble-down house. I guess I understand." And he pictured the bare house in the field, heard the laughter of the Johnson children in the flow of their unpredictable, disorderly happiness. "Peggy," he said, "all this makes you sound pretty much alone, but Foley tells me you had a – that there's a fellow in love with you. A Henry Jackson or something like that."

"That's right. And I don't think you'd like Henry."

"No?"

"You probably like people who like you, and Henry would not like you, Jim. By the way, he left New York last night. He's a commercial artist. Very intellectual."

"Does he object to your Negro friends?"

"Henry is very emancipated," she said, smiling.

"If I could only prove to you it won't work out, Peggy! A good heart can't smash a brick wall. This false idealism—"

"It's working out fine," she said, cutting him off. "And, anyway, there are a lot of things I have to see for myself."

"Peggy," he said, taking her hand, "in all of this I'm a stranger, more and more of a stranger; but in another way you're a stranger, too, if you'd only see it. When I'm with you I feel – well, I feel that neither of us should be here at all."

"At least I shouldn't be here." She stood up. "I should be on my way to work. I'll be ten minutes late, and they'll dock me about thirty cents." She got her snow boots and put them on, and then a short dark blue jacket, and a handkerchief around her head, and started toward the door. "Come on. Let's go."

Outside, the cold wind blew the snow against their faces. Taking a last puff at her cigarette, she flicked it neatly out on the road about twenty feet away.

"Can you do it that far every time?" he asked solemnly.

"I can flick it ten feet farther than that," she said.

He nodded. "Well, I'll be seeing you, Peggy."

"Sure, I'll be seeing you," she said.

She went down the street toward St. Catherine looking like an inconspicuous factory worker in her blue overalls and yellow bandanna handkerchief; and McAlpine, deeply discontented, watched her go. He stood there, frowning, close to an insight; then he got it. The little Negro section in Montreal had become for her the happy and fabulous Johnson family; and if the Johnsons, knowing her, could love and respect her, why shouldn't the Negroes down on St. Antoine? If only he could talk with some of them! Perhaps he could get Foley's friend to go down there with him...

✺ THIRTEEN ✺

Milton Rogers, the big jovial apple-cheeked photographer, lived in an apartment on the corner of Hope and Dorchester a hundred yards from a monastery whose tolling bells woke him every morning at five o'clock. He was married to a big-boned, dark-eyed girl, a painter, and he liked wearing loose tweed jackets and slacks and shirts with lowcut collars. He had the air of a rich man, but he couldn't save any money. At forty-two he had the best collection of jazz records in Montreal and a social conscience he was proud of; but it didn't prevent him from having a good time: he could go to the most expensive nightclubs and look around and say, "Isn't all this lousy! But it's the system, and I'm just caught in the system." He acted as a one-man reception committee for distinguished Negro musicians who came to Montreal.

Late that night when McAlpine called at his apartment, he was drinking Irish whisky with two friends who shared his political convictions, two newspapermen in double-breasted brown suits. They looked alike and were both exuberant. McAlpine had to have a drink before Rogers would leave with him, taking a taxi down to St. Antoine. The café manager, who knew Rogers, took them to a small table at the side of the dance floor. Peggy wasn't in the café. It was about half past one, the floor show had begun, and McAlpine, watching the performers, tried to discover in them an attractiveness, a magic warmth that might have appealed to her. He couldn't do it; it hurt him to think of her smiling at the coarse jokes.

"Do you know Peggy Sanderson?" he asked.

"Oh, sure," Rogers said without taking his eyes off the mulatto singer. "She comes around here a lot."

"What do you make of her?"

"I dislike her," he said. "I dislike her attitude. I can't talk to her any more. I think she's ignorant. A person should have some scientific understanding of the Negro's lot in America. It's economics or it's nothing. It's a matter of jobs. Only certain kinds of jobs are available to Negroes. They can't get their share of jobs. They're in an economic ghetto, which of course forces them to live in some cheap section. But if the jobs were open to them – I despise this kissing the leper stuff. It messes up the whole situation. Fundamentally, it's harmful. What good is it going to do the Negroes to have this Peggy come along and say, 'Everything I have is yours.' Particularly when she has only one thing. I no longer go for little Peggy myself," he said in a fine impersonal tone. "In fact I could slap her. Besides, she goes for Negroes, and God knows how many! I'd be scared to sleep with her myself."

"Would you?" McAlpine asked. "Are you sure she's not just – well, a friend of all of them – like you?"

"I don't get from them what she gets," Rogers said coarsely. "For another thing they still like to have me around here. And they don't like having her around."

"I think you're mistaken."

"Am I?" Rogers looked surprised. "Well, the show's over. Why don't we ask the band leader to sit down with us? You'll like him, Elton Wagstaffe. A great guy. Ask him what he thinks. He's got a great little band there. He's been right through the mill. Played with Eddie Condon and Ellington and probably knew Bix too." Calling a waiter, he asked him to speak to the band leader; and in a few minutes, Wagstaffe came to the table and sat down with them.

Wagstaffe was a quiet, patient, dark-skinned man who would never be surprised at anything that happened in a nightclub. For years in the good jazz days he had worked in Memphis, St. Louis, and Chicago; now he wandered around picking up a living in these small Negro nightclubs and hoping for a jazz revival. Polite and rather indifferent, he obviously felt friendly and close to Rogers.

He joked about how the band was developing and they agreed that no one would get rich these days playing jazz. McAlpine waited anxiously for Rogers to mention Peggy Sanderson. Instead, Rogers said, "Elton, my friend here was eyeing your canary."

"Me?" McAlpine asked, looking startled. "Well, under the spotlight she looked golden. Her shoulders looked golden."

"A pretty kid, yes," the band leader said. Standing up, he beckoned to the singer, who was going toward the bar.

McAlpine quickly ordered a drink for her. Without the yellow glare of the spotlight, her skin was greyer, the golden lustre of the flesh all gone. He praised her voice. He wanted to create for himself the feeling Peggy might have had for a Negro. The girl began to answer his questions in a thin dainty voice. She was very polite and sounded like an unprotected, helpless little girl. Gradually her brown softness and the richness of her skin began to charm him. Yes, I could get used to her, he admitted to himself. I'd always feel strange with her, but it would be a novel sensation. That soft shadowed flesh. And the charm of novelty... My God – if that's the appeal for Peggy!

The little mulatto said that she was leaving in the morning for Chicago: one splendid engagement after another awaited her. Even Café Society in New York had beckoned to her. But in the meantime she had an engagement with a gentleman at the bar. Rising, she shook hands with McAlpine and thanked him sincerely, though she didn't know why she was thanking him. When she had gone, the band leader said amiably, "You've come a couple of nights too late, my friend... She's on her way tomorrow. If you had come a couple of nights ago you might have made time."

"Oh, I see," McAlpine said. Even this quiet Negro band leader couldn't believe a man would be interested only in being friendly with a pretty mulatto – he would want to sleep with her. The normal supposition, McAlpine supposed, just as everyone assumed that Peggy wanted to sleep with her Negro friends. "I merely thought she sang very well," he said uncomfortably.

"McAlpine's a friend of Peggy Sanderson's," Rogers said.

"Is that a fact?" the band leader asked, his eyes no longer amiable. "A pretty kid, isn't she? You get along good with her, eh?"

"I think so. She has a lot of admiration – and real sympathy – for your race, Mr. Wagstaffe. I've never met anyone who's a better friend."

"Yeah, a friend," the band leader admitted. The word "friend," which was used by the Negroes to describe a sympathetic white person, had worried him. Usually he had a soft, easy flow of words. Now the right words wouldn't come. A little beer had been spilled on the table. Beckoning to the waiter, he had him come and wipe it up carefully. The glossy black-topped table had to be dry and spotless before he could choose the right words. "It's a fact, Mr. McAlpine, that my race needs all its friends," he said. "Rogers here is a real friend. Yes, maybe that little girl, Peggy, is a friend, too. Now I don't know what to say."

Not wanting to offend McAlpine, he sized him up carefully. While he was doing so McAlpine thought, When he suggested that I might be successful with his little singer it didn't matter whether I was a friend or not.

"Quiet and like a little lady, the way Peggy sits, eh?" Wagstaffe murmured, half to himself. "All by herself she sits, mister. At a table over there by the corner, sweet and round and eager like a flower somebody ought to pick. I mean just waiting to be picked. All alone and yet not so far away. Very still and yet kind of jumping right at you, eh, Mr. McAlpine? She don't get drunk, she don't even dance, she don't even clap her hands loud. She's just here like that with us. But all my boys knows she's here and kind of waiting. Yes, kind of quiet and waiting – for what?"

"I saw you sitting with her one night," McAlpine said.

"Yes, I guess you did."

"I noticed something else that night, Mr. Wagstaffe. You saw her sitting there and you looked as if you didn't want to sit with her, something was bothering you, and then you joined her and then – well, you felt good. Is that right?"

"He's got the big eye, eh?" Wagstaffe said to Rogers. "What did you say he did for a living?"

"I couldn't help noting it," McAlpine said.

"Well, it's a fact," Wagstaffe said reluctantly. "But I've made up my mind now and I don't sit with her no more."

"Oh? Why?"

"She's lousing up my band. Sooner or later she'll make trouble."

"It's not putting her in a very good light, is it, Mr. Wagstaffe?"

"No? Well, listen."

"Go ahead."

"I'm a Negro musician. I've been around a lot in my good days. Lots of little white girls have come my way." He frowned; the words wouldn't come easily, his thoughts turning inward as he groped to get his feeling right, not only for McAlpine, but for himself.

As a rule, he said, the white girls who came his way were not hard to place, for the obvious ones were crazy about jazz music and thought they couldn't understand it unless they got close to the Negro, and with most of them it was just mental. You didn't get excited about them any more than you did about those white girls with sympathy for the race who wanted to hold discussions and do field work like social service workers; and if they were real friends you liked them, and if they didn't make trouble you liked them anyway. You had nothing to lose liking them. Same with the white girls who were all political conviction and full of the class war and wanted to marry a Negro to make a point to satisfy themselves it could be done and the workers of the world could unite. But the white girls you had to watch were the odd ones who were restless and good-looking, tired of something and wanting something new that looked different and out of line. A coloured man watched himself with these women and was always suspicious, asking himself what they were after and waiting for them to make the nasty little break. With such girls, if the relationship gets intimate, you still watch, hiding the old fear, the knowledge, for even if she rolls an eye and you move in she's apt to squawk loud and outraged, and you want to run fast and break something, and you feel lonely and crazy. They were a nuisance because they were only fooling around like kids at a circus, and they hurt you deep inside; like the time when he was in Paris with a jazz band and the band was taken up by some rich people and they were at this party with these white girls, and he had played his horn a little and they were coaxing him to play some more, but he had a blister on his lip, and he was sitting cross-legged on the floor, and this little blonde came over kneeling beside him, coaxing him. "Oh, come on, Smokey Joe," she said, and she gave him a slap on the forehead. Well, he could have bust her, he was so mad. "Look out: you're not in the United States now, you're in Paris!" he said. She had made him feel like a dog, like an ape; he wanted to bust her, but instead the party broke up. It was not like that, of course, with those little white girls who came around like stuffing on a plate. They were ignorant. You tell them love is a pork chop and they eat it, and nobody gives a damn. But Montreal was a good town; things weren't so bad in Montreal, and the Brooklyn ball team made no mistake when they first broke in their coloured ball players with the Montreal team. It was important that they picked on Montreal. It's a town where there are a lot of minorities, but the French like the Negro ball players and give them a hand, and if a coloured boy kept his head, and kept his eyes closed a little and didn't want to go to too many places he didn't get into any trouble. The eyes didn't have to be closed too tight and the Negro ball players swinging around the circuit with the team were glad to get back to Montreal.

Then he smiled to himself, reflecting. He was quiet, patient and wonderfully unhurried. He would shrug with his left shoulder, and now that he had in his mind some sardonic thought his tone, when he spoke, was still mild and uncomplaining.

Maybe a girl like Peggy thought she was doing something all by herself, he said. Not that a girl couldn't do something all by herself, he grinned, enjoying his own sense of irony. Did they know Jill? Oh, sure, they must know Jill. Well, Rogers knew Jill even if McAlpine didn't. A mulatto floating around the night spots near Peel and St, Catherine, really good-looking, tall and silky and well spoken and not ignorant, a semipro. Well, the business manager of one of the visiting ball teams made a play for Jill and so he stayed a couple of nights with her and thought she was terrific and got hilarious and phoned all around saying he made a mistake opposing the clubs' using coloured ball players. "From now on he's all for them. Sure, one person can do big things, eh?" he asked cynically. "Poor little Jill. Maybe she lays down her golden body like one of those martyrs, bringing the races together; but the trouble is, Jill's golden body is like a race track." He laughed, but his laughter didn't put Peggy out of his mind.

So Peggy came along. She came along that first night when he had walked up the street with her and they had gone bowling and then sat talking in her room. That night he knew she wasn't like any of these other white girls he had been talking about. "The way I felt that night was something for the book," he said quietly. "There she was, sweet and gentle and offering something. It gave me a wallop – like a surprise. It was for me; she was offering it to me, and it was like being hopped up and yet peaceful, and I didn't have to watch myself and be scared of that bad break coming. It was there for me. I could keep it and nurse it along and have it when I wanted it all for myself. Yes, just for me. Just for me," he said softly. "Only I made a little mistake," he said, not complaining, not sad, just trying to be truthful. "Soon I see her floating around the neighbourhood. I see her coming around the other joints, sitting around the little taverns where we sit sometimes, or I see her stopping on the street with some of my boys, or some kid, or some porter or some little old guy, and she's giving them the treatment. Maybe I mean they're getting the treatment – in the way she offers herself. So they're taking it, or figuring when they'll move in and take it. So I'd say to myself maybe she was just a friend like Rogers here is a friend. Maybe it's the big church glow she's giving, so I try to talk to her about the problems, the Negro in the White world, the big intellectual talk, the brotherhood talk, the routine, but she won't listen. She don't give the slightest damn for it. She won't think about it. She makes me feel that thinking about it is bad. She don't believe in it. It hits me then that she don't believe in anything. But there she is – offering something.

"The trouble starts somewhere in there," he said, pushing his glass across the table and concentrating on his clenched hands. "I mean the resentment. You think she offers it just for you, and then you see it's no more for you than the next guy. A bum is a bum in my race as well as yours. A girl ought to have some discrimination, not make it cheap, not for every bum; you can't just throw that stuff around. Sure, you ought to be able to. That easy affection with that wonderful respect reminding you – well, like kids in the sun – the days when – well, before we all got wised up, eh? So you see her standing on the street giving some no-good lavatory attendant the same glow she gave you, and you want to push him in the mouth because you know he don't rate it. So she sets you against the little guys and maybe the little guys against you. That's bad. If we could all agree to respect her? Okay. But you know human nature as well as I do. Guys white or coloured are wise to each other and don't have that much respect for each other. We don't trust each other, do we? Well, it hits you she's like she is because she's full of love. So that old devil inside you gets to work. If she's full of this quiet love you figure maybe somebody's filling her. Maybe it's Ziggy Wallace, maybe it's Joe Thomas getting it from her good because they knew how to take it and you, like a chump, maybe the only chump, sat around respecting her. So you start watching, suspicious and watching, all the boys suspicious of each other and ready to pop, because if it's going around each guy wants if all for himself.

"Maybe she's innocent, like you say. Well, if we were all kids— But she's a woman. I can't look at her like I did when I was a kid. *Is* she so innocent though? Tell me, please. Look deep

in her eyes. Something hidden there, eh? But maybe not hidden
for some guy you know. So you want to bust loose with her, but
you can't do it; you want to get drunk with her and sleep all day,
but you can't do it. I figure it like this. She's against something.
Yeah, she's maybe against everything in the rule book; she's
throwing her stuff at the rule book, but maybe that's not so
good. Everything busts wide open when there's no rule book.

"And maybe it's the women around here that know this best.
Don't get it wrong. She's the same with the women of my race
as she is with the men, only it works out different. You know
what women are like. Six out of ten get tired and sour. It's all
poor and cheap living for them around here. The Negro women
around here can't get no dough anyway; and maybe they get fat
too quick and, just like the white women, five out of ten don't
do so well with their husbands and get sour and not nice with
them any more, and they're tired. Then they see their husbands
talking or sitting or chewing the fat or getting a skinful of little
Peggy, the husband there all loosened up and soft and taking
easy what's bright and hard to get, and so a wife hates Peggy's
guts. They think they know. Being women, I mean, they know
what's going on, they think – and they hate her guts; what
comes from Peggy doesn't come from them no more.

"Now don't get it too wrong. I'm not saying it's the same
with all women. There's right girls with right guys, right girls
sure of their own stuff and bright and happy in the world, and
they don't mind Peggy at all. Peggy's okay with them while
there's no sourness in them.

"But you see the situation, eh? These other wives turning
sour sit around resentful-like, wanting to beat Peggy's brains
out. It's no good I tell you. It means trouble.

"And the boys sit around watching each other and suspicious and sore; watching each other. Maybe each guy by him-

self would leave her alone, or believe it was beautiful having her with us just the way she is; but he don't trust the next guy. They figure they know each other. Maybe Wilson watches me, and I watch Ziggy, and I know I had it in my hand and I didn't keep it. Mind you, I ain't saying I laid her. Only I'm sure I could have laid her. Let me make up my mind tonight, and I could find her and lay her. If it would do any good. I'd want to own it, have it for myself. I guess other boys feel the same way, and you get a little tired waiting for the nod from her, and that's the trouble; and that's where there could be big trouble, and that's why I say it's no good having her around here, being against something so much, and with the boys suspicious of each other, and some of those wives knowing how to use a beer bottle."

"These women," McAlpine said uneasily. "Are any of them around tonight?"

"Let's see," Wagstaffe said, glancing around. "Well, look over there." He nodded in the direction of the bandstand at a table to the left. "That's Lily. She happens to be Wilson's wife. There he is sitting with her."

Lily Wilson, a heavy Negress in a copper-tinted satin dress, was sitting with the trumpet player and a young Negress with patent leather hair. Lily had a sullen, unhappy face. She was utterly motionless with a stillness that had silenced her husband They were a man and wife being together only because they were man and wife and could no longer find the words to pretend they were close together and so were afraid of the stillness between them.

"You could go over to her, Mr. McAlpine," Wagstaffe drawled, "and tell her Miss Peggy is a real friend of our race. I wouldn't bother myself, because – well, like the others, she thinks I've had a skinful of sleeping with Peggy myself, and she'd tell you she knows her husband better than you do, and he wants his skinful, too. Let's see what other boys are with their wives," he said, looking around again.

"Never mind," McAlpine said.

"I've been levelling with you, Mr. McAlpine, about the way I see Peggy now, understand?"

McAlpine, who had slumped in his chair, didn't answer; his eyes were melancholy. In the chatter of a hundred voices his silence was painful.

"I'm only trying to picture the situation," Wagstaffe apologized. "You see, there's another angle, Mr. McAlpine. By this time all the customers, the regulars, know Peggy. She sits there, as I say, dainty and alone in her little white blouse, making the boys come tumbling at her, and sort of queening it over the customers, see? I think by this time some of them hate her guts, too. The womenfolk figure she's moving in on them, operating. I like this town, Mr. McAlpine, and this spot here is a good one, not a hell of a lot of money in it, mind you, but the band's a cooperative set-up and it's a living, and so I wouldn't want any trouble."

"No trouble. No," McAlpine said. Every word had hurt and humiliated him, and he looked around the café. "The Johnson family," he said half to himself with a sardonic smile. "The great big happy Johnson family."

"What?"

"Nothing. A private joke," he said, smiling mechanically. "I get the point," he went on. "I know why you're talking to me. I'd like to oblige you, but it's too difficult."

"Not if you're her friend, Mr. McAlpine."

"But if I tell her to keep away from here, well, you know what will happen, Mr. Wagstaffe. Her chin will come out and she'll say I'm prejudiced. She'll say I'm cheapening your good feeling and hers, too. What shall I say to that, Mr. Wagstaffe?"

"Now don't get me wrong, friend," Wagstaffe protested.

"Then why not tell her yourself to keep away?"

"Because I can't bear to insult her," the band leader admitted reluctantly. "It would hurt me inside to insult a white friend when I've got nothing on her."

"Isn't it wonderful!" McAlpine said with a bitter laugh that startled Wagstaffe. "A girl who can't help being the same with everybody. It's fantastic, isn't it, Mr. Wagstaffe?" he asked softly. "People who think one way have an itch to spoil her because she stands for something else. And what's really comical is that we aren't hating people around here for being as vicious as they are, we're resenting her for being what she is. It is comical, isn't it, Mr. Wagstaffe?"

"So it is. So it is," the band leader admitted uneasily. "But look, if you speak to her, give me a little break, will you, Mr. McAlpine? Don't say I said anything. Believe me, I'm not stupid. You and she can make me feel I'm prejudiced. Good God, it leaves me trying to keep my race segregated. That's why I haven't got the guts to insult her. I'd end up hating myself. And believe me there's enough hate as it is jumping around this joint." Leaning back, he smiled. "Well, it's time to play again. Anything you boys would like to hear?"

"Play 'Ain't Misbehavin'," Rogers said with a neat touch of irony.

"Okay. 'Ain't Misbehavin'' it is," the band leader said as he shook hands warmly with McAlpine. "Understand, I don't like talking that way about a friend," he said. And he left them and circled the dance floor to the bandstand.

"Well, there you have it, McAlpine," Rogers said.

"Other white girls come down here," McAlpine protested. "I've seen them here alone."

"Sure. Tramps. Obvious tramps."

"Well—"

"But Peggy isn't an obvious tramp, McAlpine."

"There's the root of the matter," McAlpine said. "Why is everybody so damned eager to prove she's a tramp? So everybody can feel more comfortable and forget their own stinking trampishness? And aren't you overlooking something? Don't you notice that Wagstaffe admits he didn't sleep with her? He thinks he could do it. Well, I know what he means. He thinks she wouldn't resist, and yet he had to leave her as she was. He's black and I'm white, but we were brothers in wanting to let her stay as she is. But we all suspect each other. And Wagstaffe is suspecting the trumpet player."

"I don't know," Rogers answered. "I knew one little white girl around here who was a first-class tramp with these boys and nobody held it against her. But they know Peggy has no right to be a tramp. Say, listen to that band tonight. Good old Elton. I've never heard them as good."

His face brightened with delight, he forgot all about Peggy Sanderson and raised his heels off the floor and swayed his knees, keeping time to the music. But McAlpine turned and sought for one face among all the black and white faces in that smoke-filled room that would express kindliness and generosity and concern for a girl like Peggy. But by this time many of the patrons were drunk and noisy. The women, black and white, were loosened up and excited, and the men watched and made their little plans.

All these faces blurred into the sullen dark face of the trumpet player's wife. McAlpine forgot his own sensible unprejudiced attitude toward all coloured people and his rational good will; he forgot that they were working people out for an evening and no more malevolent than any white group in the other cheap cafés in other sections of the town. He dreaded what might happen to Peggy if ever there was any trouble over her. His heart began to pound, and when he reached for his glass his hand trembled. He avoided Rogers' eyes. He was afraid of having him discover his inexplicable unhappiness.

He became a prey to a mysterious sense of urgency. He could see all these people who disliked her circling around her in a primitive dance, hemming her in, making it impossible for her to draw back while they waited to destroy her. But he could prevent it, he thought with a strange exaltation. He was called upon to be always at Peggy's side, persuading her, then taking her by the hand and leading her out of these places where she did not belong and into the places where she would glow with a singleness of love which would bring her happiness and not destruction; and in the places where he would lead her they would share more of the innocent lazy happiness he had caught a glimpse of the day he had walked with her through the snow to see the old church.

"Well, that's about all, Jim. Have you had enough?" Rogers asked. "I'm kind of sleepy myself."

"So am I. Let's go," McAlpine said, though he was not sleepy at all.

Outside, the wind came driving down through the underpass in a monstrous funnelled blast; as they huddled together in the doorway the hard snow bit into their necks and faces. There were no gaily swooping snow ploughs down there around dimly lighted St. Antoine. A taxi came along, and Rogers offered to drop McAlpine off at the Ritz. Rogers lay back in the taxi. With a yawn he invited McAlpine to come up to his place and have dinner some night. Soon they were at the corner of Sherbrooke and the entrance to the Ritz, where the snow swirled in gusts against the closed storm doors. When McAlpine was getting out of the taxi, Rogers said, "Oh, by the way, I intended to tell you,

McAlpine. That trumpet player, Wilson, isn't exactly an Uncle Tom, you know."

"No? What do you mean?" McAlpine asked, one foot still on the running board.

"They tell me when he gets high he's a violent guy. Dangerous with a knife. Hanging around here because he can't go back to Memphis. Cut up someone down there."

"Really?"

"Sure. And if Peggy keeps on refusing to concentrate on him—"

Too shocked to speak, McAlpine grabbed at the rim of his Homburg as the wind whipped at it, and the snow blowing in the open taxi door began to powder Roger's knee.

"But, for that matter, that very dear friend of hers she likes to brag about is no Uncle Tom either – I mean the golden-voiced Joe Thomas."

"Joe Thomas?"

"Oh, she'd have to take you by the hand to meet *him*. Her very special stuff. Say," Rogers said with a laugh, "I'm freezing to death. So long."

"So long," McAlpine said, and he entered the hotel.

In the lobby, the charwoman was swabbing a spot on the floor near the elevator, while the night clerk, with his elbows on the desk, his eyes full of sleep, watched her. McAlpine had to tap on the desk and point to his box, which contained a letter. The clerk gave him his key and the letter. He stood there tapping the letter against the palm of his left hand, thinking: Spending her time alone with violent guys who use knives – counting on them being gentle and not touching her. And then the charwoman looked up. Their eyes met. She was a middle-aged woman with stringy colourless hair. Her red spongy hands were like handles on her astonishingly white flabby arms. Her unprotesting eyes showed a flicker of interest that she tried to hide with an abashed sinking of her head in her wisdom of ten years of patient charring. Her drooping head distressed McAlpine. "Good evening," he said, startling her; she moistened her lips. But the elevator door opened. The squat elevator man in his blue uniform offered no greeting; he had hard, disapproving eyes. At the fourth floor, after walking ten paces, McAlpine turned, and there was the elevator man, his arms folded, watching him go along the corridor. Not everybody around here approves of you, Mr. McAlpine, his eyes said. Where are you coming from at this hour?

In his own room McAlpine took off his overcoat and hat, but forgot to take off his galoshes. Big wet marks appeared on the red carpet. He looked at the letter he still held in his hand: it was from his father. He opened it.

His father, who had not approved of his leaving the university, was worried about not having heard from him and wanted some assurance that the job on *The Sun* was materializing. Closing his eyes, McAlpine sighed; he could see himself talking to his father and explaining what he had been doing in Montreal. "Jim, Jim, is this you?" his father would ask anxiously. "A scholar, a man of training…"

"It's just that Rogers tells me about those people at the last minute, after holding it back," he muttered, as if explaining something to this father. Then he saw the blotches made by his wet galoshes. Kicking them off, he began to undress. Stripped to his undershirt he went into the bathroom and began to wash his hands and face, scrubbing with the face cloth to wipe away the touch of a sordid life around that café. But gradually his motions lost their vigour. It's not her fault Wagstaffe thinks he could sleep with her, he thought. It's only his own vanity. And as for those other characters – their whole attention might be on her for the one reason, but it doesn't mean her attention is on them for the same reason. It's the way they live. They're men. We all have a low opinion of each other. And as for the women – what can you do about women who are frustrated and envious and embittered? If they weren't concentrating on Peggy they'd be concentrating on somebody else. Anyway, all this is Peggy as Rogers and Wagstaffe see her, forgetting she could be generous enough to think they're all her good friends and will go on respecting her gentleness and her good will. But just how do *I* see her?

If some of her friends were thugs who used knives, she was intelligent enough to have found out about them. And it hadn't destroyed their appeal. No, it might even add to it, which would mean, of course, that she had a taste for violence. His perceptions quickening, he realized he had at last put into words the emotion that had bothered him the day in the department store when he had watched her staring at the carving of the crouching leopard. She had been held in the spell of all the fierce jungle wildness the cat suggested. She had waited, rapt and still, for the beast to spring at her and devour her. He must have suspected then that her gentle innocence was attracted perversely to violence, like a temperament seeking its opposite. In fact there was some proof now that this was so.

If he himself followed her into those dives where she stirred up jealousy, suspicion, lust, and old racial hatreds, he might find himself involved. If he went on, he would be letting his curiosity get the better of his common sense; he would be forgetting that he had come to Montreal to take a job at *The Sun*, and if he got himself involved in a scandal Mr. Carver certainly couldn't afford to take him on. The job on *The Sun* was the kind of job he had always dreamed of. He had come to it after many years of waiting since the night on the Havelock beach when he had run along the road and then had stopped and looked back at the hedge, muttering, "Just wait!" That night, the end of his boyhood, he had lain awake for hours dreaming of making a name for himself some day so no one would ever have to ask again who he was. He had waited and had suffered many humiliations but had known the day would come when his talents would be recognized. Now the main chance had come. He could get his own column in *The Sun*; he would be read; he would go on from there to a bigger world. It was time, then, to realize what was expedient and what was inexpedient. It certainly would be unwise to see Peggy again.

Vowing he would put the girl and the café out of his mind completely, he got into bed. He fell asleep concentrating on a picture of himself and Catherine at the Ritz Sunday supper and at Angela Murdock's party, and in the bright picture he saw himself, free from unwanted distractions, showing Catherine how much he appreciated what she could offer him.

❧ FOURTEEN ❧

Sitting in the Ritz lounge with Catherine, who was so attractive in her pale green dress with the Mexican earrings and silver bracelets, he tried to find in her fresh glowing face the promise of all he wanted in a woman. Her tone, her style, her sympathy were just right for him. She showed her approval in her slow happy smile. She offered him not only an intensification of all those pleasures he had ever enjoyed in the company of a pretty woman, but something more, which he felt especially when their conversation trailed off and there were silences; it was a reminder that he had within his grasp not only all the familiar delightful emotions that could come from a woman in love but the success he had sought since his boyhood. How could he have let anyone get in the way and blind him to her attractiveness? he asked himself. By concentrating on all Catherine offered, he believed he could keep Peggy out of his thoughts. He joked and laughed, he confused and charmed Catherine. He gossiped with her about the guests entering through the swinging street doors, making it clear they were the kind of people in Montreal who interested him. They came in with snow on their shoulders and fur hats and headed for the big table in the dining room that was set up like a Swedish smörgasbord. The French, unlike the English, came in family groups; but, French or English, those who looked most prosperous and distinguished bowed to Catherine.

Then Claude, the headwaiter, with the manner of an emperor looking after his own people, glanced at his reservation list, beckoned to McAlpine and Catherine, checked off the name, and announced, "Yes, indeed, Mr. McAlpine," and they joined the line moving around the long table. There were hot roasts, cold cuts, turkey, chicken, ducks, salads, hot meats in steaming silver bowls, mushrooms, and pastries and sweets. If the hand of one guest touched the hand of another, both reaching for a last napoleon, both hands were withdrawn deferentially and the watchful waiter whispered, "I will bring more at once."

But McAlpine drank too much wine, he ate too heartily, he laughed too boisterously, his face flushed. "I suppose most of Angela's friends are also your father's friends," he said.

"Oh, my goodness, no, Jim! Daddy doesn't take some of Angela's enthusiasms very seriously. But everybody will be there. Maybe your friend Ernest Havelock will be there." And then she noticed that he was not really listening; his eyes now were melancholy, and he was slowly rubbing his left cheek with his fingers. "Jim? Where are you? What's the matter?"

"Why, nothing at all, Catherine."

"But you didn't hear a word I said."

"Why, I could repeat every word of it."

"What's on your mind, Jim?"

"Nothing. Nothing at all. What makes you think there is?"

"You always seem so sure of yourself, yet now – well, one minute you seem close to me – with me – happy, and I love it, Jim. We seem to be soaring along. But the next moment you're worried."

"Me worried?" he asked, looking astonished. "I suppose I'm full of wine and brandy and lighthearted." His hand reaching out for the salt brushed against hers, and he doggedly dwelt on her long fingers; in the silent moment he looked up at her hair line; his eyes met her candid blue eyes, and he nodded in recognition of each attractive part of her.

"Sometimes I don't seem to know you, Jim," she said shyly. "I don't know what goes on in you. Maybe there's a side to your nature I don't understand. At first I didn't think so. I felt I knew you about as well as you knew yourself. I thought I knew what you wanted, and we seemed to want the same things. I mean all the way down the line."

"We do, we do," he said. "We don't open up enough to each other, Catherine, that's all. It's my fault. I don't want it to be that way. Come on, let's move. It may be hard to get a taxi."

In the crowded lobby while Catherine was getting her snow boots from the checkroom, McAlpine looked for a taxi. When she joined him at the door they smiled at each other; they both felt they were at a point where their lives could change, and she reached for his hand.

"What's the matter with that doorman?" she asked. "Here I thought he was getting us a taxi. Look how he's playing favourites." Then she laughed. "Let's forget him. It's only a few blocks away. I'm in an Alpine mood. I like climbing in the snow. Come on, Jim."

They went out and crossed the street and began to climb tree-lined Drummond with its old houses, and he held on tightly to her arm. Snow banks lined the slippery sidewalk, the slope got steeper, and they had to go more slowly. At the top of the street they came to the high steps which were like a dark web against the snow; and, holding on to the railing and laughing and lurching when they slipped against each other, they went up the steps, resting awhile on the platforms, breathing hard, then going on to the top where they sat close together to rest and look down over the city.

All round were bare, snow-laden branches of trees, and the wind sighing through them blew clots of snow on their shoulders. The exertion of the climb had warmed them, and they felt exhilarated. Rows of bare trees below them dipped down the slope in a fantastic netting strung across the glowing street lights, and the roofs of the houses were blanketed with snow. The street lights threw a brilliant winter glow over the whole white sloping city. The sounds of autos on Pine Street above and the streetcars and the jingle of sleigh bells below broke the sigh of the cold wind. Linking their arms tight, they swung their knees together for warmth; they were still breathing hard, and it was this catch in their breathing and the thumping of their hearts that gave everything Catherine said a broken eagerness.

"I don't very often go to these parties of Angela's," she said. "You see, they are mainly Daddy's friends. They're the kind of influential and intellectual people who would have bored me to tears a year ago when I wasn't interested in anything. I had no mind then, I mean." She laughed with a puzzling excitement. "Daddy always said I had a good mind but I never used it. I liked all my friends to be amusing, and we just played around. What happened in the world didn't matter, as long as we all had some money. In those days I would have laughed at the women at Angela's place all standing around by themselves. Nice busy women, but all drabs, really. I still don't like the women, those energetic wifely women, Jim." As she caught her breath he wondered why he was moved. "But going along with you, Jim, knowing it's important to you – well, it's different. It becomes fun. I want to be bright and intelligent so we'll both make a good impression." Her tone changed, her rapid and incoherent talk ended in a soft laugh. For the first time she felt that he could be content in being always with her.

He felt her happiness, and it soothed and charmed him. What a fool he had been, he told himself, not to see that he could be more truly and freely himself with her than with any girl he had ever met! He groped for her hand, wanting and yet not daring to tell her that she had been in his thoughts all week, warning him not to spoil his life. "Everything changes a little, then looks right when you're with someone who – well, when you know someone seems to be keeping in step with you," he said. "Someone helping you go the way you've always wanted to go. Nobody can count on meeting anyone who seems to have been with him from the beginning, Catherine," he said, wondering if she would remember how he had stood outside the Havelocks' dark hedge years ago, feeling the power of his own will. He didn't have to explain it to her; she felt it herself; it added to his own fine awareness that she fitted perfectly into his ambitious plans. More than that; with her own life she could carry him forward lightly and effortlessly in the direction he had mapped out for himself; she beckoned and prodded him along with an enchanting ease.

"I think I was a lonely kid," he went on. "That's why I don't open up, Catherine. I think I've always been hiding something of myself, waiting until the one I could be sure of would come along."

"I know," she said gently.

Their silence only bolstered his sensible conviction that everything could go smoothly for them, and he looked down over the snow-laden roofs to the streets, ghostly in the pallid gleam of the lights reflected in the sky. If he hadn't come to his senses, he told himself, he might be down there now in some dingy little quarter by the railroad tracks or in a bare room in some side street, worrying irrationally about Peggy and exhausting himself in violent protests against his own wrongheadedness in trying to cope with her difficult nature; and, even while protesting, he would be foolish enough to let her go on complicating everything for him with the mysterious disorder of her life. He had let her knock him off balance – not in the head, no, never in the head, but by touching something in his nature like a hidden shameful wild recklessness. She could destroy his self-control; she could heap on him jarring fragments of a strange chaotic experience. To be with her would be to be jarred always, to be hurt strangely in the heart whenever he tried to be sensibly disciplined. All so difficult, so difficult and mystifying, he protested within himself, starring down at the white city where Peggy still called to him, trying to compel him to follow and understand the quick darting changes in her life; to follow till he caught the disturbing glow of a poetry in it he could never understand, alien as it was to his nature and shattering to his soul. Even to think of her now was so difficult and so upsetting that he turned to Catherine, seeking the tranquillity and peace he found in her presence.

A gust of wind blew a snow pad from the branches overhead, and it plopped down on Catherine's neck. Jumping up, she squealed, "Ouch, it's cold! Oh, Jim, my poor neck!" Drawing off his gloves he tried to scrape the snow from her warm skin before it melted.

"Well, that's enough of that," she said, laughing. "Come on, Jim."

The Murdock house, only a little way east along Pine, was a vast square brick house with an iron fence on the street, and many trees at the back of the house, all perched on the rim of the mountain. Cars were parked along Pine in front of the great lighted house that had been built by Judge Murdock's father, a lumber merchant who had made a fortune. In the old days the Murdocks had entertained only their merchant friends; but when Judge Murdock, at the age of sixty-five, had married Angela the house had become a brightly lit place with the doors always open.

The party had overflowed into the big panelled hall, where Angela Murdock waited at the drawing-room door. A tall, warmly plump, auburn-haired woman of forty with lovely shoulders, a slender waist, milky skin, and graceful movements, she had a warm, tolerant word for everyone.

"Ah, Catherine, you and Commander McAlpine," she said gaily. Not for months had anyone called McAlpine "Commander," and he liked it. "I was talking to Catherine's father about you, Commander," she whispered. "Or rather he was talking to me about you. My, you've made an impression!" And she led him across the crowded drawing room to the corner where her husband, the Judge, sat contentedly by himself. For two hours he would sit there and then retire unobtrusively to his own room so he would feel fresh and keen-minded when he took his place on the bench in the morning.

The diningroom buffet was loaded with the choicest whiskies and brandies. Catherine took a small brandy, and McAlpine a stiff Canadian Club. Why he poured himself such a stiff drink and felt he needed it, he didn't stop to figure out. The drink had a peculiar effect on him. Of course he had drunk too much wine at the Ritz anyway, and had just come in out of the cold air, but as he glanced around, none of the blurring faces looked attractive; yet they were the faces of important people who could be valuable to him. He caught snatches of familiar conversation.

"I don't agree, Perkins," said the economist: "I'm not at all alarmed by what you call this Catholic puritan pressure..." Another voice, an investment banker's soft voice: "We buy from the States. We sell to England. Ground in the middle..." And the French Canadian lawyer's voice: "That old conception of the power of the sterling bloc…"

And McAlpine thought, What makes them sound so incredibly pompous and dull? He had determinedly reached a pitch of nervous expectation, but these voices did not belong to the expectation or the secret excitement of his soul; he felt let down, then on edge, then reckless as he had never felt reckless before. It's only that drink, he thought.

Catherine tugged at his arm. "Look, over there. Your friend Mr. Havelock," she said, indicating a mild little man with a graceful air and a scrawny neck who was smiling to himself as Angela said to him, "Why is it, Ernest, that I never want to listen to symphonies these days? Only quartets."

But his father and mother had once stood outside this man's gate. How could he now seem so unimpressive? he asked himself. As a gesture to his boyhood he wanted to speak to Havelock, but again someone touched him on the arm.

"Ah, here you are, Jim," said Mr. Carver. "Look, you know all about Henry McNab," he whispered. "Over there by the refreshments. Come on."

The big-shouldered, white-haired cabinet minister was at the end of the diningroom table helping himself to celery sticks stuffed with cheese.

"Very good celery, McAlister," he said, after their introduction.

"McAlpine, not McAlister, sir."

"Well, try the celery anyway."

"I was talking to Jim about your United Nations speech, Henry," Mr. Carver said blandly.

Playing along with him recklessly, McAlpine said, "I read it, McNab. Of course I know you have to do a certain amount of shadowboxing." Mr. Carver's startled expression jolted him, and he tried to concentrate on McNab's blurring face. "I mean you did throw a little cold water on the hot heads of those idealists." And then he lost track of what the cabinet minister said until he heard the words, "stupid self-deception."

"Stupid self-deception. Why, of course," McAlpine repeated. The words offered him a disturbing illumination accompanied by a bewildering pang, and he was unaware of McNab's and Carver's blank expressions. Had he been frantically trying to achieve some stupid self-deception all evening? But he refused to deal with his own question. It was easier to ask, What if Peggy, too, had been deceiving herself, not only about her life but about her true feeling for me? Maybe only a few words were needed— And then Mr. Carver said, "You were saying, Jim?"

"I was thinking I knew the kind of person Mr. McNab had in mind. I mean," he faltered, "these idealists who deceive themselves. I was talking to one the other day."

"Really?"

"Yes, an intelligent young girl, a charming creature," he said with a melancholy smile. "It was like talking to a brick wall. All idealism, no prudence – ready to hurt anybody who got in her way. No, I don't think she'd care," he said. Again he faltered. "A passionate longing for the impossible, eh?" he asked.

The feeling behind his words astonished both McNab and Carver. The liquor had loosened his tongue; he nodded dreamily, and in his thoughts went hurrying out of the Murdock house down to that bare room on Crescent Street and sat beside the iron bedstead and talked to Peggy. "A soft heart is all right if it goes with a hard head," he said aloud to McNab in a gentler tone; then he blinked, cleared his throat, momentarily confused, realizing he had begun to make the speech he had wanted to make to Peggy the time she had cut him off. Behind him on the wall was a portrait of Judge Murdock's father done in browns and blacks and burnt sienna tones, and against this sombre portrait, as he stood with folded arms, his own face looked pale and melancholy. My God, he thought, what am I saying? It's that last damned drink of whisky. I'm supposed to be talking about international affairs and the United Nations. Recovering himself he went on, "I mean, sir, you for one see clearly that these idealistic people misunderstand the whole structure of the United Nations. A cynical structure really, sir, but you have tried to explain it for what it is, eh?"

"I like – well, I like your sincerity, McAlister," the cabinet minister said uneasily. "Let's all be hardheaded."

"Hardheaded, of course," McAlpine agreed. He still felt a little drunk, but the familiar phrases had got him into the swing of things again. He was back where he belonged, after sitting up last night in a garish Negro nightclub feeling desolate over a little girl he hardly knew. He was where he belonged, and, more than that, his head was clearing; he could concentrate on the wrinkles at the back of Ernest Havelock's thin neck. The head kept twisting, a hand came up to the neck. The draft from the open diningroom window was bothering Mr. Havelock. "Mr. Havelock is going to have a stiff neck in the morning. Now wouldn't that be a pity?" he asked sardonically.

"I beg your pardon?"

"That draft from the open window. Why don't we all close the window for Mr. Havelock?"

"I'll close it, Jim," Mr. Carver said, and as the cabinet minister turned to get another celery stick he whispered, "It's fine to be independent, Jim, but don't be foolhardy."

At that hour at the Murdocks' the guests, exhausting all the possibilities of formal conversation, began to feel lonely and wandered away from one another. The party began to break up into two groups. The French Canadians gradually retreated to the drawing room, where they could relax with one another, and the English-speaking Canadians moved toward the dining room and possession of the cakes and sandwiches. The cabinet minister, alone with McAlpine and apprehensive, said with a false heartiness, "I have to put in a phone call – I'll be back, McAlister," and hurried away.

McAlpine was left alone, feeling discontented; he had never felt so discontented, and he didn't know why. In a little while he heard Wagstaffe's voice: "I don't want no trouble around here." Then Roger's voice: "Cut a man in Memphis." But the voices faded. He wasn't sure he had heard them. Then he saw it; of course it was only the liquor, but he saw it with a brilliant clarity: the carved leopard. And while she watched it, fascinated, it sprang at her, and he cried, "Look out!"

"Jim, oh, Jim!" Catherine called.

"Hello, Catherine," he said, his tone full of relief.

"You look positively distressed, Jim."

"I'm left alone."

"Is that such a calamity? Everybody suddenly gets left alone around here. What have you been saying, Jim?" she asked with an anxious expression.

"Very little. Talking politics. Why?"

"Daddy was a bit worried."

"What's worrying him?"

"You didn't insult McNab, did you? Or Havelock?"

"Not for the world would I insult him. Why should I?"

"Play along a little, will you, Jim? I mean, don't be too outspoken. Not tonight. Not here."

"I'm an outspoken man," he said grandly. "Isn't that why your father wants me to work for him?"

"But you haven't got the job yet, Jim. Don't boot it out the window."

"No. That's right. No. I'll be careful. I'll get you a drink."

"No, I'll scoot along. Don't drink any more, please."

"I certainly won't," he said firmly.

People were going home; now that the room had thinned, he could see the pictures on the walls and the rugs on the floor. In the drawing room was an immense Chinese rug. An oriental rug was in the dining room. But Catherine had worried him. What possesses me? What compels me to smash it all up? he thought. And he moved into the drawing room among the French, where there was a solemn argument about André Gide. All these French Canadian Catholics spoke with enthusiasm about Gide, the Protestant. They were captivated by the Gide style. It bored him. It put him more on edge. Near by, Carver and a young French Canadian lawyer who had a cynical smile and a perfect English accent were arguing, Carver saying, "But obviously your people don't produce enough engineers and technicians. All the emphasis is on the liberal education, the arts, the humanities."

"Yes, we do need more engineers and fewer lawyers," the French Canadian teased. "But we neglect other things, too, eh? Vitamins in tomato juice." And he laughed and moved away.

Mr. Carver turned to McAlpine. "Education! Try and talk to these pea-soupers about education, and see how far you get," he snorted with contempt. "But I shall go on trying, just the same."

"That's right," McAlpine said in his best sardonic tone. "The white man's burden, eh?"

"What's that, Jim?"

"I mean trying to do something for an educational system. Taking the burden on yourself." McAlpine was bewildered by his own imprudence.

"Oh, I see."

McAlpine expected him to go on, I know what you mean, all right – you and that girl and those Negroes. But Mr. Carver smiled, offering nothing but good will. "A very neat touch, Jim," he said complacently. "The white man's burden – very good. I must remember it."

Voices came from the hall: Good night, Angela – I always have such a good time – Good night – Good night, my dear.

"Just look at Angela," Mr. Carver said as they sat down together. "A little light from her lamp for everybody. All that's womanly and warm and gracious! H'm. Yet I find myself wondering... Oh, well—" Then he put his hand on Jim's knee. "By the way," he said confidentially, "I had a good talk with Horton this afternoon. Mentioned that you and I were going fishing on the ice."

"Does he want to go fishing with us?" McAlpine asked.

"Horton? I don't think he'd know one end of a fish from the other," Mr. Carver said, smiling broadly. "Jim," he said, his tone changing, "the job is yours. It's all settled. A column three times a week. When could you start?"

"Any time."

"Good! How about going on salary next Monday? Horton suggested a hundred a week. We can do better than that, of course, if it goes well. If I were you, I'd take a week to get two or three columns done you can show me; and we'd start printing you, say, in two weeks. There's a desk at the office if you want to use it; or, if you'd feel freer, more independent not coming down, it's all right with me."

"I'll try working in my own place, Mr. Carver."

"Just as you say, Jim." Their eyes met. Mr. Carver waited for approval. His smile was gentle and wistful; his eyelids red from the smoke in the room. But McAlpine felt only a grim satisfaction. The expected elation was absent. But it would come, it would surely come when his head cleared; he could hardly follow the flow of Mr. Carver's relaxed, philosophical conversation: "… the editorial page… rational persuasion… I'm not a belligerent fellow… the method of old Plato. Life… life, a long series of crushing losses, the impermanence of everything beautiful and dear to us… the compact we enter into to protect our way of living… the economic and aesthetic barbarians always at the gates trying to hasten the end of things…" It got all mixed up for McAlpine until Mr. Carver said, "What do you say, Jim?"

"I say— I say Plato would like it, sir."

"We should have a drink to Plato, Jim. You and me and Plato here in Montreal!"

From the hall voices were calling: "A lovely party – Remember me to the Judge, Angela – I'll see you at our place, Angela – Good night, my dear—" Angela was shaking hands with one of her guests, and this guest was that tall, thin, bald Professor Fielding whom McAlpine had planned to get in touch with. He was twisting a white scarf around his scrawny throat, the light gleaming on his bald head. No, no, I should not see Fielding now, McAlpine thought. It no longer matters what he would say about Peggy. Not now. Not anymore. And he turned to Mr. Carver, wanting to feel himself held there, and yet he twisted around again; he had to turn, though crying out within himself, Don't be a fool! He smiled thinly at Mr. Carver, wishing he might take him by the arm and walk him far away. "Why, there's old Fielding," he heard himself say in surprise. "I've been trying to get hold of him. Excuse me just a minute, Mr. Carver." And he headed for the hall.

"Fielding! Fielding, old man," he cried.

"Why, hello there, McAlpine."

"Have you been here all evening, Fielding? Where were you?"

"Sitting in the corner of the drawing room. I didn't see you either."

"You see what a bad hostess I am," Angela said, laughing, and she turned to speak to someone else who was leaving.

As he shook hands warmly, McAlpine tried to find something to say about Peggy Sanderson that would sound easy and natural. "An odd thing, Fielding," he said. "I was talking about you only the other day. Ran into one of your former students with a friend of mine. A little girl, rather pretty, too. What was her name now?" he said, alarmed by the sudden pounding of his heart. "Singleton. Yes, that's it. No, no, wait a minute. Sanderson."

"Singleton – Sanderson," Fielding repeated, frowning.

"Sanderson, that's it. About four years ago."

"Is that so? Wait. No, I don't seem to remember her. What does she look like?"

"Small and fair and delicate. An air of innocence. Like a little flower girl at a wedding. If you know what I mean."

"H'm. Let me see. Ah, yes, yes, I *do* remember her now. Yes."

"Strange how it takes a while to remember even the best of former students," McAlpine said helpfully.

"Now that I remember her, she wasn't much of a student. Mediocre. Definitely."

"Then she – well, she didn't make much of an impression?"

"No impression at all," the professor said with a shrug. "Just one of those vague unimpressive featherbrained little girls that drift through a class and are never remembered."

"Ah, I see." McAlpine's expression was incredulous.

Angela, who had only half heard, waited till Fielding had gone and then turned to say, "Was it Peggy Sanderson you were asking about, Mr. McAlpine? Is she a friend of yours?"

The glint in her eyes shocked him. The name Peggy Sanderson had aroused in her a personal resentment. Yet she was too tolerant to be disturbed by a woman merely having sympathy for Negroes. It must be something more.

"No. Not Sanderson. The name was Singleton. Betty Singleton," he said, for he knew that Angela, if she had an antipathy for the girl, would gossip with Catherine.

"Oh, I'm sorry. Excuse me." She relaxed and smiled. "Come on," she said, taking his arm. "I insist you have one more drink. Just one for the road."

But his denial of Peggy had left him stricken with remorse. "I'll be with you in a minute, Mrs. Murdock," he said. And he turned and walked swiftly up the stairs to the big blue tiled bathroom and locked himself in and leaned heavily against the door.

The tiled room was like a cell. He stood there trying to understand why he felt so ashamed of himself and so insignificant, and why he felt he had lost all his integrity. It wasn't only that he had denied Peggy; but with the denial he had yielded up his respect for his own insight which had always been his greatest strength. Someone came up the stairs, tried the door, and delicately hurried away. While he listened to the retreating footsteps he wondered if, in spite of himself, his faith in what he believed Peggy to be had really wavered. For hadn't she been there all evening to haunt him? Hadn't she followed him up the steps like a wraith from the white winter city to worry him when he wanted to feel gay and successful, to arouse in him that peculiar anxiety which had really been guilt? For last night and all day and all evening he had tried to abandon his faith in her. Yet he hadn't been able to do it, either last night or here at the party: all evening he had been wanting to watch over her and to be always with her. To be always with her...

In the bright, immaculate, tiled bathroom he whispered, "Where are you tonight, Peggy? Go home, please go home. Go back to your room and be there by yourself tonight, Peggy. I'll see you in the morning, and we'll go our own way together." He cried it out in his heart because he understood at last that he loved her.

When he went downstairs where Catherine waited, she suggested they walk home. She had been talking to her father and felt happy for Jim, and she wanted to prolong the glow of success for both of them. The wind had dropped, and it was easy going down the steps. "But the best part of the evening really was when we were here on these steps," she said. "The part I'll remember, Jim."

"Yes." He longed to find words that wouldn't hurt her and yet would correct the wrong impression he had given her. "It's odd how you can suddenly realize how important a friendship has become."

"Yes. Oh, it is, it is," she agreed, waiting anxiously.

"I'd count on your friendship, Catherine," he began awkwardly, "no matter what was happening to me."

"Yes, I think you could count on me," she said faintly, frightened by his apologetic tone. "You could, Jim."

"Comrades, always good comrades, eh?"

"Oh," she said, hiding her pain. "I'm the good comrade, the best in Montreal, in fact. Your very good comrade."

"In our own way we'll always feel important to each other," he went on wretchedly. But she knew what he meant; she knew he was implying she had got a wrong impression. Yet she chose to tell herself that he was still shy and afraid of himself with her, and that it need not be so.

She understands, he thought. If his job depended on his relationship with her, it had no dignity. He had made his own decision; he knew now with whom he belonged. He could hardly conceal his vast relief. At last he felt elation.

☙ FIFTEEN ☙

Her door was open and he went in. He had been there earlier in the afternoon, when Mrs. Agnew had told him Peggy was on the day shift. While he waited he paced up and down making eloquent speeches to her. Pausing, he listened; he went to the window and watched the lighted street. He sat down slowly on the bed, his thoughts racing wildly.

Then the street door opened and he heard broken steps in the hall and voices low and faltering. As he stood up, apprehensive, the door burst open; there was a whiff of the cheap factory perfume, and Peggy lurched in with Walter Malone, the big grey-haired editorial writer, just behind, his big hand jerking at the bandanna handkerchief on her head. Her white stricken face frightened him. Malone's grey face, ugly and contorted, loomed up behind her. They both saw him.

"What is this?" he said. Malone's mouth gaped open and the bandanna handkerchief fluttered from his fingers. Peggy stood there, too surprised to move toward him. And Malone, with time to control himself, grinned, the vicious hardness still in his eyes. "I see the professor gets around," he sneered. "How should I know you had moved in?" As he turned to go McAlpine said, "Take your time," and took a step after him.

"No, let him go, Jim," Peggy whispered. She sat down on the bed and tried to smile.

Malone's angry footsteps receded down the hall and Jim closed the door.

"What happened? What's wrong?" he asked.

"Where did you come from, Jim?"

"I've been waiting here. What went on with Malone?"

"It's all right," she said. "It's nothing." But her nerves were tightened up and she couldn't sit still; and as she stood up and walked around, her arms folded, she looked at him again and again. Finally she burst out, "Oh, the smug complacent fool! That phoney understanding. That stupid, stupid vanity. I feel dirty all over. His wretched arrogance! Big-hearted enough to come my way, and not mind! And not mind, do you see, Jim?"

"You haven't told me what happened," he said soothingly. "Take it easy, Peggy."

"You're right. Why should I let that embittered failure frighten me? Why should I be surprised at anything he does?" She sat down and tried to relax and took the cigarette he offered her. She rubbed her left shoulder. In a few minutes she was calmer. "I was coming home from work with Willie Foy, the shipper. Remember him? The boy who taught me how to work the crimping machine? Only eighteen and he wants me to go out with him. It was fun tramping through the snow with him." Her tone changed as she remembered, and she smiled.

"Yes, I remember Willie," he said, marvelling that her recollection of the boy could free her so quickly from her anger.

"Willie wanted me to go to a dance with him and we were kidding each other," she said. "The cold air, you know, heightens the smell of the cheap perfume that's all over us, and I said we were like two winter flowers, and he was saying I wouldn't know him when he took a bath and put on his new drapes. This was on Dorchester Street. Malone must have been standing there by the restaurant. I didn't see him till he stopped us. It was easy for him to scare Willie away. I mean he overawed him with his grey hair and his expensive overcoat, and then he took me by the arm to walk me the rest of the way."

Her changing face made him want to put his arms around her. The break in her calmness had brought her wonderfully close to him. "I sort of knew what was coming," she said. "He was kidding me about working in the factory, but with that awful sleazy understanding of his. I'd stay there two weeks, he said. "Then a new experience, always the new experience. The charm of novelty. He had known women like me in France! Throwing that stupid tolerance of his around me like a big moth-eaten coat. France! France! Ah, the life he had led in France! In France a woman could have Negro lovers. Anything for a kick! And he was about the only man in Montreal who could understand and be sympathetic with my little sophistications. I wasn't arguing with him. What do I care about his stupid sympathies? I wanted to get home and get rid of him. Well, he insisted on coming in, and in the hall, then – Well," she went on unevenly, "he tried to kiss me and I guess he saw I hated it, and then – then it happened."

"What happened?"

"Just – just what I saw in him."

Her eyes were stricken again, and McAlpine, waiting, was sure what he had dreaded had touched her at last. "Maybe I pushed him away," she went on shakily. "It's dark in the hall with only that small light. He had pulled me against him. My face was against his coat. 'You go for those jigs,' he said. 'They can touch you, but when I try and touch you— Am I such scum?' It was the way his head shot back in the light, and the glazed sparkle in his eyes, sort of crazy white and wild, crazy with humiliation as if – as if I had left him nothing, nothing in the world to be superior to, and he was like a savage, and he raised his hand to – to – well, to beat something out of me, to beat me until I was dirtier than he was and he could feel big and proud again. Do you see?"

"Sure," he said, his own heart beating unevenly.

"I had never seen anything like it in a man's face. Never in my life, Jim."

"He's sick – defeated," he said, soothing her. "Maybe he can no longer bear any kind of a rejection."

While the snow from her boots melted on the floor she dwelt on the brutality of Malone's resentment. Normally, he was too lazy and indolent a man to go berserk, she said. But he had it in his mind that she had friends down on St. Antoine, which was all right with him, providing – well, if she had friends down on St. Antoine it should have made her feel he was superior and desirable – willing to give her a break. "Yes, you're right, I think," she said, meditating. "When he felt himself rejected, the last remnant of his pride was rejected, and he couldn't stand it. If he couldn't retain his belief in his superiority over a few Negroes, then he would go wild with hate, and rape and destroy everything." She offered these explanations tentatively. What had really terrified her, she said, was her belief for the moment that she was being overwhelmed by vindictiveness from everyone Malone had ever known or admired. "I think that was what was so horrible," she said, looking up.

"Sure. He turned into a thug. You're lucky you didn't get beaten up," he said. "I could see it coming."

"See what coming?"

"This trouble. It's better it should come from Malone in your own hall."

"Who else would bother me?"

"It could happen down in St. Antoine, couldn't it? If Malone can get violent and become a thug because you're a white woman, maybe there's more violence coming your way from some of those Negroes, who can be thugs, too."

"You don't know anything about those people down there and I do. You don't know how they feel about anything."

"I only know the gossip I picked up."

"Gossip about me, of course. Oh, it's a laugh!" she said vehemently, and she did not laugh; she was too exasperated. "If people can't destroy you one way they try another." Her cheeks reddened, and her eyes were angry. "Try doing something in your own way sometime, Jim. Try having your own notion of your own integrity, and see what happens. Everybody takes a turn cracking at you. They'll break their backs trying to bring you in line again, and if you won't see things the way everybody else does, you're crazy or perverse or pig-headed or stupid. Everybody's willing to give you a hand if you'll only string along and quit. And if you won't quit— Why don't I feel sour about people?" she asked bitterly. "All that's the matter with me is that I'm what I choose to be. Does anyone think of trying to help me? Oh, Lord, no! Everybody wants to put a hole in my head. Look at you. You've heard some gossip and you're wondering if I don't attract corruption. How do you know I don't attract what's corrupt in you?"

"That should put me in my place," he said, but after an embarrassed moment he went on doggedly. "But if the trumpet player is actually more violent than Malone—"

"Who says so, Jim?"

"Rogers. He says Wilson has a police record down in Memphis."

"That Memphis business," she said. "It was some trouble over a crap game, wasn't it? You don't understand such people, Jim. They're not like Malone."

"Peggy, you're not in love with Wilson, are you?"

"Oh, dear! There you go!" she said wearily. "You mean, do I sleep with him? The one important question!"

"I only asked if—"

"Why don't you ask if I sleep with Wagstaffe? Or Joe Thomas? Joe's a pullman porter, the most eloquent man I've ever met. You haven't heard them talk about these things down around St. Antoine," she said, contemplating one worn spot on the floor where the paint had been scraped off, and her smile was as serene as a nun's, rebuking him for his lack of charity. "I've sat in dirty little back rooms down there; men and women, all poor, just neighbours, patient and troubled, listening to Joe Thomas, and trying to understand this very same thing that bothers you. You ought to see those Negroes just sitting around together, listening and wondering while Joe tried to explain how a good-natured human being like himself can suddenly go berserk. Just listening was wonderful. I loved the way he put it. It went something like this: 'If a white man, even a bad one, is getting kicked around, he knows he can call a policeman. It's a feeling deep inside him. From the time he was a kid the authorities have pounded it into him. *His* authorities! Justice will always have one eye open for him. But when a Negro has a crazy, angry moment he wants to close his eyes, he wants to go blind, he doesn't want to see the face of justice. It'll be a white face, so he's alone with nothing to fall back on but his own blind anger and he has to make a crazy violent protest before he opens his eyes. He knows he'll hate what he sees when he opens his eyes, and so he likes the angry darkness. Then, of course, he comes to himself, and he's frightened and on the run, which is no news for him because all his life in one way or another he's been on the run in a white world. See, Jim?"

"Yes, I see." But he pondered, then asked, "Peggy – all this stuff— What are you trying to do with yourself?"

"With myself?"

"Yes. What are you up to?"

"Look, Jim, who's being inhuman? The supercilious people who have charge of this world, or me? In one way or another there are a lot of people on the run from what's inhuman. If they rap on my door – well—"

"Yes, I see." He wanted to say, "Black or white, a thug is a thug," but he was helpless when she sounded so sweetly compassionate. Even if the man was a thug it was right that at some ultimate moment in a thug's life someone should find something good to say for him. "Who knows?" he asked with a sigh. "There might come a time in my own life when I'd need someone like you to put in a good word for me. I think I'd be satisfied if I could hear you." Then he smiled. "Well, you'd better take those snow boots off. Here. Let me help you."

She thrust out her feet and he knelt down, avoiding the little pool of water, and pulled off the boots one at a time, his hands getting wet from the soles.

"How are they standing up?" he asked, inspecting one of the boots.

"I think I'll have to stuff a little paper in the toes."

"If they're too long why not put in an insole?"

"An insole? Why, of course," she said. "My slippers are over there by the bed."

When he had brought the slippers and was putting them on she said, "You worry a lot about me, don't you, Jim?"

"I suppose I do."

"I know you do. I'm all right, Jim. I'm fine. I think you worry about me too much," she added, going to the closet to get her dress. "I don't want you to worry about me." With a black dress over her arm, she returned to the bureau and knelt down, pulling out the lower drawer. "I'm going out for dinner with Henry Jackson," she said apologetically. "Do you want to wait here till I get dressed?"

"Why, sure," he said, his pleasure so plain she smiled to herself. She took stockings and underclothes from the drawer and laid them over her arm. She took a few steps toward the door and then, compelled, she turned and looked at him and frowned. His white cuffs shone below the sleeves of his expensive blue suit; the light gleamed on the toes of his well polished good shoes.

"Why did I turn and look at you?" she asked.

"I don't know."

"I think I wanted you to stay."

"Did you?"

"You look so reliable and secure. I feel – well, as if it might be nice to stay and relax with you."

"Why not?" he asked, for he knew she had felt herself being taken in another direction than the one she had been following in dirty factories, narrow dark halls, and shabby rooms. She was making a pattern with her toe on the floor.

"Well?" he said.

"Well what?"

"Were you going to say something?"

"No, nothing. But when I picked up this dress—"

"Yes? Go on."

"Why did I remember another dress I wore one summer in my second year at college? It was a lovely dress, pale Nile green. I had a rakish green straw hat, too. I wore the hat and the dress one day in the park with a student. I remember how we stood on a little bridge and I was looking at our reflections in the stream and I thought he was, too, and then I looked up and he was watching me, and I felt beautiful. Why did you make me remember such things?"

"I don't know."

"It's odd, isn't it?" she asked solemnly. Again she made that pattern with her toe; then she opened the door and shuffled along the hall in her slippers.

His heart took a heavy, slow, painful beat, and he stared at that spot on the floor; he understood what she had wanted to say: she had a doubt about the life she was leading. It didn't matter whether he himself or Malone had put that doubt in her mind. It was there, it was what he wanted, and he could afford to be happy. Her acceptance of his presence in the room when she came home meant she felt committed to him and knew he loved her. His surprise and his joy blinded him. And he did not realize she had kept her own opinion of the trumpet player.

When she returned in a simple black dress, her hair combed and twisted into a smooth knot on her neck, he nodded and smiled. "Why, you look beautiful," he said. Now he knew she had always belonged in his own world. She looked like an exquisite little figurine done with a delicate grace and belonging in some china cabinet. "Those overalls, that bandanna handkerchief you've been wearing. Why, it's all masquerade!" His laugh was so boyish she put her head back and laughed, too. She looked proud; it was the first time he had ever seen her show any pride in her beauty.

"Oh, by the way," she said, going to the dresser and opening one of the drawers. "Have you a lighter?"

"Why, yes."

"Here's a couple of tins of lighter fluid from the factory. The foreman told me to take it any time I needed it."

"Thanks. Thanks, Peggy," he said.

It was an odd little gesture; she was offering him a gift as he had offered her the snow boots.

"You can walk me down to the corner anyway," she said. "I was thinking you might like to meet Henry later in the evening. If you're around the Chalet about eleven or later we'll probably drop in there."

"I'll be there," he said.

❧ SIXTEEN ❧

At midnight he was with Foley in the Chalet sitting at the corner table in the alcove where the draft from the open window hit him, as usual, on the back of the neck. He kept his scarf on to protect his throat. "I want to look like one of those French intellectuals," he said. Wolgast was behind the bar, his sleeves rolled up, his bald head shining brightly, and at the other end of the bar Malone and Gagnon, the cartoonist, were having a subdued conversation.

"Well, I go to work for *The Sun*, Chuck," McAlpine said quietly.

"You do?" Foley looked surprised. "It's definite?"

"It's definite."

"Starting when?"

"I'll be working on a couple of columns this week. I'll let Mr. Carver see them, of course. I get a cheque at the end of the week."

"How much?"

"A hundred. More later."

"On staff?"

"On staff. Come on, man, relax. You can believe it. And I don't have to go down to *The Sun*. I can work at my own place. Turn in three columns a week."

"H'm. Not a newspaperman, a journalist! You should get a pair of striped trousers and a cane. Well, you know what it means?"

"Go on."

"You're a teacher's pet. Teacher down there always has a pet."

"Don't be such a wise guy, Chuck."

"Or maybe it's just Catherine's hand I see in there. Well, okay, I'm wrong. Maybe you know people better than I do. Where are you going to live?"

"That's it. I need a typewriter and an apartment."

"I may be able to help you. I know a fellow in my building who's moving to Miami in ten days. You could sublet."

"Well, that's that," McAlpine said. Now he wanted to find out all Foley knew about Henry Jackson.

Foley found it amusing to talk about Jackson. "Little Henry," he called him. Not too much of a success as a commercial artist, he said, but an entertaining kid. How could a boy with a beard be taken seriously? Of course Henry was never quite sure whether he wanted to be a successful commercial artist or a dramatist like Bernard Shaw. He wrote radio plays, and they weren't so bad either. In fact he was a bright little guy with a chip on his shoulder, and the boys around the Chalet liked him until he got drunk and annoyingly Shavian. The trouble with Henry was that he had been a sickly child; when he was in a good mood he would tell how he had been kept away from school because he had bronchitis twice a year, but those times in his boyhood when he had lain in bed had been important, for his mother, a clever woman apparently, had read Flaubert to him in the French; Henry could recite whole paragraphs from *Madame Bovary*. Those sick periods had shaped his whole life; he had cultivated a taste for the witty writers of other periods, and naturally had come to believe he was a great wit himself... What was his particular attraction for Peggy? It couldn't have been his splendid appearance... You should see him. He hadn't cleaned his shoes in seven years. Everybody in the joint was surprised if he ever came in looking dressed up. McAlpine would know him as soon as he saw him. Was he Peggy's lover? Well, everybody had taken it for granted he was, and Henry seemed to think so, too. In the last year Peggy and Henry had been together a lot, but whether he was sleeping with her or not, how could you say? One took it for granted they slept together because they both took so much pride in doing exactly what they wanted to do. On the other hand, maybe they regarded it as a novelty not to go to bed. With a couple of inverted exhibitionists a simple love relationship was sometimes difficult, and it was possible they got such excitement out of their spiritual emancipation that a warm embrace would be too vulgar for them. But certainly Henry had been eating with her, reading his plays to her, and staying up all night with her and sharing her interest in primitive African art and Negro musicians. It would be astonishing to everybody if she had only been leading him around by the nose. For the record, then, Henry was her lover, and as to what she got from the bearded boy McAlpine would have to make up his own mind. "And don't look too eager to do it," Foley said, with a slow grin. "Here's the boyfriend now."

A young fellow of twenty-four with a wispy reddish beard, wearing a sloppy loose brown tweed jacket and grey trousers, the jacket and trousers hanging on his thin body like a tent, had come in and was staring at Foley and McAlpine. But is he alone? McAlpine thought. Where's Peggy? Henry Jackson had fierce, bright blue eyes and the weakness of his chin was concealed by his untidy little beard. He went limping to the end of the bar to join Malone and Gagnon. On his left foot he wore a special shoe with a built-up heel.

"Look, that foot," McAlpine whispered.

"Yeah, he's lame."

"You didn't tell me he was lame, Chuck."

"Didn't I?"

"No."

"Is it so important?"

"Well, yes, if you had only told me he was lame…" McAlpine said, protesting Foley's concealment of a fact that would have helped explain Peggy's sympathy for Jackson.

Jackson and Malone began to whisper; their heads bobbed together, then bobbed away, and Jackson, turning slowly, glowered at McAlpine. He put his elbows on the bar, meditated, and finally swung full around and regarded McAlpine morosely. Challenging questions were in his eyes: Where did you come from? What makes you think it's important to you that I'm here alone? You're an utter stranger. You don't belong in this at all. She's nothing to you. What makes you think you can have any right to try and understand what's happened between me and Peggy, or believe that a guy like you could take my place with her?

Then he slid off the stool and approached the corner table, taking four limping, solemn-faced strides, courting a humiliation.

"Hello, Chuck. Mind if I sit down?"

"A pleasure, Henry," said Foley, now full of vast good humour. "I think you and Mr. McAlpine should know each other."

"Yeah, I think so," Jackson said. All his movements were jerky and irritable. When Wolgast came from behind the bar with one drink, which he put in front of McAlpine saying, "This is special – for you, Mr. McAlpine, because you held me up the other night," Jackson scowled unhappily.

"In fact, Henry," Foley said slyly, "it looks to me as if you and Jim already know each other."

"I think Mr. McAlpine has heard of me," Henry said.

"Sure I have," McAlpine said.

"Sure you have," Jackson repeated sourly, and then looked puzzled. "I feel like hell," he said, trying to laugh. But McAlpine's intense interest fascinated him. Long explanations could be dispensed with; they understood they had been in the closest communication. "If you and I were contemporaries, McAlpine," he said arrogantly, "I would try and explain to you; but we're not contemporaries. The gap is too great. You're not in my world." Foley chuckled with vast secret amusement and Jackson scowled. "I think Mr. McAlpine understands," he said.

"What are you trying to tell me?" McAlpine asked.

"I said my generation can't expect much from your generation."

"But why are you so belligerent?"

"I'm making a point. You get it, I think."

Smoke curling up from the cigarette on the ashtray at Jackson's elbow made him blink his eyes; he kept on blinking at McAlpine. "Yeah, you get it all right," he said.

Clenching his fists McAlpine felt his whole body tightening up, and he was afraid of the force of his own inexplicable hostility.

"I seem to bother Mr. Jackson," he said to Foley.

"I think you have a point there, Jim," Foley agreed. "Something about you bothers the guy."

"Nothing about him bothers me," Jackson said. "I was making an intellectual point – about his generation. Guys like him in colleges in his time chased around reading about the lost ones. All crap. If you'd ever get down and rub your face and hands in the mud—"

"The mud?"

"Yeah, the mud." His little red beard wagged fiercely; his pale cheeks and his vehemence were comical. Foley smiled broadly and winked at Wolgast, who polished the bar and listened with a knowing grin, speculating on what McAlpine would do when sufficiently insulted.

A waiter entered and gave an order to Wolgast. "Who for?" he asked.

"Tom Loney," the waiter said.

"Tell Loney to come and speak to me," Wolgast said, still watching McAlpine. "I don't mind carrying Loney on the cuff, but last night he insulted me. I don't like to be insulted."

"Say, Henry," Foley said, with mock earnestness.

"What?"

"You'd better admit it."

"Admit what?"

"You didn't write the Shaw plays, Henry."

"Leave Shaw out of this."

"No Shaw then. Go on."

"I don't take professors seriously."

"Neither did Shaw," McAlpine said, smiling.

"Are you trying to needle me, McAlpine?"

"Take it easy, Henry," Foley kidded him. "He's only saying you didn't write *Saint Joan*. Shaw did."

"Don't try and needle me about Shaw or *Saint Joan*. Your friend couldn't even understand a girl like Joan."

"'A girl like Joan,'" McAlpine repeated, and then it struck him: Does he really mean I don't understand a girl like Peggy? He quickened, and leaned forward, waiting to see what Jackson had meant. He waited jealously for Jackson to reveal that he, being close to Peggy, was aware that she, like Joan, lived and acted by her own secret intuitions. Joan had shattered her world, and Peggy shattered people, too. Not only Malone, but Mrs. Murdock; even Foley. She would shatter all the people who lived on the mountain and the people who prayed on the mountain. Joan had to die, he thought with a sharp pang, simply because she was what she was. And there had been terror in Peggy's face as Malone's hand reached out for her; she had sensed that there were many others like Malone, who would destroy her. His intent stare only puzzled Jackson, who glanced questioningly at Foley. It was plain he hadn't intended the comparison, and McAlpine was relieved. He felt sorry for Jackson. "You'd rather talk nonsense about generations, wouldn't you?" he asked in a bored tone.

"I see," Henry Jackson said in a whisper. "I ought to sock you."

"Don't overmatch yourself, Henry," Foley said.

"No," Jackson whispered. "I won't." Turning to Foley he begged silently for some help, not because he was afraid but because he had been seeking a humiliation and now it had come.

The distress in his eyes worried McAlpine. "Look, Henry," he said. "We're not really talking about your generation or mine, are we?"

"No," he whispered.

"Nor about Shaw."

"No."

"Nor any of that stuff."

"I know."

"So do I," McAlpine said. "Have a drink with us, will you, Henry?"

"I don't know why I insult you," Jackson said. "I don't feel good, and I got talking."

"A drink for Henry," McAlpine called, and Wolgast brought them drinks.

For the next few embarrassed moments Foley made it easier by switching the conversation to last night's hockey game, and

Henry Jackson was able to finish his drink, say he had an appointment, shake hands with elaborate politeness, and leave without a glance at Malone and Gagnon, who were coming toward the table. Malone disregarded McAlpine's hostile aloofness. He had a twisted, cynical, understanding smile, and McAlpine hated him.

"Mr. McAlpine," Wolgast said, "I want you to understand that Henry is not always a jerk. I heard him talking to Malone and Gagnon. He has his own little problem. It's that girl of his. You know her."

"I know her."

"I think Henry is now on his way to break her neck."

"Oh!"

"Yes. You see, Mr. McAlpine," Wolgast said tolerantly, "the girl is a nigger lover. I knew it the other day. Saw her myself going along Dorchester with a jig."

"That's not news to Henry," Foley protested.

"Mr. McAlpine, You're a friend of Chuck's and, so to speak, a friend of the house." Wolgast glanced at Malone and Gagnon. "You see, Henry just had a fight with her and she called him a 'white bastard.'"

"Very comical," Gagnon said sourly. "Little Henry, so very proud of being tolerant and understanding."

"If it's so comical, why don't you laugh?" Foley asked.

"I'm laughing."

"I don't hear you."

"I don't laugh out loud at myself."

"Oh, Peggy and you – too?"

"I once toyed with the idea of going to bed with her, yes. A good dinner, much sympathetic intellectual discussion – I do it well. For her to call Henry a white bastard – well, it offends me," he said angrily.

Gagnon was not one of those French Canadians who had a fanatical pride in race. He had lost his influence with prominent French Canadians after he had permitted his brilliant cartoons, always satirical about French Canadian life, to be printed in a New York magazine. His compatriots said he had mocked his own people for the edification of strangers who wanted to see them as Gagnon drew them. So his indignation astonished them all. "I know what she implies when she calls Henry a white bastard," he went on scornfully. "The remark implies a sympathy with the oppressed. Racial sympathy! From her? As you say, 'boloney.' I fell for it. It seemed to be the way to her bed, I admit, but I talked about the low wages of the French Canadian industrial workers. Ah, that little toss of her head! My compatriots can look after themselves. She likes dark meat. We're not dark meat," he said, sounding vindictive. "Why didn't Henry ask me to go with him? I could hold her while he booted her in the pants."

"All you mean is that she brushed you off," Foley said cynically. Then he turned to Wolgast. "Wolgast, why does a girl like that go for jigs?"

"Why? Well, I think I can tell you," Wolgast said, his cigar ash falling on Malone's shoulder.

The others leaned close to Wolgast with profound respect, and McAlpine waited, pale and desolate. He wanted to go; but to strut out with an air of offended dignity would be to cheapen her. Nothing they could say could destroy his faith in her, and it was like the night when he had been in the Café St. Antoine talking with Elton Wagstaffe and he had known he was called upon to be always with her, even while she was being viciously misunderstood.

"Go on, Wolgast," he said quietly.

"Why does a girl like that become a nigger lover?" Wolgast began, with a beautiful expression of philosophical detachment. "To get at the main reason, as Gagnon says, you've got to know a little about the girl. But when you get to know her you'll find she's always wanted to be in the spotlight and has never been able to make the grade. What's that big two-dollar word I'm looking for, Chuck?"

"'Frustrated'?"

"Frustrated, that's it. Who's got a match?"

"Here," Gagnon said, lighting his cigar.

"She's the little girl who wants to sing when nobody will listen to her, the piano player everybody walks out on. Hell, you guys have been around here, you've met some awful earbenders, haven't you? Why, the poor guys will start saying anything just to get hold of somebody's ear. A little attention, see? We all want this attention. I don't think any of us get enough attention. And it makes those little girls I'm talking about get desperate. They'll do any god-damned crazy thing to make them seem a little different. Well, the ones that go for the coons are showboating in a big way. Everybody turns and looks at them. Everybody talks about them. It's like travelling with a brass band. You should agree with me, Mr. McAlpine. You're a historian."

"Better than that, he's about the only white guy Peggy bothers seeing these days," Malone said slyly.

"Oh, they went to college together," Foley said, brushing him off.

"Just the same, now that Henry has gone, I will move in," Malone said. "I will lay her."

"You're a fool," McAlpine said.

"I want to know if McAlpine agrees with me," Wolgast insisted. "I have just made a speech. I have asked his opinion. He's a scholar."

"Well, I don't agree with you, Wolgast." McAlpine longed to be able to throw a cloak of splendid protective words around her. "I think you all make one little mistake. If she were merely fascinated by Negroes – an exotic taste, yes – that would be a kind of perversion. But supposing she is interested in them only as human beings she has come to know and like – as she might be interested in you or me? If I were a Negro and I liked her it would hurt me to know that I couldn't have her friendship because I was coloured. I know this, too," he said, toying with his glass, "if I had some Negro friends and liked them as one human being likes another I think they'd get into the habit of talking frankly in my presence, and I'd hear them talking about little incidents of discrimination going on all over the country in restaurants and trains and hotels. A lot of them are porters and they have these stories of one humiliation after another. Well, if they were friends of mine and I liked and respected them I'd feel ashamed. As a human being, I'd be apologetic. I might sometimes feel contempt for my own race if I had any sense of justice. If I were young and ardent I'd feel guilty and perhaps overly sympathetic. What she's doing around here may be imprudent and impossible. You might all agree that it's simply an adventure. But with her I'm sure it's a noble adventure."

He had spoken with such dignity and good faith they were all embarrassed.

"He makes speeches like music," Gagnon said finally. "Beautiful speeches in a pleasant tone. The right kind of music for Peggy. You follow me? There she is, lost in the dark underworld. Montreal's Plutonian shore. Like Eurydice. Remember the lady? Remember? How did Eurydice die?"

"Bitten by a snake," Foley said.

"And certainly our little Peggy has been badly bitten."

"So McAlpine becomes her Orpheus."

"Ah, yes, there you are. Her Orpheus."

"Orpheus McAlpine!"

They were all alert, watching him. He called for a round of drinks, but when the drinks came and their attention was diverted he wondered why Jackson had resented him so much. He felt restless. "Sorry, Chuck," he said, patting him on the shoulder, "I have an appointment," and he left them. But he stopped just outside the door, waiting; and of course it came: the burst of derisive laughter.

A gust of wind sprayed snow from the roof onto his face and he had to take out his handkerchief and wipe his eyes. He strode up the street, looking up only once at the barrier of the mountain. It was there, of course; it was always there. On St. Catherine, where he slowed down, the moonlight glinted on the steeple of the stone church at the corner of Bishop, and the steeple was a white snow cone thrust against the night sky. All he could think of was that Peggy had got rid of Jackson. He remembered the intimate moments in her room and hoped she might have quarrelled with Jackson over him. That would explain why Jackson had been so resentful.

He turned up Crescent; he looked along the alley to see if there was a reflection of light on the back fence from her window. At that angle it was hard to decide. Going in, he tapped apprehensively on her door. At first there was no answer; and the door, for the first time, was locked. Again he tapped, and then she called, "Who is it?"

Sighing with relief, he said softly, "It's Jim. It's not late, Peggy."

A light appeared at the crack under the door and it just touched the toes of his galoshes. She opened the door and stood there in a light blue silk kimono around her white nightgown. She had a black eye.

✦ SEVENTEEN ✦

"Your eye! What happened to your eye, Peggy?"

"It's nothing. What do you want, Jim? I was in bed," she said impatiently.

"What happened to your eye?" he asked, raising his voice as he pushed his way in and closed the door. She was in her bare feet, which were so surprisingly small that he couldn't take his eyes off them. "You're in your bare feet," he said. "The floor's cold. Where are your slippers?"

"Here." She went to the bed and put them on. "You don't have to worry about my eye," she said, watching him take off his coat.

"Somebody should. What happened?"

"I was having a drink with Henry. And I had a little disagreement with him, and he got pretty sore. Well, he punched me." Her eyes were bright, vindictive, and hard. "It was something I said to him," she added tentatively, waiting for him to ask what she had said.

But he didn't ask. Instead he put his hands gently on her head and turned her face to the light. "It'll be all blue tomorrow," he said. "It's closing now. What did you do for it? I think I'd better put some cold compresses on it."

He got a face cloth from her dresser and marched resolutely along the hall to the bathroom to soak the cloth in cold water. Against the bathroom window lay the shadow of an icicle. Opening the window he knocked it off and broke it into lumps which he wrapped up in the face cloth, and then he returned to the room where she waited, sitting cross-legged on the bed, smiling to herself.

"All right, put your head back on the pillow," he said. And when she lay back he tried to tell her all the secrets of his heart in the way his fingers touched her cheeks, touching her with a gentle reverence that made her smile. He caressed her head and stroked her hair. All his motions were full of tender concern. And gradually the bruised and swollen eye emerged in a fantastic contrast with her other eye and her dainty fair head and tranquil body. The bruise was a mark of wildness on her; it was a glimpse of a strange mixture of peace and wildness, and his heart began to swell and he stared at the shadow under her chin and the shadow between her breasts. Then he trembled and looked again at the bruise and he put his hands on her head and he held her and kissed her. His right hand slid down boldly under her nightgown, and cupped her breast, and when she squirmed they were both lost in a pulling, tearing ecstasy, trying to hold each other in some embrace that eluded them.

He whispered, and she answered him in a savage whisper, neither hearing what the other said. Then her soft little body was convulsed. He couldn't hold on to it, and she slid away from him and off the bed where she stood facing him, trembling.

"No! I say, no! Don't, Jim. Don't," she said doggedly. She backed over against the dresser. On the wall behind her was the drawing he had done of her – "Peggy the Crimper."

There were two red spots on her cheeks, his finger marks on her shoulder, and a flush mounted from her neck while she held her kimono tight across her breasts. He took a slow step toward her, his eyes on the clenched fist holding the kimono, waiting for the fingers to open, the arm to drop, the sudden agitated yielding. And his hand went out, thinking she needed only to feel the compulsion of his own desire in order to believe she had been persuaded against her will and so could do what she wanted to do.

"I love you, Peggy," he whispered. "I've loved you all the time. I have to be with you, darling. Don't fight against me. Let it be easy, darling."

"Oh, stop it!" she cried, wheeling away in anger from his outstretched hand, and he thought she was going to hit him. "If I wanted to let you touch me I would. What's the matter with you? Can't you see I don't want it?"

"Oh!" he said, feeling stupid. "I thought—" he began, stammering awkwardly.

"I don't care what you thought."

"I got it wrong. I can see I got it wrong," he said. His humiliation blinded him to the meaning of her anger. He did not realize that his kindness and love had broken through the passive indifference she had shown that day when he had tried to kiss her, and that now she had to resist and struggle not only against him, but against herself. He knew he had hurt her, but he did not see that he had done it by arousing her own desire. He did not see that, if she yielded, she yielded also to him her view of her life and of herself. He was also too bewildered to realize that she was now afraid of his gentle concern and his passion, and that it tormented her more now than any pressure all the others could bring to bear against her.

"I apologize," he said, feeling miserable.

"Oh, all right, all right," she said grudgingly. "I like you. Like being with you. You're sort of there to rely on. I do rely on you. You're clumsy, but gentle. Only it doesn't mean that..."

"I know," he said. The little motions he made, fumbling with his tie, adjusting his coat, reminded him of his unattractive love making and he blushed. If only she weren't watching him fumbling with his coat! Then there flashed into his mind a picture of Henry Jackson and the faces of Wolgast's grinning clients; he heard their jeering laughter: "You see, you're not dark meat." And the cords in his throat tightened and his head began to sweat, but in his heart came one pathetic cry. Why couldn't she be a virgin? Virginity would be so becoming to her.

"I talked to Henry Jackson," he said, trying to smile.

"Oh!"

"He talked as if you were his girl."

"Well—"

"As if you had been in love with him."

"Henry has to feel someone is in love with him."

"I don't like to think of – well, tell me on thing, will you?"

"What?"

"Are you a virgin?"

"Oh!" She smiled faintly. "How about Catherine Carver?"

"She was married. Will you tell me? Are you?"

"What do you think?"

"I don't know."

"That's the way it should be, isn't it?"

"Yes, I suppose so."

"You certainly take a direct method of trying to find out, don't you, Jim? Yet it's interesting. Very interesting."

"What do you mean?"

"I seem to remember a little conversation about whether I was corrupt – or was it whether I attracted brutality and corruption?"

"I – I remember."

"I do seem to bring it out in you, judging by your performance just now," she said dryly. "I think some of those Negroes you worry about would agree with me, don't you?"

"I made a mistake. I make mistakes with you because I love you. I thought Jackson had been your lover. People think so, Peggy."

"I told you I had been very fond of Henry."

"I still don't know what it was like between you. What made you take to him?"

"It's hard to know sometimes," she said, "but I think I know why Henry appealed to me. He has a chip on his shoulder. But I knew why, Jim. Henry has pure feelings, and he gets hurt so easily. He's always angry but he doesn't want to be."

"And he's lame."

"Yes, he's lame. And he's always in flight."

"Always on the run."

"On the run. Yes, in a sense," she said, looking surprised. But he believed he could see where Henry fitted in with the Johnson family and the St. Antoine people, and he was glad.

"Maybe I still seem a little like a stranger," he said. "Maybe later on, when you get used to me, it could be easier for both of us."

"You worry me," she said. "Why the hell I keep having you around, I don't know. In heaven's name please don't be so humble! I hate it."

"I – well…" he began helplessly. Then the wind rattled a loose window pane and he turned. "The glass there is loose. Isn't there always a draft on you?"

"It rattled all last night," she said, going toward the window. "I had a piece of paper in there to tighten it."

"Has it come out?"

"I think I can fix it," she said, pressing the folded paper tighter between the frame and the glass. "There."

"I'm sick of this zero weather. I'm sick of the snow," he said.

"So am I. Aren't we due for a January thaw?"

"It'll come. It always comes."

"I like the summer better. I like the hot summer in the city," she said.

"That's odd. I like the city in the summer, too. It doesn't get too hot for me."

"Me neither," she said. "Well, I might as well make some coffee."

She put on the kettle, and while it was boiling she went to the mirror to examine the bruise. Her face was close to the mirror, and standing beside her, he showed her that the bruise was really under the eye. "Maybe it won't blacken at all," he said. "What a break that would be!" she said hopefully. The kettle began to boil. She measured out the coffee. He poured in the water. Doing these things with her delighted him, and he knew that he only needed the right to share this part of life in the room to have her under the siege of his love. When they were drinking the coffee he grew cunning. It was difficult for him to do any work at the Ritz, he complained. Phones rang, maids walked in, he wandered down to the lobby. "I don't see how you get anything done there," she said. Nodding, he led her on. What he needed was a little place he could use as an office, a place where no one would bother him. When she agreed he said, "Say, why couldn't I come here in the afternoons, Peggy?"

"You mean use my room?"

"I wouldn't be in your way. You wouldn't be here."

"What do you think I am? Why, you'd be moving in on me."

"But only when you're not here."

"Do you think I live my life on the sidewalk?" she asked, exasperated. "Just because you've found the door open a few times, is this room supposed to be a hangout?"

"I've just said you wouldn't know I was here."

"Why, you'd be living in my pocket, Jim. I don't know what impression you have of me, but the fact is I have a private life. This room, damn it, is my castle. Well," she added, looking around the bare room, "at least it's my cottage. It's the only place where I can be alone."

"I know," he persisted. "I wouldn't bother you. I'd get out before you came home."

"And you'd wonder where I had been."

"No. Honestly I wouldn't. I'd never ask."

"And you seem to have taken a fancy to that bed."

"I swear I wouldn't bother you, Peggy," he said, eagerly. "I'd do my work. It's quiet here. Nobody would know I was here. I'd go before you came back."

"In a funny kind of way I think you feel I need you here. Isn't that it?" she asked, and when he shook his head vigorously she added, "I don't need anybody around here." But what she had just said surprised her. Maybe she suddenly remembered Malone barging in with her. Maybe she had some sudden doubt of herself and a remembered awareness that she liked having him around and in touch with her. "Well, if it's so important to you," she said reluctantly, "if you wouldn't bother me, if you'd get out when I came home—"

"Thanks, Peggy," he said, quietly exultant. He had wormed his way into the room, he would worm his way into her life and into her heart and take her life into his.

At two o'clock next afternoon he was back in Peggy's room taking off his overcoat and overshoes and putting them in the cupboard. First he tidied up the bureau, dusting off the spilled face powder and the hairpins. He made an orderly arrangement of the face cream and nail polish so he would have space for writing. Opening his briefcase, he spread out his papers on the bureau. It was too high for writing comfortably. He put a layer of books on the chair seat and then a cushion on top of the books and sat down. It was awkward and uncomfortable.

He wanted to get down some background material for his first three columns. He tried to work with the air of a man who had come to the one place where he could think with beautiful clarity. But the light from the ceiling was not good; he would hear a whirring noise from the floor above and jump up: it would be Mrs. Agnew's vacuum cleaner. The woman had a passion for the vacuum cleaner. If she were unhappy or lonely or restless she ran her vacuum cleaner, and he would listen nervously to the whining until he wanted to scream. He would look around and frown, wondering how he got there. Instead of working in such a dump he could have been in his comfortable hotel room, or he could have used Foley's apartment; yet he had let himself be chained in this musty-smelling basement with the odour of stale food seeping through the cracks in the door.

He had only one visitor, a strapping, good-looking young Negress who came to the room accompanied by a five-year-old boy. It was at five-thirty, when Peggy should have been home. The smart young Negress, who was abashed at encountering McAlpine, said that she was in the neighbourhood and wanted to take an hour to have a drink with her boyfriend and knew Peggy would mind the boy for her for that hour. McAlpine offered to look after the boy. She refused, and was puzzled by his obvious approval of her visit. But her visit for him was a vindication of his own judgment of Peggy. Not only Negro men but Negro women liked and trusted her.

Those moochers who used to come must have heard he was there on guard. No one came to disturb him. He would write grimly until his eyes got tired, then he would get up and stretch and saunter to the little back window and look out at the snow-capped fence and the cat's footprints in the snow leading to the three garbage pails by the gate. Then he would turn away from the window and stare morosely at each stick of shabby furniture and hate it for its cheapness. The smudges on the wall, the bare spots on the floor, and that odour of lighter fluid perfume she brought into the room every night filled him with disgust, and so did the little discoveries he made every day of her untidiness. Toast crumbs would be left on the burner, toast crumbs and cigarette butts, and the dregs of coffee in a cup; a stocking would dangle from a drawer or be tossed on the floor in the closet. His loathing of the room became a dull ache in his brain. His sense of order would compel him to tidy up the place as a gesture to the dignity of his work and his own self-respect; he would wipe off the burner and take the coffee cup along the hall to the bathroom to wash it. He kept asking himself bitterly why she hadn't the sense to let him take her somewhere where they could lead an orderly life.

Each night when she came home from the factory she would look around, smile brightly and thank him for tidying up the room. She began to take it for granted that he was willing to play housekeeper for her and hardly bothered to make the bed. She was trying to provoke him, he thought, and drive him away. With all the resources of her slovenliness, she was cunningly protecting herself against him by inducing him to believe she was a slut. But the true sluts, he told himself, were meticulously clean on the outside. This flaunting of her untidiness was her way of repelling him.

He prowled around the room, searching in drawers and closets for scraps of evidence to prove that her carelessness with her clothes was part of her defiant resistance. On his knees before the lower drawer of the bureau he pulled out a silver bracelet, a little discarded beaded bag, and a pair of satin pumps saved from her college days. He got up slowly, the beaded bag in his hands, an exultant smile on his face, and stood in a trance. Then he hurried to the closet and looked at her black dress. Again he smiled. In that black dress which was so beautifully and simply cut she had true elegance and knew it; and when she put on that white silk blouse and black skirt she had her own peculiar distinction. Good style was instinctive with her as was her gentleness and the lovely tone of her voice. All the untidiness, the overall mess was her gesture of contempt for those who were passionately concerned with these things, for she knew she could emerge effortlessly with her own kind of superior elegance.

When she came home from work he would have the coffee made and serve her a cup, then sit in his chair by the bureau, crossing his knees and holding his cup while they gossiped and she stretched out on the bed. She would always love him for his coffee, she said. It was as if they were living together.

She would move around the room, and sometimes he would reach out and circle her hips with his arms and put his head under her breast, listening to the beating of her heart, and she would stand still, unprotesting, but uninterested, till her stiff stillness gradually took the heart out of him. Then she would smile to herself.

It was his privilege to stay there until she got dressed to go out for the evening. He did not ask where she would go. Nor did she ask him whom he would see. There were no strings attached.

He had to go to the Carvers' in the evenings for conferences with Mr. Carver, and with those visits he believed he was clarifying his position. Mr. Carver was helping him with his work. They would adjourn to the library; they would remain alone there, and he would be so businesslike that Catherine hesitated to interrupt them. Mr. Carver became his editor; he himself was simply the conscientious newspaperman. He had drafted three columns, each one a development of the same idea. He wanted to express these ideas as stories. He wanted to tell of the lost men of Europe, the mass men who were driven by some death wish to surrender their own identity and become anonymous parts of a big machine: he intended to make the point by devoting each column to one character, one lost man. The plan and the treatment delighted Mr. Carver, who had some shrewd suggestions. "Keep it lively and personal. Always put flesh on the bones, Jim, and you can't go wrong," he would say. Then they would have a drink and Mr. Carver would talk about ice fishing. In two weeks he would be able to get away for a weekend, he said. It would be nearly midnight when they came out of the library, and Catherine, who had got bored waiting, would have gone to bed.

Going back to the Crescent Street room was like going home to his work, his happiness, his love, and that dream he had about four o'clock in the afternoon when his eyes grew tired from the bad light and he had to lie down on the bed, cupping his eyes with his palms and focussing them in the darkness behind the palms to rest and strengthen them.

In the dream he would give himself the time he needed before the Carvers heard of his attachment to Peggy. Sooner or later Catherine and her father would hear of it; but, given a little more time, he would be prepared. Given time, he and Peggy would be ready to emerge from the dark cellar world of illicit relationships and meet the Carvers. As yet they were not ready, and he could only pray his job wouldn't be jeopardized by Catherine's premature shocked discovery of his love for a girl like Peggy. But when the peculiar fury of Peggy's defiance was exhausted they could emerge together.

In his scheming dream of breaking her resistance and remolding her, he failed to see that he was pitting himself against her; that he was justifying her instinctive resistance. He went on dreaming of her as she would be when she had yielded to him. He dreamt of the two of them meeting his friend Sol Bloom, the Jewish gynaecologist, whom he had called when he first came to town. Sol had been in New York. The short round-faced little doctor, with only a fringe of hair around his head, was one of the wisest and kindest men he knew. He could see Sol having a cocktail with him and Peggy. And Sol in his wisdom would say, Yes, she had those rare childlike qualities that the Chinese sages used to admire, she was spontaneous, acted only on impulse, never reflected, cared nothing for her circumstances, took no stock of the future. And after the cocktail he would take her to the theatre, to His Majesty's if a play from New York were there, and between acts Catherine would be in the lobby, and, of course, there would be one shy diffident moment. But as a token of her own self-respect Catherine would invite them home for a drink and Mr. Carver would meet Peggy. Mr. Carver would be shrewd and worldly enough to make it plain he sought talent and energy in his employees, value for his money, and not the right to pick wives for them; the only vital question for him would be whether Peggy would do the newspaper and McAlpine credit, and of course he would soon succumb to her gentle charm. The first meeting with Angela Murdock would be more amusing; but even that meeting could come off easily with a warning word to Peggy. That expression of disapproval thagt had shone in Angela's eyes when old Fielding had mentioned Peggy's name was born no doubt of wounded pride. A spoiled woman like Angela had been unable to endure Peggy's indifference; that had been the trouble. But if Peggy were friendly and enthusiastic Angela would like her. On a weekend he would take her to meet his father; yes, he could see them walking up the path to the house. And there at the open door would be his father in his best suit, restraining his natural eloquence as he tried to remember he was the dignified father of the columnist of the Montreal *Sun*. But her refinement, her simplicity and fresh intelligence would be too much for his exuberant father. "You have chosen a fine girl, Jim. She has poise and charm," he would whisper enthusiastically. "Your mother would have liked her. Why don't you get married here at home?" And that night of their marriage with her at last in the bed beside him: the incredible surprise of having her lying in the dark beside him, his hand on her breast, her neck, the curve in the small of her back...

His dream would be broken by the heavy beating of his heart. But he would go back to it to watch her turning to him, her lips parting, her head back and her eyes closed; and again the dream would break, always breaking like that before they entered the darkness and peace of their being together.

NINETEEN

With his clients big Wolgast had always made a joke about the fact that he was a Jew. Nothing was upset. It was very important that his relationship with the whole town should not be upset. None of his clients called him the "Jewish Lush" to make him something less than he was. Nor had French Canadian hostility to the Jews disturbed him. It only made him smile complacently. On St. Catherine East, the French Canadian shopkeepers and the restaurant owners and the tailors hated the Jews for encroaching eastward and for growing rich. But that kind of hostility was something you laughed about; everybody knew the French Canadians were hostile out of envy; it was a mark of respect. Amiable French Canadian sporting writers or a distinguished cartoonist like Gagnon came to his bar and joked about his race and theirs, and, besides, he had always had the cooperation of some French Canadian politicians when he needed to get his license renewed.

But no one who couldn't go anywhere else had felt free to come into his bar just because he was a Jew. No one had ever shown that much contempt for him, he told himself – until today.

It was all clear to him. He was the one bartender in the whole Peel and St. Catherine neighbourhood that Peggy Sanderson had felt sure of, the only one who wouldn't be able to feel insulted if she walked in with a dinge.

Rolling down his sleeves, he buttoned the cuffs, did up his shirt collar and took his coat from the hook and went back to the washroom to put on his tie. He had heard Peggy ask the Negro boy to walk her home. He took an address book from his pocket, got Henry Jackson's phone number, and went to the phone and called him. He simply asked where Peggy lived; he wouldn't offer any explanation. In the restaurant his partner, Doyle, was playing gin rummy with Tony Harman, the barber from along the street; and English Annie, the pretty fair girl with the bad teeth who was in love with Tony, sat there getting sore as usual when Tony lost.

"Take over for a while, will you, Derle?" Wolgast said. "Heh, you lug, where are you going?" Doyle protested. But Wolgast didn't answer; he went out, and walked slowly up the hill on the way to Crescent Street; he walked with a slow solemn step, a big clumsy man in ill-fitting clothes who now had an extraordinary air of dignity.

With each big slow step he thought, All I want is that things be left just the way they are. It's very little to ask. I have a right to ask that much. His mind was in turmoil.

As he turned up Crescent Street he thought of his boyhood and a white horse he had loved. At the Crescent Street house he began to climb the flight of stairs to the main door, then remembered that Henry Jackson had told him to enter by the basement door, and he went along the hall to Peggy's room and knocked.

McAlpine in his shirt sleeves opened the door. He had been sitting at the bureau making some notes in a big flat notebook.

"Oh!" he said, looking startled.

"Mr. McAlpine!"

"Why, hello, Wolgast."

"What are you doing here?"

"I was just going to ask you the same thing, Wolgast."

"I wanted to see this Peggy. I didn't know that…"

"I've been waiting here for her myself," McAlpine said, blushing. "As a matter of fact I was just going," he added quickly. "I don't think she's going to show up."

"Oh, she'll show up," Wolgast said with a knowing smile as he watched McAlpine tuck his books in his briefcase, and tried to appraise his importance in Peggy's life. "I should have seen you were thick with her. It's a good thing though, a very good thing." And he sounded relieved. "Walking down my way, Mr. McAlpine?" he asked mildly.

"Why, sure. Let's go. Wait. I'll put out the light."

Again Wolgast smiled faintly, recognizing in the gesture the act of a man who had been in the room many times.

On the street it became embarrassing, for McAlpine wanted to ask why Wolgast was looking for Peggy and Wolgast himself wanted to talk about her; but as soon as they fell in step they realized that they did not know each other. They had never met outside Wolgast's bar, and now they were two strangers from different cities trying to capture a hearty intimate relationship they were supposed to enjoy.

A fierce wind blew down from the mountain and the thin snow on the wind stung their ears. The temperature was dropping rapidly.

"Looks like the coldest night we've had so far," Wolgast said. "If I had whiskers I could knock them off like icicles. I wouldn't need to shave."

"They say it's ten below right now."

"Twelve below. Which way are you walking? Why don't we have a cup of coffee somewhere?"

"I don't mind," McAlpine said. "I'm walking over to Peel." But he wondered why he didn't ask Wolgast to walk up to the

Ritz with him; it was where he was going, and he tried to assure himself it was because Wolgast would not feel comfortable in the Ritz; for that reason he was walking all the way over to Peel.

"Fine." Wolgast said. "Why don't you turn up your collar?"

"It's a good idea. Your chin down and your hat down and your collar up. That's right."

"Funny things pop into a guy's head when he's going along with his head tucked down like this and his eyes half closed against the wind. Ever notice, Mr. McAlpine?"

"Yes. Yes, I have."

"On the way up here I got thinking of a big white horse I used to ride when I was a kid. Cockeyed, eh?"

"You on a horse! I imagined you were always a city man."

"I was a kid once – just like you," Wolgast said mildly. "How about this place?" he said after they had walked along silently for a couple of blocks and were at the soda fountain near the corner of Peel.

"What's on your mind, Wolgast?" McAlpine asked when they were sitting at the counter.

"It's a little hard to explain, Mr. McAlpine. You've got more education than I have. But you and Foley aren't like some educated drips I know. I'd do anything for Foley. And I think you'd get my point of view, too. You see, I like Montreal very much, Mr. McAlpine."

"It's a fine city."

"A big town, a good town. Lots of different kinds of people. A man has a chance to make a buck for himself and mind his own business. Yeah," he went on profoundly, "I like it better than Brooklyn or New York or Chicago. Got more real character than those towns. And, besides, it's now my home."

He was taking his time, undisturbed by McAlpine's puzzled expression. Wolgast had always been proud of the way he could keep his voice down and take his time. They looked out at the hard snow streaming across the window, and both thought about Montreal. For Wolgast it was the city where his life could be easy and enlarge a little more every day in an atmosphere of pleasant tolerance. But for McAlpine it was a place that had always beguiled him; a rock of riches with poverty sprawling around the rock, and now a place that had inexplicably brought turmoil to his heart. They were both moved by their own thoughts, and Wolgast stirred his coffee methodically.

"A little while ago I said I was a kid once just like you. Remember?"

"Sure. Why?"

"That was wrong. I wasn't a kid like you were."

"Well," McAlpine began, grinning, "I never owned a big white horse."

"Well, neither did I," Wolgast whispered. "It was a funny thing, though, remembering that white horse. Maybe it explains the way I feel now. How would you like if I told you about it?" And when McAlpine, baffled and curious, nodded, he said that he had been born in Poland in a village on a wide flat stretch of land near the Russian border, a forlorn little village of about a hundred homes where everything and everybody belonged to the landowner, who had a fine big house about a mile away. The village houses were windswept and bare. They had old barns and lean-tos, and in the winter the village was bleak and lonely. It was hard to be a Jew in that village. But there were good times in the summer, especially when soldiers were on army manoeuvres. They spent money and the girls danced and got pregnant, and young husbands were often ashamed of their wives; but the kids all had fun with the soldiers.

His father lived in an old shack that had one big room, the kitchen where they lived, and two little rooms where the children slept. In the winter they lived their life in the kitchen around the big stove. It was a hard life. His father, a short powerful man, strong as a giant, was stern and fierce with his wife and children. His mother was a meek woman who never dreamed of having a better life than she had in the village. It was the kind of life her people had known for five hundred years. They were little better than serfs. Everything they got out of life, the money, the suffering, the poverty and a few hopes, they got from the landlord and the big house where his father worked around the stables. He had always been afraid of his father, who scowled and scolded and grumbled and slapped him; yet somewhere, maybe around the big house, the father had learned to read; his son had to learn, too, and sometimes at night he would bring home a discarded book from the big house and toss it at his son and make him read it before he went to sleep. It didn't matter what the book was about. He read by candlelight, his eyes always ached in the flickering light. He had to stop reading because they said he was losing his sight.

In the summer he worked with his father around the landlord's house and in the fields, working from dawn to dark, helping around the stables, feeling happier when working alone because his father scolded him and bossed him. He liked the stables, he liked the warm smell of the horses in the winter and hitching the horses to the sleighs for the long journey along the lonely roads. Sometimes a horse and sleigh would get snowed in on one of those roads. People from the village had been frozen to death travelling from one village to another in a snowstorm.

A few miles away from the landowner's village was a town where his father had to go once a week to haul home supplies for the landlord. On this journey he always accompanied his father. It was his job to hitch up the same white horse to the wagon. It was a fine proud white horse, not a show horse, and not a heavy work horse, just a beautiful white horse for pulling a boy on a wagon. The journeys to town became the happiest part of his life. After they had gone a piece along the winding dirt road with the deep ruts twisting into the sunlight his father would solemnly hand over the reins while he lit his pipe, and then forget to take them back; and he would doze in the sunlight, breathing heavily with his cap pulled down over his eyes. The white horse knew who had taken the reins; it would swish its tail a little and trot along briskly all the way to town. He wouldn't wake up his father until he had driven down the main street because he wanted everybody on the street to see him on the driver's seat with the reins in his hands.

They would spend three or four hours in town going from store to store, and those hours were an exciting part of the ride, for his father was more like a human being, chatting with the shopkeepers and the street loafers. Not that he paid much attention to his son, but he would laugh and make jokes with men in the stores as if he owned those few hours in his life. Nor did he look so much like a big-shouldered, slow-moving, bearded serf. At nightfall, when they drove back to the big house, he let his son look after the horse, feeding it and bedding it down. In the poverty-stricken life of a small boy, that white horse was a magic horse, able to carry him to places that were gay and free. It was like nothing else he had ever known. It got so that he was the only one who ever looked after the white horse. He came to believe it belonged to him.

One day they drove into town to the livery stable where his father met a merchant from another town, and this well dressed merchant inspected the horse and the wagon. The merchant and his father had an important conversation; he didn't listen to it. Then his father took him by the arm and walked him out of the livery stable and told him they were walking the five miles home; the horse and wagon had been sold.

Not until they were out of town and going along the road together did he understand that he would not see the white horse again. He began to cry and yell that it was his horse. He turned and started to run back to town. His father had to chase him and catch him. The landlord had ordered him to sell the horse, he said gruffly. They started back along the road again. It was the hot part of the afternoon and his father, holding him by the arm, walked fast. There were no trees along the road, and in the sunlight big beads of perspiration began to roll down his father's face. He noticed the red sweating face even while he trotted along trying to keep up, bawling at the top of his voice, stumbling in the ruts and pleading with his father to go back and get their horse and not let anybody take it from them. While he cried and pleaded his father never answered, just kept plodding along looking straight ahead. So he dropped on the road, howling and refusing to get up; then his father wheeled around, jerked him up, and began to pound him. After he had hit him the first time he couldn't stop. He was like a crazy man. Grabbing a stick from the roadside he beat him furiously, his eyes blazing, the hatred in his eyes terrifying, and the little stick broke, and then he looked at the stick, bewildered, and tossed it away. Without saying a word he went on down the road alone.

He always remembered the figure of his father plodding on down the road, big-shouldered, stooping a little and never looking back, his big hands hanging loosely at his sides. He wanted to call to him to come back and pick him up but was afraid of what he might see in his face if he turned.

The rest of the summer and into the autumn, whenever he went into town on another wagon and with another horse, he looked for the white horse. He dreamed of going into the nearby town when he grew older and finding the horse, but he never mentioned this dream to his father. The cold weather came and he did not go into town. His father was helping some workmen build a stone barn on the estate. He himself was lending a hand. On the first really cold day, when the ground was frozen and there was a little snow and the masons were trying to get the job finished, his father, the most powerful man on the estate, was carrying stones from a stone pile to the masons working on the walls. All day, like a beast of burden he carried these big stones, two at a time, one under each arm, from the stone pile to the scaffolding, and it was getting dark and they wanted to finish and he hurried. Then his knees wobbled, he dropped one of the stones and looked surprised; then the other big stone fell from his hands. He sat down slowly, then rolled on his back, both his hands over his heart. His eyes were closed but he said to the workmen who ran to him, "My son. Where is my son?"

For a little boy it was awful listening to his father gasping for breath, and remembering at the same time that he had always been afraid of him. His father, opening his eyes, smiled at him. It was the first gentle smile he had ever seen on the big bearded face; the effort to make the smile gentle was there in spite of his pain. "I'm sorry about that white horse, my son," he whispered. "Try and own a white horse of your own some day, son. Try hard." And he died.

Wolgast turned and watched the snow drifting across the window. "Did I say it happened the day of the first snowfall in our village?" he asked mildly.

"I think you did."

"Today's the coldest day of the year, too. Not much snow either. Maybe it reminded me of all this." He offered McAlpine a cigar. He took one himself but didn't light it. "We had an uncle in Brooklyn who got me and my mother and sister out of Poland," he went on. "My mother died in Brooklyn. Well, I've been awfully poor, but there's nothing I haven't done, Mr. McAlpine. I learned how to look after myself, and most of the time I was in a cheap business that wasn't legitimate; but I always wanted to get on the legit... I carried water pails for crooked fight managers, I was a lavatory attendant, I was a doorman in a whorehouse in Buffalo. But you know something? I always remembered that white horse and the way my father smiled at me and what he said. I think that's why I always wanted to go legitimate. To get something of my own – on the legit. Well, Montreal has been my dish. I got a nice class of customer now. For the first time in my life I'm legit. I got friends. I got influence. I got wholesale connections. I can borrow a buck or loan a buck; yes, up to twenty thousand any time I want to. It's a grand town. Even when it's twenty below I say it's a grand town. You should move here, Mr. McAlpine."

"It's been in my mind."

"Sure. Well, as I say, I like it the way it is for me. I want everything to stay just the way it is," he added slowly and carefully as he made his most important point, his pale blue eyes on McAlpine's. "I'd get sore if someone spoiled it for me. Wouldn't you?"

"I think I would."

"I'm a little sore right now, Mr. McAlpine. I'm a little sore at your friend Peggy."

"Peggy? Why?"

"You see, she came into my spot with a jig this afternoon."

"Oh! Oh, I see."

"It's a fact, she did. Now look, Mr. McAlpine," Wolgast went on softly. "Your friend's an educated girl. She knows what she's doing. She makes up her mind to select a spot away from St. Antoine where she can drink with a jig. Why did she pick on my place first?" When McAlpine only sighed, he repeated angrily, "Why did she pick on me? Go on, why don't you answer? Do you understand my question, Mr. McAlpine? All right, then answer me."

"But you think you have the answer, Wolgast."

"I want to hear you say it."

"No," McAlpine said wearily. "It would be too heartbreaking."

"Heartbreaking?"

"Yes. The way you feel, you couldn't believe she went into your place with this Negro because she knows you and likes you and thinks you have no prejudices. Maybe it was her tribute to you as a human being. Do you see, Wolgast?" Wolgast did not interrupt because he knew McAlpine was not reproaching him; his tone was too sympathetic and understanding, and he knew he had been harmed. "But what may have been a tribute to you has to be taken inevitably – oh, the whole of history compels you to take it – as an insult. I agree, Wolgast," he said. "She has no tact. If she only had a little prudence—" He leaned back and sighed. "What bothers me is that this lack of prudence of hers always brings out the worst instincts in us, the stuff we try and hide, the stuff that's inhuman."

He was so troubled that Wolgast too, for a moment, was disturbed, appreciating as he did McAlpine's sympathetic understanding of his position.

"I like you, Mr. McAlpine," he said finally.

"Me?" McAlpine asked, surprised.

"You're a good guy. But I understand a dame like that better than you do," Wolgast went on grimly. "She wants to move out of St. Antoine with her jigs, and we both know why she picked on me. Well, I've got nothing against the jigs. So let's say she brings one, then another and another, counting on getting away with it with me. So what? So soon I'm running a nigger joint and I lose my fine class of customer and I'm through. Am I right?"

"I suppose it's the way it would work out," McAlpine agreed unhappily.

"I don't want any trouble. I like it the way it is, Mr. McAlpine," Wolgast said. His smile was almost kindly, but his whispering gentle tone and his pale hard eyes made him sound frighteningly persuasive. "If little Peggy walks in on me again with a jig I won't say anything to the jig, understand? I won't insult the jig, because the jig won't be belittling me. But I'll hit your friend over the head with a gin bottle. Better still, I'll break the bottle and cut her with the jagged edge, and not even a jig will ever go for her again. You'll tell her that, won't you, Mr. McAlpine?"

"Oh, I'll speak to her," McAlpine said hastily. "Don't worry about it, Wolgast."

"Just keep her out of my joint. I like it the way it is, a friendly place," Wolgast said, and he smiled gratefully when McAlpine nodded.

They finished their coffee, got up and went out, and stood on the corner feeling embarrassed. They clutched at their coat collars and shifted on their feet and shoved their hands in their pockets. At that hour on Peel and St. Catherine the lights had come on and women flitted by with their faces hidden, their shoes squeaking on the snow. But the window of the newsstand was open; the four touts were in their places, shifting around to keep warm. A scrawny horse pulling a sleigh clopped by. A little man in a big overcoat dashed across the road from the cigar store to take his place among the touts on the corner. "I couldn't get in a phone booth," he complained. "It was a hot tip and I almost didn't make it." Across Dominion Square the Sun Life Building loomed up against the darkening sky.

"Well, how about coming down to my place for a drink?" Wolgast said, taking McAlpine by the arm.

"I've a little work to do before dinner," McAlpine said. "I'm going to the hockey game tonight."

"I'll take a night off myself sometime and go with you," Wolgast said. "Maybe you'll be around later tonight with Foley, eh?"

"Maybe I will."

"I'll look for you. So long."

"So long."

He patted McAlpine on the shoulder, and went on his way down Peel, loafing along like a slow amiable man and leaving McAlpine on the corner still shaken by the power of the ominous anger he had felt in him.

Wheeling sideways from the wind, McAlpine grabbed at his hat and hurried away, wanting to get to Peggy before Wolgast could do anything about her. But he didn't know where she was. When he got to his hotel room he paced up and down. He couldn't go to the hockey game with Catherine until he spoke to Peggy, even though he knew there was no use speaking to her. Glancing at his watch, he saw he would not have time to go out and eat. He stood at the window looking along Sherbrooke toward Catherine's apartment house. And at last he picked up the telephone. Peggy was at home. "Maybe this won't impress you much," he said, and he told her about the conversation he had had with Wolgast.

"Oh," she said. He had to keep talking. "Oh, I understand," she said finally. "Well, you can tell Wolgast something for me. He has a public license in that joint of his. Any time I go around there and behave quietly and the people with me also know how to behave, he has to serve me. You tell that to old Colonel Wolgast, or better still I'll make it clear to him myself."

"But Peggy, don't— Oh, hell, nothing I can say will make any difference, will it?"

"No, but thanks, Jim. Thanks anyway." And she hung up.

ᵜ TWENTY ᶜ

At the Forum the sustained roaring echoing along the streets compelled Catherine to take his arm and go plunging into the cavernous corridors and up the flights of stairs, half running with the other late stragglers. The fact that he had been late and had come offering apologies had made her feel important to him. All week she had been wanting him to ask her to forgive him for some breach in their intimacy which she couldn't define; now she liked the way they were rushing up the stairs together. A fine blue homespun woollen scarf embroidered in pink and yellow trailed over the shoulder of her beaver coat. "Hey, not so fast! I'm out of breath," she gasped.

"Where were you this afternoon, Jim?" she asked, reaching for his hand at the turn.

"Well," he said, hesitating, "what time?"

"About four o'clock, when I phoned." They began to ascend the second flight of stairs.

"Oh, I must have been downstairs having a drink," he lied.

That it should be necessary to lie shocked him and made him realize how false his relationship with her had become. And soon she would learn of his relationship with Peggy. Wolgast had walked in on him; it meant that word about him and Peggy had probably already got around, and soon Catherine would hear of it. Everybody would know about it. It was happening too soon. He and Peggy were not yet ready; they couldn't as yet be truly together. They would be dragged into the open while everyone was against them. If word did get around to the Carvers and they rejected him and he lost his job, well, he could take it. If it had to happen – to hell with them – let it happen. He had made his choice. It would be all right if he had Peggy. As yet, though, he didn't have her. Maybe he would never be able to count on her love. If that were so and he lost the Carvers and his job, and with his university post gone, too, he would be left with nothing. His life would be ruined. It frightened him, and his head began to sweat.

Their seats opposite the Ranger blue line were in the centre of the section, and they had a little luck; as they started along the row, mumbling apologies, the Canadiens threatened the Ranger goal, everybody stood up and they got to their seats between a stout florid French Canadian in a brown overcoat who was eating a bag of peanuts and a short French Canadian priest with a pale bony face. The roaring came like waves rising, falling, breaking, and always in motion. "Oh, that Richard!" Catherine screamed, pounding McAlpine's shoulder. "Who says he isn't the best right winger in the business? Look at him go!" Then the play shifted to the Canadiens end, the lines were changed and the roaring subsided, with the background of gigantic humming always there. Behind them, three rows up, a fight broke out. A fair-haired boy in a leather jacket started swinging wildly at a prosperous-looking middle-aged man in a hard hat. They couldn't reach each other and flailed the air. So the fair boy grabbed the brim of the prosperous citizen's hard hat and jerked it down over his eyes. Everybody laughed.

McAlpine remained standing, apparently waiting for the fight to break out again, but really gazing at the rows of grinning, exuberant faces. They would all be with Malone. They would all agree that Wolgast, too, no matter what he was, had really spoken for them.

They were fairly prosperous people, for the very poor didn't have the money to go to hockey games. Some of the men wore fur caps and coonskin coats; others, pink-faced and freshly shaven, wore hard hats; but most of them had on snap-brimmed fedoras. The women in their fur coats huddled happily together with their men, row on row, the rich men looking like rich men, and doctors and lawyers with their wives, and the merchants and the salaried workers and the prosperous union men. They came from all the districts around the mountain; they came from wealthy Westmount and solid respectable French Outremont and from the Jewish shops along St. Catherine, and of course a few Negroes from St. Antoine would be in the cheap seats. There they were, citizens of the second biggest French-speaking city in the world, their faces rising row on row, French faces, American faces, Canadian faces, Jewish faces, all yelling in a grand chorus; they had found a way of sitting together, yelling together, living together, too, and though Milton Rogers could shrug and say, "Our society stinks," even he had his place in this House of All Nations, such as the one they had in Paris, and liked it. And Wolgast! Wolgast, their bouncer, would whisper as he grabbed Peggy to throw her out, "You goddamned amateur. Don't give me that tenderness and goodness routine. Our cheapest whores have lost of that stuff to throw around, too."

"Look! Look!" Catherine screamed, tugging at his arm. The sea of faces rose around him, and it was rising around Peggy, too; the waves washed over both of them.

"Hey, you in the hat! Sit down, you bum," somebody shouted at him.

"Sit down or go home!"

"Jim, Jim," Catherine said. "What's the matter with you?"

"Hit him on the head! Sit down! You're a better door than a window!"

"Hey, you! Get out of the way!"

"For heaven's sake, Jim," Catherine called, grabbing at his arm. As he sat down she screamed, "Oh, look, look, look!"

A beautiful passing play had been set in motion by the Canadien goalie. Blocking a shot, he passed the puck to a defenceman on the right who sent a long pass across the ice to a forward who raced up into position, circled and feinted his check out of position, then shot another long pass forward across the ice to a wing coming up fast from behind the blue line. The wing trapped it neatly, swerved in on the defence, shifted to the right, then backhanded a pass to the trailing Canadiens centre coming in fast on the defence, now split wide open. He faked his shot to the lower right corner; the goalie sprawled for it, did the splits, and the centre calmly lifted the puck over his prone body.

"They score! They score!" Catherine cried ecstatically. "Oh, it was beautiful, Jim, wasn't it? What a pretty pattern! It's just like the ballet, isn't it?"

In the din his answer couldn't be heard. The florid man with the bag of peanuts sitting beside McAlpine, leaping to his feet, emptied the bag on McAlpine's coat, then slapped him on the back and hugged him, and the French Canadian priest, both hands raised in rapture, burst into eloquent French. Everybody was filled with a fine laughing happiness. But McAlpine, staring at the ice in a dream, thought, "Yes, Catherine's right. A beautiful pattern. Anything that breaks the pattern is bad. And Peggy breaks up the pattern."

The siren sounded, and they crowded out into the crush of people seeking hot dogs and coffee. Soon they were all jammed together, shoulder to shoulder, swaying back and forth, unable to get near the coffee counter. Catherine saw two of her Junior League friends and she called to them. McAlpine found himself thrust chest to chest against the thin bony-faced French Canadian priest who had been sitting near him. The priest, who came only up to his shoulder, wore his hat square on the top of his head. His elbow was digging hard into McAlpine's ribs.

"Nice game," he said politely with a slight accent.

"Not bad."

"But the way the game is played these days, I don't like it. No?"

"It's skate, skate, skate," McAlpine agreed. "A long pass, and skate into position."

"Like watching moves on a checkerboard. No?"

"That's true," McAlpine said. The priest had a homely, intelligent face. Surely he was the one man who at least would have a professional interest in an amateur like Peggy. It would be good to talk to him and get his professional understanding and not feel so completely alone. But no! In the end he would line up with his flock and Wolgast. "When I was a kid they had those beautiful short passing combination plays. It used to look wonderful."

"It's a different game today," the priest agreed. "It's still all combination. But some of them can't hold on to the puck."

"That Richard can at least do that."

"From the blue line in. Yes."

"With great drive," McAlpine said. He was certain the priest would be against them, too. Sure! Get her into a confessional with him: "I confess to the Almighty God and to thee, father. I confess to having no sense of discrimination. I confess to not keeping my love for the right ones. I confess to bringing out the worst in people and turning one man against another. Why do I bring no peace to anybody, father?" ... "My dear child, it's complicated. You must not be a nuisance. Guard yourself against the opinion that those who stand for law and order are always at war with those who stand for – well, this uncontrolled tenderness and goodness of yours. Examine it carefully, my dear child, in the light of the greater harmony. St. Augustine would say—"

"It's the coldest night of the year," the priest said vaguely, feeling he no longer had McAlpine's interest.

"How cold can it get around here?" McAlpine asked. And then the siren sounded, ending the intermission, and Catherine, who had been pushed four feet away from him, called, "This way Jim," and they went back to their seats.

In the corner to the left of the Canadiens goal a Ranger forward was blocked out and held against the boards by a Canadiens defenceman, who cleared the puck up the ice. The Ranger forward, skating past the defenceman, turned and slashed at him, breaking the stick across his shoulder. The official didn't see it. The play was at the other end of the ice. The defenceman who had been slashed spun around crazily on his skates, dropped to his knees, and circled around holding his neck. The crowd screamed. The other Canadiens defenceman, dropping his stick and gloves, charged at the Ranger forward and started swinging. The Ranger forward backed away, his stick up, trying to protect himself. The official, stopping the play, made frantic motions at the fist-swinging defence man, waving him off the ice. Another Ranger forward came out of nowhere and dived at the defence man and tackled him; then all the players converged on one another, each one picking an opponent in the widening huddle, fists swinging, gloves and sticks littering the ice. Some of the players fenced with their sticks. The crowd howled in glee. The referee finally separated the players and handed out penalties. He gave a major penalty to the Canadiens defenceman who had first dropped his stick to attack the Ranger forward who had really precipitated the brawl; he gave a minor to the Ranger who had dived at this defenceman and tackled him.

And the forward who had broken his stick over the defence-man's shoulder, the instigator, the real culprit, was permitted to escape. He skated around lazily, an indifferent innocent.

"What about him?" the priest asked Catherine as he pointed at the Ranger. "Yes, what about him? Look at the fake innocence," Catherine cried. She thrust out her arm accusingly. Ten thousand others stood up, pointed and screamed indignantly, "Hey, what about him? Why don't you give *him* a penalty?" The Ranger skated nonchalantly to the bench to get a new stick. His air of innocence was infuriating, yet the referee, the blind fool, was deceived by it. The players on the Canadiens bench, all standing up, slapped their sticks on the boards, screamed at the referee, and pointed. The referee, his hands on his hips, went right on ignoring the angry booing. He proposed to face off the puck.

"Boo-boo-boo-boo!" Catherine yelled, her handsome face twisted, her eyes glazed with indignation. "He's letting him go scot-free. The one who started the whole thing."

The stout French Canadiens, who had been standing up shouting imprecations in bewilderingly rapid French, suddenly broke into English. Twelve thousand people were also screaming, but by shifting to English he imagined he would get the referee to listen to him. His jaw trembled, his eyes rolled back in their sockets, he was ready to weep; then his face became red and swollen, and he cried out passionately, "Blind man! Idiot! All night you are a blind man! A thief, a cheat! You're despicable – go on back home, go out and die! I spit on you!" He cupped his hands around his mouth and let out a gigantic moan.

The ice was now a small white space at the bottom of a great black pit where sacrificial figures writhed, and on the vast slopes of the pit a maniacal white-faced mob shrieked at the one with the innocent air who had broken the rules, and the one who tolerated the offence. It was a yapping frenzied roaring. Short and choppy above the sound of horns, whistles, and bells, the stout French Canadian pounded McAlpine's shoulder; he jumped up on his own seat, he reached down and tore off his rubbers and hurled them at the ice. A shower of rubbers came from all sections of the arena and littered the ice as the players ducked and backed away. Hats sailed in wide arcs above the ice and floated down.

"They've all gone crazy," McAlpine muttered to Catherine. "Just a crazy howling mob." Their fury shocked him. Only a few moments ago he had imagined himself and Peggy facing the hostility of these people. Aside from the rule book, that player was guilty, he thought. I'm sure Peggy's innocent. That's the difference.

Someone in the row behind grabbed at McAlpine's hat and sent it sailing over the ice. His hands went up to his bare head and he whirled around belligerently.

"Jim, Jim, what's the matter with you?" Catherine cried, and she laughed.

"What's the matter with *me*?" he asked indignantly.

"Nobody's got anything against you, Jim. They way you're going on you'd think you were rooting for the visiting team. Aren't you with us?"

"What? Why do you say that?"

"Why quarrel with the home crowd?"

"I'm not," he muttered. "It was my hat. What am I going to do for a hat?"

"Oh, what's a hat at a time like this? Maybe you can get it afterwards. Ah, look," she cried, pointing at the referee, who was skating toward the Ranger bench to have a conversation with the coach. "Now we'll see." The coach beckoned to the fugitive, who came over to the bench, and the referee, tapping him on the shoulder, raising his arm dramatically, pointed to the penalty bench. But only a two-minute penalty, mind you! Oh, the fantastic ineptitude of the authorities! The pitiful mockery of justice! But everybody was pacified, and the boys with the snow ploughs came out to clean the debris from the ice.

The game was played out with the Canadiens keeping their lead and winning by two goals. McAlpine made little jokes about recovering his hat. On the way out he agreed with Catherine he would have no chance of finding the hat and he might as well forget about it. They had the good luck to get a taxi at the stand across the street.

In the taxi, with the excitement of the game all gone, they were really facing each other for the first time since McAlpine had acknowledged to himself the falseness of their relationship. Now he accepted with relief the fact that he might soon be revealed to her in a fantastic light. Well, to hell with them all!

❧ TWENTY-ONE ❧

Sitting beside McAlpine, she felt their separation in his silence. Even if she talked about each step he would take in his career and dazzled him with predictions of success, it would not bring him back to her. Something had happened. Something he concealed from her. What had really happened to him? Who had been taking him so steadily away from her? He *had* been taken, because it seemed to her he had found nothing wrong with her. And nothing *was* the matter with her. When she woke up in the morning everything was in its place – her clothes, her food, her furniture, the maid's soft respectful voice, and the telephone calls coming from her friends. When she attended a Junior League meeting and spoke in her firm cultivated voice, she knew by the envious faces of her friends that there was nothing much the matter with her. Her sense of style, the way she wore her clothes, her laugh, the way McAlpine in the beginning had shown his eagerness to have her love – it all added up to the same thing. Night after night now, when she left him she would undress and sit by her window looking out at the street; and she would know someone was taking him from her.

She would be alone in her room. It would snow. And she would sit by the window wondering where McAlpine had gone and with whom, and then she would be reminded of one lost thing after another. She would remember how, when she was a little girl, her mother had wanted her to study ballet and she had refused, and ten years later when she had wanted to be a ballet dancer they had told her she had lost her opportunity; she was a little too old. One lost triumph after another, all trivial and irrelevant, would float in her mind; the time when she had bought a brown suit for a tea party and three other girls at the party had worn brown suits and so, of course, no one could notice hers; and the boys she had once quarrelled with, whose affections she had lost; and her mother, who had died young.

All the lost things of her life would fill her thoughts on those nights when it snowed and she sat by the window wondering if McAlpine had really gone back to his hotel after leaving her, and if he would dream of having her in the bed beside him. Or if, instead, he would be meeting Foley somewhere, more likely than not in that awful Chalet Restaurant, which was open all night, where he would sit around in the company of alcoholics who wanted to get rid of their women. Or maybe they would tease him about having been with her. She would be talked about. How unbearable it was to be talked about! But how much more unbearable that he should persist in having a place in his life where she could not enter, a low-brow drinking place for men which represented, no doubt, a taste he had picked up in the war. She longed to sweep it out of his life, but as yet she couldn't; and yet any fool could see that she and her friends could do more for him in one hour than such a low-brow crew could do in six years. In her own bed, watching the shadowed corners of the room, she would twist and turn and assure herself that the only thing wrong with her was that she didn't have enough to do. She could join a dramatic group, she could study interior decorating, or found a political study club, and yet really be working for Jim. And even now in the taxicab, why couldn't he see that she only wanted to help him in the smallest details of his life, and that if she couldn't she was lonely and that her cool Carver style only concealed her loneliness? She longed to feel his arm come around her.

"I'm hungry," she said in that hearty clear tone she couldn't help using. "I'd like some seafood. I know a place on Dorchester. No décor, Jim, but it serves the best lobster Thermidor in town."

It turned out to be a barren little room. A draft came from the swinging doors every time they were opened, and they had to eat with their coats on. And the lobster Thermidor wasn't remarkable, either.

"Nothing is right for us these days, eh, Jim?" Catherine asked pointedly. But McAlpine laughed. In such weather nothing was right for anybody, he said; and with that remark he fled from intimacy with her, and she knew it and frowned and watched his eyes. There were no tablecloths on the tables. The cutlery was like kitchenware. But the cheque would be solid and substantial, and he would resent it, thinking of his bill at the Ritz.

"Jim, what is it?"

"What?"

"I don't know. You're not really with me, are you? Where were you at the hockey game?"

"Sitting beside you," he said, trying to laugh.

"No. Your thoughts. In your thoughts where were you?"

"I don't know what you mean."

"I can tell by your eyes. I can always tell, Jim. They're always looking over my shoulder, and you're not really listening."

"Oh, come now! That's nonsense."

"Well, right now, for example."

"I was thinking of a horse."

"A horse? Whose horse?"

"Wolgast's," he said, with a little smile. "Wolgast's white horse."

"Wolgast? That mug. Is he your bookie now?"

"No. But there was a white horse once he wanted to own."

"If he owned a horse it would soon be ruled off the track. Every race would be fixed."

"No, it wasn't a race horse. Just a white horse that took him places."

"Who cares where Wolgast goes?"

"I mean it had just struck me that there's a white horse for everybody. Call it possessions – security – a dream… There's such a horse for your father – one for me – the guy, the girl next door."

"So?"

"So, it's bad if someone takes your horse."

"And that's why they used to shoot horse thieves," she said lightly. "You're downright strange tonight, Jim."

"The chances are," he said half seriously, feeling his way, "I might always seem like a stranger to you, Catherine."

"And you and I might never really meet," she said quietly. And she remembered that night at the Murdock party when he had said they could always be good comrades; a fine intellectual friendship; the pain she had felt at those humiliating words! And now, whether he complained about the lobster Thermidor or the icy draft from the door, he tried to withdraw from her still further. She ached with desire to possess his secret so she could deal with it – so she could struggle fiercely against whoever it was that had taken him from her. But not to know who was defeating her was to be shut out of his life completely and to have the emptiness in her mind and heart deepened and the intolerable anguish made more intolerable because she had to hide it.

Going out, they crossed the road, ploughing through the snow, wheeling helplessly against the mountain wind and waving at taxis sweeping by. The wind moaning and the air heavy with unbearable cold forced them to hang on to each other, weaving along the sidewalk. It was twenty below. McAlpine never wore heavy underwear, and Catherine had on her nylon stockings; they huddled together and became one form. And while they held on to each other for warmth the tension between them became a vast unbearable irritation, and finally Catherine suggested that they duck into the old Ford Hotel. They hurried into the warmth of the lobby and smiled with relief at being able to let go of each other.

They waited by the door, watching for a taxi bringing passengers to the hotel. It was really no trouble at all. In five minutes they were at the Château. Catherine insisted he come in and get a hat. Her father appeared in a blue polka-dot dressing gown and chuckled and produced a black Homburg of his own. It was the right size, too. He said, "The men in the black Homburgs can all wear each other's hat. Keep it, my boy." They had a few stirrup cups because it was so cold out. McAlpine had four stiff drinks from a bottle of Dewar's, two for each block on the way to the hotel. He left wearing Mr. Carver's hat.

On the street he felt warm and exhilarated. But he was afraid he might go down Crescent Street and humiliate himself if Peggy had company, so he entered the Ritz lobby and telephoned the Chalet and asked if Foley was there. Of course Foley was there, and he explained to him that he didn't want to see Wolgast, and Foley offered to meet him in the Chicken Coop on St. Catherines and have some coffee.

It was extraordinary how warm and exhilarated he felt in the cold air on the way down to St. Catherine. And there was Foley waiting in the Chicken Coop with Commander Stevens, and they seemed to be exhilarated, too. They sat down and ordered chicken pies, and a coffee for McAlpine, who was grinning brightly.

"You didn't notice my new hat," he said. The restaurant warmth had hit him; it was the warmth and not Mr. Carver's excellent whisky, he was sure, and he said, "Excuse me," and got up to go downstairs to the washroom. The stairs were steep, yet he didn't fall. It was incredible how easily he got down the stairs and locked himself in the washroom. But he couldn't vomit; he could only sit there in deep meditation. Someone shook the door angrily. Finally he opened the door and stepped out and bowed to a pale-faced stranger supported by a powerful sailor who eased him gently into the chamber and glared at McAlpine.

McAlpine looked at the flight of stairs and knew he could never climb them, and so he leaned against the wash basin and waited and smiled thinly at the hostile sailor.

In five minutes Foley came hurrying down the stairs. "What's the matter, Jim? The waiter brought our chicken pies,"

"I still think I should go in there," McAlpine said, nodding at the privy.

"Then go in," Foley said, and he rattled the handle of the door.

"Just a minute, friend," said the sailor, the companion of the pale-faced incumbent. "Someone's in there."

"Well, my friend here has to go in there." Foley said, shaking the door irritably.

"Well, I've got a friend in there."

"My friend's not going to stand around here all night," Foley said angrily. "Tell you friend to get the hell out."

"Tell your friend to take his time," the sailor said.

"The hell you say! Your friend's certainly taking *his* time."

Foley and the sailor bristled and glared and elbowed each other belligerently. Foley wanted to fight. But McAlpine tugged weakly at his arm.

"I've been in there, Chuck," he whispered. "It didn't do any good. I'm just waiting here till I can climb the stairs. Don't let your chicken pie get cold."

"If you're all right, Jim."

"My respects to the Commander. His pie will be cold, too."

"I'll give you about five minutes," Foley said, and he hurried up the stairs.

McAlpine waited until the pale man had come out and had been assisted up the stairs by his own devoted friend. Alone at the foot of the stairs he looked up longingly. It was the steepest flight of stairs he had ever seen. If only he could climb those stairs, everything would be all right. Peggy would not get into trouble. She would quit her wandering. She would turn to him.

And while he reached out for the banister and put his foot on the first step, looking up and concentrating, he had a moment of beautiful clarity. Since he had talked to Wolgast he had been confused in his thinking. It was not a matter of reasoning with Peggy or frightening her. That wouldn't save her. If she was indifferent to the opinion of Wolgast or Wagstaffe and the fact that the whole town was turning against her, nevertheless she was not indifferent to him, James McAlpine. And how did he know she was not indifferent? The hours he spent in the room on Crescent Street were becoming a part of her life. Each day in his secret struggle with her, he was making gains so imperceptible and subtle that he himself had underestimated them. The main thing was to be always in that room when she came home from work. He began to climb the stairs. His head raised, his eyes fixed fanatically on the top step, he climbed with a slow, heavy, powerful determination, as if he were on his way to her room.

✎ TWENTY-TWO ✎

In the room he had worked out a scheme for the subtle penetration of her imagination. At night he would leave his notes on the bureau, and these notes would be in a kind of shorthand. He left them there deliberately, as a bait for her curiosity. Each day when he returned to the room he looked at the notes, and one day he found she had scribbled in a margin, "What on earth does this mean?" In his joy he cried out, "I knew it would work!" When she came home he was there to explain it to her. In the argument that followed his eyes glowed, he spoke out of his heart, and though it was supposed to be a rational discussion it was really his argument of love.

When she came in next day she was ready to take up the argument before she took off her overalls. She relied only on her own insights. She would take nothing for granted. It was wonderful and exasperating. He would find himself thinking. If Henry Jackson really wanted to write plays, how stimulating it must have been for him, talking over his ideas with her! One was compelled to look at everything freshly.

She was always broke and therefore willing to let him walk her down to the cafeteria where he could buy her something to eat. A little way along St. Catherine was an art shop, its window bright with large Matisse prints. The window ledge coated with snow and the corners glazed with ice made it look like a big white picture frame holding the light on a warm gaily coloured print of a ripe pumpkin on a fence. The blotch of gay warm colour was fantastic on the winter street. It made them laugh. They linked arms and laughed, and wisps of snow drifted across their faces. The gay colours and the bold design delighted them. There was a painter! she said. But of course! He had always had a passion for Matisse: couldn't he buy her some prints and hang them in the room? Certainly he could, she said; he didn't have to coax her. Now he saw how he would open her mind again to harmonies and rhythms that were in her own tradition and foreign to St. Antoine and keep her moving further and further away in her imagination from St. Antoine, in the true direction for her nature, toward what was light and gay and bold.

It would be so easy to do, he reflected one night when they were taking a ride in a barouche along Sherbrooke Street. They were huddled under the old buffalo robe, the sleigh bells jangled, her knees pressed against his, and the severe cold made their faces burn. She teased the beery old driver. Her teasing had affection in it, and the driver knew it and chuckled. That warm affection would touch McAlpine when she grabbed his arm to attract his attention to someone passing. This affection for little moments and casual people made him jealous; he wanted it for himself. He tried to get it with extraordinary eloquence, talking about Paris and New York, and she responded so warmly he longed to be in those cities with her. Oh, the fun he could have opening up those cities to her! he said. They talked of Baudelaire and Villon, and his ears nearly froze. He couldn't understand why she didn't feel the cold. She only had on that light belted coat.

They drove out to the east end, and she agreed to have something to eat at Chez Pierre. She had an enormous steak which she ate with enthusiasm, and he tried to assume the role he had always found so successful in the past with young girls. He got her talking about herself, and he bought a bottle of champagne;

he tried unobtrusively to make her believe he could understand the dreams of her youth far better than anyone her own age, but despite all the eating and drinking and talking he was convinced that the tenderness and affection he evoked in her meant no more than response to the fur-capped sleigh driver with little icicles from his running nose forming on his big moustache.

But the Matisse prints could be like strands in a web he would cunningly weave around her. She would be living in a room he would change a little every day. What gripped her imagination would change as the tone of the room changed.

He bought four Matisse prints for twenty-six dollars – which he couldn't afford – and that afternoon he met Foley for a drink before dinner in the M. and A.A. Club on Peel Street. They were joined by the garrulous navy man, Commander Stevens, who was indeed very navy. The whole country had betrayed him. He got drunk and told him he had lost sixteen ships in a convoy. The politicians had betrayed him. A Jewish tailor had betrayed him. A shirtmaker had betrayed him. He showed them his shirt. And McAlpine wanted to get away and go over to Crescent Street. At last, with his prints in a big manila envelope, he left the club and started down Peel Street with a brisk military stride. He had on Mr. Carver's black Homburg. It was dark out, the street lights were lit, and there was no wind. The temperature had risen rapidly; it was now twenty above. The weatherman had said he could foresee the end of the cold snap, but snow clouds were moving down from the Laurentians.

Coming down the hill he approached the liquor store. A group of people were waiting around the entrance. A Negress who stood there with another Negress watched him coming down the street; she stepped out and touched his arm. "Excuse me, mister," she said.

"Me?" he asked in surprise.

"I've seen you down at the St. Antoine," she said abruptly. She had on a muskrat coat and a golden toque; she was fat and heavy; she had aged too soon, and her face was no longer attractive. Though her gesture was humble and timid, her face in the street light was full of dogged resolution. "I'm the trumpet player's wife," she said.

"Oh! Oh, I see," he said, becoming too elaborately polite. He was shocked to think she had stopped him on the street. He looked around, expecting people standing on the hotel entrances steps across the road to be watching him. He felt a chill. He had feared that Wolgast's visit to the room meant that he and Peggy would be dragged into the open when they were not ready. And now it was happening in the open street. This coloured woman believed she had a right to stop him. "What is it?" he asked.

"It's about that little girl, mister," she said. "I know you'll excuse me. I know you're with her."

"Oh, you mean Miss Sanderson," he said vaguely.

"I speak to you, mister," she said, "because you're her man."

"Oh, no!" he said.

"It's what I hear, mister. So you'll know how I feel. No. Listen," she said, growing sullen, her tone bitter as McAlpine twisted away awkwardly. "Ain't you got no pride, mister? Can't you keep your woman away from my man? You could do it easy. I'd do it the hard way; but, hard or easy, I'd make it stick. Only you could do it easy, mister, and leave me something, leave me with something. I want to get rough, but right now I can't do it. I want to get wild and smash things up, but I can't do it. Only maybe I get liquored up like you or anybody else and I find I can do it," she said grimly.

He was appalled that he and someone he loved could have become so important in the alien life of this stranger with the big soft sullen black face. "Of course, of course," he muttered stupidly. But the sound of his own voice broke the strangeness of the encounter. She was only an aging woman who was troubled and poor; he wanted to comfort her. "You exaggerate, I'm sure," he said, touching her arm. "Take it easy. Your husband really means nothing to Miss Sanderson. It's just a friendship. It will only last a little while. I know it for a fact. In a little while you'll never be seeing her again. Don't worry, Mrs. Wilson." Raising his hat, he bowed stiffly; he fled before the misery of her married life could tumble down on him. He wanted to look back, but he knew she was there watching him, with no faith in what he had said. On his way to Crescent Street, he began to upbraid Peggy. He accused her of seeking trouble; he called her names. He kept it up until he got to the room.

She was in front of the bureau mirror dressed in her white blouse and black skirt, her knees crossed, one foot bobbing up and down as she polished her nails. "Oh, hello, Jim," she said. The light fell on one side of her face and touched the calf of her leg rounded out from the pressure on her knee. It might have been the light, or her sudden smile, giving her face indescribable glowing freshness, or her slow lazy greeting, but he was sure she knew how she looked; she knew a man couldn't help wanting to reach out and feel his fingers touching her blouse and sinking into the soft flesh; she knew how provoking she was and how triumphant over all tired and aging women.

"Well, who do you think stopped me on the street?" he asked, tossing the envelope containing the prints on the bed.

"Someone I know?"

"The trumpet player's wife."

"Ronnie's wife? No, you're kidding, Jim."

"Just fifteen minutes ago. Right on Peel Street."

"Right on Peel Street," she repeated, and then, incredulous, she put down her nail file. "Why did she stop you? Why you?"

"I'm your friend. The woman's worried about her husband. Is that news?" he asked sarcastically. "Oh, Peggy, for God's sake Peggy, how can you have such a thick skin? Do you have to have your little triumph over a poor fat middle-aged woman – have a poor woman like that hating you? To be telling it to a stranger on the street—" He broke off, white-faced, for she had stood up, her hands on her hips, the corners of her eyes wrinkling with amusement.

"I knew you could be indifferent," he said angrily. "I didn't think you could stand there and laugh."

"But I'm not laughing at poor Mrs. Wilson. I'm laughing at you."

"I'm used to it," he said.

"If you were only being honest, Jim!"

"I'm the one who's not being honest? That's funny!"

"Is it, Jim? Well, I'm not being taken in by your high moral tone," she said. "I know you're not really angry out of concern for Mrs. Wilson. I know why you're sore. You've been humili- ated. A fat coloured woman stopped you on the street. What an outrage! You, the man who's going to do the global thinking for *The Sun*, a friend of the Carvers, were publicly waylaid and drawn into the love life of a fat coloured woman. And who knows who was watching? How humiliating it must have been!"

"It was," he said sharply. "Indeed it was."

"But surely you were sympathetic."

"I was, I hope."

"Of course you were. I'm sure you had a friendly chat. Real chummy. Did she seem like a sensitive soul, Jim? Would you say, for example, that she would like our Matisse?"

"What are you driving at?"

"You can't tell about these Negroes," she said. "There's a Negro elevator man around here, and his wife likes Matisse." She was deliberately wounding him by implying that the little world he had created for himself and her could be invaded easily. But the pain in his eyes and his resentful glance as he sat down on the bed filled her with contrition. "Jim, listen," she said. "I don't want Mrs. Wilson's husband."

"You may say you don't want him now—"

"Who says I ever did want him?"

"But if he thinks you want him—"

"You mean, if his wife thinks I want him."

"She'd know if he thinks he's not through with you."

"What he thinks. What she thinks. What you think. Never what *I* think. Well, I am concerned. How unhappy that woman must be! Of course, I'm only a scapegoat. Well, Jim," she said firmly, "I'll try and see that there's no more trouble about Mrs. Wilson."

"You mean you're really concerned about her?" he asked doubtfully.

"Of course I am, Jim."

"But you weren't at all concerned about what Wolgast thought of you."

"No, I wasn't."

"But why? What's the difference?"

"I don't care for anybody's opinion of me. But with Mrs. Wilson – well, it's something that goes on between her and her husband, about me. And it's not good. I ought to do something about it."

"And I think you will," he said. She had lightened his heart and he was amazed that he could have confused her indifference to the town's opinion of her with indifference to what happened to other people. "I did feel humiliated," he admitted. "I wanted to drive her away from you and me and having anything to say about you and me."

"No, you weren't annoyed at Mrs. Wilson," she protested, turning his hand over and moving her finger on the palm. "You'd be sympathetic, Jim. A little embarrassed, of course, and worried about me, but good-hearted enough to be concerned about Mrs. Wilson. That's why I like you, Jim."

The touch of her hand was gentle, and her eyes were tender. She was confessing for the first time his importance to her; for the first time she was offering him a physical caress, and he was moved.

"I'm worried about Mrs. Wilson," she said. "I've wanted to be friendly with her, but you have to understand her, Jim. She's one of those possessive women who make a man's life completely intolerable. She wants every moment of her husband's life to belong to her. A woman who can't stand a man having a sympathetic friendship with anyone, not even another man, not even a fellow musician. If he brings a man to his apartment and seems engrossed she has to destroy that friendship. If he's out playing cards with two of the boys she's insanely jealous, and I think she cowers in a corner trembling until he comes home. Have you known women like that, Jim?"

"I have," he said uneasily, thinking of Catherine. He still wanted to argue with her but believed that if he did he would be still quarrelling as usual with her one fault, her malignant innocence. "A woman like that can be dangerous," he insisted. "A couple of extra drinks of gin and a little brooding, and Mrs. Wilson could blow her top. Well," he said with a sigh, "if you see it, that's fine. I'll leave it to you. I won't worry about it. I see you're going out—"

"Yes, I'm a little late as it is," she said, looking at her wrist watch.

"I won't keep you then." He picked up his hat. "Those Matisse prints are in the envelope there. Pin them up when you get time."

"No," she said, stepping out to the hall with him, "I'll wait till you come around, Jim. We'll do it together." She followed him along the hall, reached for a button on his coat, and started twisting it in her fingers. "You know something, Jim—"

"What?"

"I'd just as soon I didn't have a date." She looked up, surprised by what she had said. "Oh, well, you'll be around, won't you?" she said, brushing aside the impulse to have him stay with her.

"Yes." His heart throbbed. It was the first time that she had ever admitted that she might be happier remaining with him. If he had coaxed or insisted he might have made her feel he had prevailed on her to stay with him for the evening. But he was afraid she would instinctively resist if he argued with her. "I wish you didn't have a date," he said, brushing his lips against her cheek. Her hand went up slowly to her cheek and she nodded. It was a secret agreement made in the dimly lit hall, and he felt happy.

"Good night, Jim."

"Good night," he said.

He stood in the shadow of the steps, feeling exultant. It was much milder, but the weatherman had been right, more snow was falling. It fell on him in the shadow, pulling on his gloves, and on a man coming up the street. As he moved out of the shadow the man must have seen him, for he slowed down, then stopped, lit a cigarette, and turned his head, apparently shielding the lighted match. He was waiting for McAlpine to go. But he made a mistake: he began to saunter back the way he had come.

McAlpine noticed him and strode toward him. Whoever he was, he increased his pace; he didn't want to be recognized; it meant that he had intended to call on Peggy. It didn't matter whether he was white or black; he was someone intruding too quickly on that moment of understanding shared with Peggy in the hall, and McAlpine felt bitter about him.

But Peggy wasn't expecting a caller, she had said she was going out; and, gaining on the intruder, he thought, Maybe Mrs. Wilson sent him here to threaten her. Violent guys. No Uncle Toms. He kept his eyes on the man's broad back, getting closer. He was sure it was someone bringing her the trouble he had always dreaded. Something about him was familiar. Twenty paces of thick falling snow screened the man from him, and he couldn't tell whether it was Malone or Wagstaffe or Wolgast or a complete stranger. Then the man turned the corner on St. Catherine and was lost among other snow-covered figures.

Who was it? Maybe he'll come back, McAlpine thought. He went up the street beyond Peggy's place, then across to a lamp post where he stood watching her door. He had forgotten to turn up his coat collar and the wet snow melted down his neck, but he watched and waited and didn't notice it.

In a little while Peggy came out and hurried down to St. Catherine. She vanished on the corner where the street lights shimmered behind the veil of snow. In his excited imagination all the whitened figures crossing the street down there loomed up like ghosts wandering in the world of the dead into which she had vanished, and his heart pounded, and he was sick with anxiety.

❧ TWENTY-THREE ❧

The more he thought about it the more he wondered if it was Wolgast that he had seen on the street; but in the morning he was able to forget for a while because his first column appeared in *The Sun*. He got the paper at his room door, and it was there at last, his own column, on the editorial page, the eighth column, under the heading "One Man's Opinion." There was a note to the effect that the column would appear three times a week; he was to stay on that page for some time to come. He read the column carefully, then he got dressed and went out and had another coffee and read it again and walked around feeling light and satisfied, the paper tucked in his overcoat pocket.

His anxiety about Peggy, suppressed for the time being by his satisfaction with his work, must have contributed to his persistent excitement. At the Peel and St. Catherine newsstand he bought six copies of *The Sun* and went back to the hotel. He cut out a column to send to his father and one for old Higgins, the head of the History Department at the U. of T. Then Mr. Carver telephoned to congratulate him. Two or three friends at the club had praised the column, he said. It was attracting a lot of attention. Day by day it would build its own following. They congratulated each other. After the telephone conversation he took another walk, wishing he could see Foley and share his satisfaction with him.

He went into the Chalet at midnight, and Foley, who was there, started kidding him. "All the other global thinkers are folding up, Jim. They just haven't got your stuff. They all sent wires here to Wolgast. Read that wire from Dorothy Thompson, Wolgast," he shouted.

"I'm giving him a drink on the house instead," Wolgast said.

When he had finished the drink McAlpine leaned over the bar. "How's the white horse?" he asked.

"Going strong." Wolgast smiled a little.

"Well, don't fall off it, eh?"

"I never do," Wolgast said. After meditating a little he whispered, "Thanks for giving my message to your friend."

"Oh, then it's all right?"

"No, not exactly."

"Were you talking to her?"

"Yeah, she was around here. Marched right in and had her little say. But some other people were here and I couldn't make my point. Didn't have a chance. I'll make it, though, don't worry."

"Oh!" McAlpine said uneasily. His suspicion had been verified. "Did you go around to see her?" he asked, trying to sound casual.

"No. Why?"

"Well, you did once before."

"I don't do the same thing twice." And that was all there was to it, and McAlpine had to sit down wondering if Wolgast had lied to him.

The bar was a quiet friendly haven. The white-haired stockbroker in the beautiful grey suit who had been there the first night was sober and serious now; he had half an hour to relax before an appointment with a client. Malone and Henry Jackson, at the bar with Gagnon, tried to join in the table conversation, wanting to be friendly. They offered diffident and placating smiles. Only McAlpine was subdued. But gradually the respectful friendliness of the little bar touched him. Everybody was good-humoured. No one was noisy. There were no insults. They were all polite and all at home, and he too began to relax and feel secure.

Milton Rogers, flushed and jovial, came in and sat down at the table, ordered a round of drinks and rubbed his hands together in high glee. A new little singer was down at the St. Antoine: a high yellow girl with a mean low wail in her voice who could do things with her arms and shoulders and waft you right out of this stinking society. "Right from the pants, she sings. Right from the pants," he said rhapsodically. "You never heard anything like it."

Rogers's enthusiasm was understandable even if a bit boyish. They took turns insulting him, belittling his taste in women and his callow instincts. In spite of his laughter his face got red; he was wounded and he offered to buy them all a round of drinks if they didn't agree with him about the girl. They could all get a taxi and go down to St. Antoine at once, he said, looking hopefully at McAlpine.

"Why not?" McAlpine said. He wanted to go. He tried to appear indifferent, yet he was eager to have this legitimate opportunity of seeing whether Peggy was in the café. But Foley complained that he had just ordered a steak, which he intended to eat right there at the bar; he didn't care whether the lady sang from hunger or the pants. The days when he would rush out into the night to hear a sultry singer were gone. But he had said the wrong thing; he had exposed himself to insult, and Rogers joyfully accused him of being a sterile old man. Even Malone and Henry Jackson gibed at him. Everybody but Foley became exuberantly enthusiastic. Glowering at them, he complained that he hadn't had any dinner, and finally he said with a deft air that since Wolgast was his only friend he wasn't going to walk out and leave him alone. Of course he would go if Wolgast did. It was a mistake. Wolgast, with a glance at McAlpine that im-plied he was absolutely impersonal about Negro night-clubs, offered to go along with them.

"What about your bar?"

"Derle hasn't done any work all day. He can look after it," Wolgast said.

They all got up to get their coats and hats, Malone and Jackson trailing along, not quite sure that they were in the party. Pushing one another and snickering, they piled out of the restaurant. It was a peaceful mild winter night. The snow was wet and slippery. The moon shone and the stars were out. Rogers ran to the corner and got a taxi. Wolgast slipped and sprawled in the snow, and they all gathered around him, doubling up with laughter. At the corner, Rogers began to throw snowballs, and one big wet blob landed on McAlpine's neck as he bent to grab Wolgast's arm. It was all very jolly. They were like a bunch of boys playing around in the snow. No one really felt drunk.

The taxi, backing up the street, churned the snow and sprayed it over them. When they piled in there was one delicate moment – Malone would be left sitting on McAlpine's lap; but Jackson, with poetic awareness, suggested that he and Malone sit in the front seat with the driver.

It was only a little way down the hill, and McAlpine was the first one out.

"Listen!" shouted Rogers, who was paying for the taxi. From the open upstairs window came the sound of a girl singing. "My God, there she is! We're missing her!" he shouted wildly, and they all rushed at the entrance, brushing aside the doorman and crowding one another from the checkroom and confusing the girl with their laughter. Rogers threw her a bill. They all went pounding up the stairs. Foley tripped and cursed, and Gagnon had to grab him and yank him up.

They charged into the nightclub, all out of breath. The manager, a hard-faced mulatto, tried to stop them, but was not too belligerent. He wasn't sure of himself; he had heard the heavy pounding on the stairs and had thought it was a raid.

"Out of the way," Rogers cried. "Can't you see she's singing?" And he led the way back to the chromium bar. The manager, relieved, let his hands drop, and turned and looked blankly at the singer.

She was a good-looking mulatto in a white dress; her hair, parted in the middle, fell on her bare shoulders. There was something delicate and yet untamed in her face, and the delicacy of her features contrasted with her husky voice, which was, as Rogers had said, mean and sensual. She knew it and smiled a little; she could do things with her arms and shoulders like a ballet dancer.

"Okay," Rogers said softly. "What do you think?"

"For my money she's just another hot broad," Wolgast said.

"I say nuts," Foley growled. His barked shin was hurting him.

"She has to sing too loud in here," Gagnon said professionally. "It's not fair to her. She has to sing above too much noise. It will spoil her. You can't fight the beer, no matter how good you are. She should have an intimate little club on Peel Street."

"I like my own joint better than this one," Wolgast said, looking around. "Too many beer drinkers. A joint where they drink so much beer gets a bad name quick."

"It's not the joint, it's the dame," Rogers said. "What about her, McAlpine?"

"Not bad," McAlpine said absently. But he had hardly looked at the girl. His eyes had wandered hesitantly around the crowded room, seeking each familiar object and fitting it carefully into his memory of the place. There was Wagstaffe, his horn in his right hand, his head half turned away from his band as he watched the singer. And Wilson, the trumpet player, who had been listening, had just raised the trumpet to his lips. To his left at one of the tables close to the bandstand was Mrs. Wilson in an elaborate copper-coloured gown with two other women also in copper gowns and two broad-shouldered Negroes, light in colour, who were appraising the singer. Sometimes the two men whispered to each other. And across the floor in the shadow, well back from the band and not more than twenty paces away from McAlpine, sat Peggy in her white blouse. He hadn't wanted to look first in that direction.

She sat there by herself, untroubled and secure, her drink hardly touched. Not once did she glance over at the bar, and it may have been that she had not seen McAlpine come in.

The singer finished her song, and Gagnon, Rogers and Wolgast applauded so boisterously that many turned and looked at them, and the singer herself bowed in their direction.

"I'll get her to have a drink with us," Rogers said. "That white dress is like a sheath around her, isn't it?"

"We've seen her, now why don't we go?" Foley asked sourly.

"I was to buy you a drink if you were disappointed. Remember?" Rogers asked. "Okay. Call the roll. Who didn't get his money's worth? Professor Wolgast?"

"The babe's a nice little dish," Wolgast said judicially. "As them dames go, you're right about her, only I don't go for them dames. You don't owe me any drink."

"Professor Foley?"

"I want a drink."

"Professor Jackson?"

"She's terrific, I'd say."

"Professor Gagnon?"

"Bring here over here and I'll buy you a drink."

"Professor McAlpine?"

"Yeah?"

"Do I owe you a drink?"

"What for?"

"What for? The kid with the vaginal voice."

"Oh, no, no, no!"

"Professor Malone. Hey, where's Malone going?"

Malone had left them and was slowly making his way across the floor toward that one table in the shadowed corner. The band was playing, and there was a loud hum of conversation. Waiters moved from table to table, and Malone's path was blocked by couples who got up to dance. Not only McAlpine, but the others, too, were watching Malone.

"Ah, I see," Wolgast whispered. "Our little friend, the nigger lover, over there." And Jackson, blinking and tugging nervously at his pathetic little beard, said, "Sometimes I hate Malone's guts. I talk to him a lot now, but I hate his guts."

Confused by the pounding of his heart, McAlpine remained with the others, watching Malone and assuring himself it would be wiser not to intervene unless he were offensive. It would be wiser not to embarrass Peggy, who could rebuff Malone herself. But the dancers kept blocking his view of her table. For a moment he could not see Malone. When the way cleared again he saw him sitting at her table and beckoning to the waiter.

Peggy shook her head and turned away, but Malone, leaning closer, grinned and went on whispering. You could see Peggy's hand on the table. If he as much as touches her hand I'll move over there, McAlpine thought. But Malone didn't touch her hand. Leaning back, his legs crossed, he talked to her while she watched the band. The musicians were putting down their instruments beside their chairs. Dancers drifting off the dance floor hid Malone from those at the bar.

Then they could see him lean close to her. He grinned and whispered, and his hand went to her shoulder. She slapped it away. McAlpine took two steps toward them, but everything happened too fast for him.

The Negro waiter spoke to Malone, who answered contemptuously with an arrogant gesture as he shifted his chair closer to Peggy. He put his arm around her shoulder. The waiter touched the arm. Malone wheeled around, half standing, shot out the heel of his hand and caught the waiter painfully under the nostrils, snapping his head back. Again he turned to Peggy, trying to get her to leave with him. McAlpine now was only twenty feet away from them. Wilson jumped down from the bandstand and came forward, not running, but in a hurried businesslike stride, hard-faced and grim, brushing past the tables and reaching Peggy's table before McAlpine, whose way was blocked.

Wilson jerked Malone away from Peggy. He looked extraordinarily competent. He swung a left hook and caught Malone on the head. Malone lurched back. Wilson waited, crouched like a professional fighter, and Malone put up his own hands. He posed like an old-time fighter, his left out and his back stiff. It looked oddly comical. Wilson moved in and hit him with three hard left hooks and knocked him down.

It was all happening in a tight little circle formed by those who were at the adjacent tables. McAlpine tried to push his way through. "Peggy!" he yelled. She had stood up; she was lost and frightened. On his feet now, Malone whirled around. The waiter whom he had insulted was beside him, held by the manager. Ignoring Wilson, Malone smashed this waiter in the eye. There was a moment of silence. Nobody moved.

Everybody waited. This was the dreadful moment McAlpine had been anticipating ever since the first night he had come there; he felt a strange exultation and he stiffened, ready to leap to her side, but he had the sense to wait and not break that silence with a violent gesture. He wanted to get Peggy quietly out of the café. Even one body lurching against another might break that strained silence.

Wagstaffe, standing frightened on the bandstand, swung around, grabbed his horn, and started to play. The other musicians hurried to their chairs and picked up their instruments. They followed Wagstaffe in his own version of the St. Louis Blues, and he had never had so much stuff on the horn as he did then. Some of the customers who knew what he was trying to do sat down and applauded. Those who had been circling around Malone and Peggy and the two Negroes milled around, trying to detach themselves.

While the Negro waiter expostulated vehemently with the manager who was pushing them away, Malone wiped his bleeding mouth and Wilson argued with his wife. They were in a half-circle around Peggy. She was too scared to back away. She couldn't move. Supplication was in her lonely eyes. A thin, sad young Negro with gleaming hair put out both hands to her. "Come here with us, Peggy. Come away, girl," he called.

"Keep out of this, you filthy black swine," Malone yelled at him, and he sucked in blood from his bleeding mouth and spat it into the sad young face.

The young Negro swung at him. The waiter broke away from the manager and jumped Malone, and three of his colleagues who had been standing behind him also jumped Malone.

McAlpine roared, "Peggy! Peggy! Here!" and lunged toward her desperately, for her head had turned in his direction. It was extraordinary the way Wagstaffe played on so beautifully; but the other musicians had stood up, and their music was a discordant wail. That little old guy, the flashy old Negro porter whom McAlpine had seen the first night, came out of nowhere and threw his arms around Peggy to shelter her.

"Look at the nigger after that girl!" a white woman screamed. "Stop him!"

None of the white men had sympathized particularly with Malone when he insulted the waiter. They were all embarrassed. And they had made no move when three waiters tackled him and he rolled on the floor. But the first waiter made a mistake. He got loose and staggered to his feet; he saw Malone's greying head rolling on the floor and he put the boots to him. He kicked him over the eye. A powerfully built white man, a truck driver who had been watching doubtfully, aware that his white pride and superiority were involved, shouted, "They got him down and kicked him!" His own moral problem had been settled. "Are we going to take that?"

He jumped at the little waiter, who backed away from him, sparring, swinging, lurching against tables and knocking chairs over. The waiter was no match for the big fellow. A lonely coloured girl wailing for her beaten boyfriend ran across the dance floor. McAlpine could no longer see Peggy. As he lurched around, hurling people aside, he saw Gagnon standing at the bar, his hand up to his head; someone had thrown a salt shaker at him. Gagnon picked on a Negro in a light brown suit. He swung at him, dazed him, and drove him along the bar. He hoisted him onto the bar. They were reflected in the big mirror, the flash of the Negro's body sliding along the bar sweeping off all the glasses. The crash of splintering glass above the melancholy wail of Wagstaffe's horn was terrifying. Other fights broke out. "Peggy!" McAlpine roared again.

Then he saw her. She tried to come to him. He knocked over a Negro, clawed at the mass of swaying bodies. A brown fist swinging at him caught him high on the forehead. Amazement was in his eyes as he rocked on his heels, then the wall of bodies closed in front of him. Women shrieked; the white ones struggled to get to the stairs. Some of them were weeping.

At the end of the bar Foley, who had sat down on the floor, was fumbling with his glasses, then adjusting them on his nose. Most of his body was hidden by the bar; only his red head stuck out, and he was full of profound and bitter disgust that he was there at all. Then Wolgast's head rose above the level of the bar and he looked around with caution. Feeling secure, he stuck a cigar in his mouth; no matter what happened, he felt more at home behind a bar.

He watched McAlpine crash through the wall of bodies swaying around him; he heard him roar like a bull, swinging and clawing and cursing, trying to get to Peggy. The more he struggled, the more they clawed at him. Someone cursed him; he tripped, fell to his knees, and grabbed at the legs around him. A table crashed on the floor beside him and rolled away, and he was on his feet again. In the little clearing where the table had fallen he stood all alone, looking so big and threatening that the Negro waiters backed away, thinking he was crazy-drunk. He caught a glimpse of Peggy's white blouse. He knocked over a little white man in a blue suit. They're trying to keep me away from her, he thought. Then someone leaped on his back pinning his arms – a powerful white man who had an arm lock on him. The man yelled, "Take it easy, pal, take it easy before there's murder. Break it up. The cops are coming, pal."

"Let me go!" McAlpine shouted. He couldn't see the man's face, he could only feel his vast weight and his great strength.

The manager and Wagstaffe, yelling at waiters and Negro clients, tried to herd them into a corner, and a big uniformed doorman with a false nervous grin wedged himself between Negroes and white men. "Break it up, boys," he urged them. "Break it up. The cops are coming."

The fighting had stopped abruptly, and there was Peggy back against the wall, half stooped, her arms folded across her breast, her hands clutching her shoulders, trying to hide herself, and on his knees beside her was Wilson with a bleeding head.

Malone, who had been crawling along the floor, stood up, his torn face like a smeared white mask, his eyes popping. "There's the little bitch that started it!" he yelled, pointing at Peggy.

"Yes! There!" screamed Mrs. Wilson, her voice a high quavering wail as she lurched toward Peggy. She spun around with an hysterical moan. "No good trash, no good trash!"

Wolgast had come from behind the bar with a slow calm step, his face impassive, an impressive solid man above the little tumult, a man on a horse.

"She's a troublemaker," he called out, "a first-class troublemaker." And it sounded like a calm impersonal judgment as he stood there with his hands on his hips.

"That's right," Wagstaffe yelled. "Get her out of here!"

"Go on, get out of here, you floozie!" the manager shouted at Peggy.

"Let me go!" McAlpine shouted wildly at the giant whose face he still hadn't seen, but whose grip and heavy weight were drawing him farther away from the circle around Peggy. "Take it easy, pal," the giant whispered consolingly. "You'll be thanking me in a minute."

Peggy took one slow, frightened step from the corner, then another, not seeing anybody, hiding within herself from their contempt; she stooped to pick up her coat and, while stooping, looked at the door. She straightened up; there was an effort at dignity in her first few steps, a wavering, uncertain dignity, but when Mrs. Wilson yelled, "Slut!" and snatched a catsup bottle from a table and threw it at her she began to run. The catsup sprayed from the bottle in a blood-red line toward her, and she screamed. Beer glasses thrown at her broke at her feet and scraps of sandwiches fell around her.

At the head of the stairs the Negroes and white women who had huddled there for safety made way for her; but as she brushed past them they jeered. A Negro woman tugged at her coat. "You've had it coming, you trash," she rasped. Peggy turned around blankly. Then her fair head disappeared down the stairs.

"God damn you," McAlpine said quietly to the giant. The threat was all in his suddenly relaxed body, and the giant said good-naturedly, "I'm your pal, buddy. I've saved you some trouble." He relaxed his grip, and McAlpine slipped away from him without even looking at his face. He dashed toward the stairs, stumbling down and tripping. He whirled around, facing the hat-check girl. "The girl," he said. "Girl with a light coat."

Before she could answer he lurched out to the street, but there he stopped and drew back. A police car had drawn up to the curb. Four policemen jumped out of the car. Leaning idly against the door, he smoothed the sleeves of his coat and straightened his tie and brushed back his hair. He tried to convey the impression that he was waiting for the police. Each one of them glared at him suspiciously as they dashed one by one up the stairs. Then he stepped out to the street and looked toward the underpass. No one was on the sidewalk between him and the underpass. She got a taxi, he thought. If a taxi were out here she'd have jumped into it.

From the café across the street and from the little shops and the upstairs rooms came the neighbours, some in shirt sleeves, some in bathrobes and slippers, all looking up with curiosity at the windows of the café. It was like a crowd watching a building on fire. McAlpine made his way among them. No one noticed that he wore no hat or overcoat, for they had run out to the street without their own hats and coats.

He hurried across the intersection and up the street; when he got into the shadow of the subway he started to run.

Maybe she's just on the other side of the underpass, he thought. Coming out of the underpass, he stopped. No one was ahead of him on the hill. There had been no snow in the underpass and running had been easy, but now that he was in the open again, he started to slip and skid. He spun around, one shoe deep in a snow bank, his foot soaking wet; but he came down heavily on both feet and kept his balance. He stared at the pink neon lights on Dorchester.

Fearing a policeman would see him and stop him, he slowed down to a walk. He darted out to the road and waved at each passing taxi. He got sprayed with slush. Finally a taxi stopped; he gave the Crescent Street address and leaned back in the cab, holding his head in his hands. His fingers touched a big bump on the back of his head and the feel of it astonished him. He could not remember being hit. His breathing sounded to him like a loud sobbing.

"Here you are, bud," the driver said. McAlpine, paying him, was casual and polite. "Good night," he said, thinking he was concealing from the whole city what had happened. "Nice and mild, isn't it?" He waited from the cab to pull away, then he hurried in and along the hall. Her door was open.

ஃ TWENTY-FOUR ஃ

She was sitting on the bed, looking so bewildered and untouched that McAlpine couldn't speak. He swallowed hard.

"Oh, it's you," she said.

"Me. Yes."

"Well – well, that's good, Jim."

"Who else did you think it would be?"

"I – I didn't know," she said, closing her eyes, and then, still bewildered, she asked, "Where's your coat and hat?"

"My coat and hat?"

"Yes."

"Oh!" His hand went to his pocket for the cloakroom check as if to give it to her. "Yes. Here's the check. I'll have to get that hat. It's Mr. Carver's. I can get it tomorrow. How did you get here?"

"A taxi – right outside the door," she said, her voice breaking. "I just jumped in. It was right there. It was odd how it was right there, wasn't it?" Before he could answer she got up, tried to smile, and went over to the bed. She was no longer alone, and she did not have to hold on to herself, and she lay down and began to cry. Her hands kept working the pillow around her face, and he could hardly see her head, just her shoulders shaking with her heartbroken sobbing. The sound of her sobbing filled him with a peculiar poignant gladness, for he knew she wept out of shame and over the failure of her judgment of herself and others and her bitter humiliating disappointment.

The ceiling light shone on the short fair hair at her neck. He sat down beside her and comforted her; he stroked her head, saying nothing, and his understanding, his soothing and unprotesting affection compelled her to mutter a desperate defence of herself: "It was Malone. It was all Malone's fault. That awful man! A man like that could start trouble anywhere," she insisted. And when he didn't remonstrate with her, she whispered, "Oh, no, no, no! Why don't you say it was my fault, Jim? It's me! You saw how they all turned on me?"

"It was awful, Peggy." He said gently. "But a fight over a girl could happen in any café."

"Oh, no! Not like that."

"Yes. If a drunk makes himself offensive anything could happen. It could happen to any girl. It was the circumstances, that's all. I don't know how it started. What did Malone say to you?"

Turning on her side and looking at him gratefully, she said, "Well, when he came over to the table and asked me to dance with him, I refused. Then he asked me to go home with him, and I wouldn't. Well, he called me a name and started pawing me. All the waiter did was ask him to go back to his own table. Any waiter would do that, wouldn't he, Jim?"

"Of course he would."

"Oh, Jim!" she said miserably. "You sound as if you still had such respect for me."

"I love you, Peggy."

"But you shouldn't, Jim."

"I can't help it," he said.

His gentle manner made her turn away. "Oh, keep on talking to me," she pleaded, for his words soothed her, restored her, and entitled her to possess herself again. They went on talking incoherently. They told each other that something was finished.

By repeating it again and again they made what had happened seem remote; they used it to help them understand why they were together in the room.

Yet they were still nervous and excited. They spoke of the inexplicable suddenness of the violence, of the way Wagstaffe had tried to get the band playing and of Malone's viciousness. Soon they began to sound like two people who had been watching a fantastic brawl in a far-away café, and the girl they were talking about was not the girl who was lying beside him, and he was not the man who had struggled so wildly to be at her side. There in the room they were safe and unharmed and close together.

"I heard you cry out," she said. "I heard you the first time."

"I didn't think you heard me."

"Yes, I heard you," she said, nodding and reflecting. "And yet it was strange. I had known all along that at some terrible moment when I was alone I would hear you cry out to me."

"Yes, that is strange," he agreed, walking up and down, feeling happy.

"Those yells and curses. Such irrational fury, the frenzy of people possessed. And the awful faces – like demons. All unnatural and inhuman."

"It was horrible for you, Peggy."

"Yet your voice, Jim. A human voice. I knew what it meant. I knew what it said. I didn't want to hear anything else. Just that one voice."

"Well," he said, smiling a little, "now you can hear it to your heart's content."

"Yes, yes, of course," she said. "And everything becomes normal again. Oh, so sweetly normal! See, I hear your shoes squeaking. Your feet must be soaking wet, Jim."

"I slipped in a snow bank. I left my overshoes back there in the café."

"Why don't you take off your shoes and put them on the radiator?"

"I think I will." Sitting down, he took off his shoes and put them on the hot radiator. "Now I'll make some coffee," he said.

She crouched on the bed, watching him move around in his stocking feet. At the stove he turned, grinning, and asked if she had seen Foley behind the bar. "I did," she said. "But I wonder why the Negro women didn't run like the white women did." And he said, "Maybe they felt it was their café." But, whatever they said, they were comforting to each other.

"You've got dust all over your coat and pants," she said. Of course he had; he had sprawled on the café floor. Getting up quickly, she got a whisk from the cupboard and had him stand still while she brushed him. She did a thorough job, examining each smudge on his coat intently, then brushing it with vigour. It seemed to be important to her that he be cleaned up before they had coffee together – that not one smudge from the café should remain on him. "Stand there. Don't move," she said. Then she hurried along the hall and got a basin of water and she wiped his face with a cloth, almost apologetically, as if she had put the smudges on him herself and wanted him to forgive her and look as he had always looked in that room. "There. Now we can have coffee. My, it's a good homely, friendly smell, isn't it?"

When they had finished the coffee and he was putting the cups on the table, she lay back contemplating the picture he had drawn of her in her factory overalls.

"Remember the day you drew that picture?" she asked.

"I remember."

"Bring it to me, will you, Jim?"

"Why?" he asked, getting the drawing for her. Without answering, she held the picture out at arm's length, regarding it with an ironic smile.

"Peggy the Crimper," she said. "Me down there in the factory! It seems just as incredible, doesn't it? Well, I have a feeling that's gone, too." She watched him, wondering about him, feeling that she was nothing now, yet knowing she still had the security of his faithful devotion.

"Come here, Jim," she said softly, and she put out her hand to him, letting the picture flutter to the floor half under the bed. And when he bent down she put both her arms around him, drew him to her, and held him hard against her. They lay folded in each other's arms. For a long time they lay there tight against each other, hardly moving, hearing the smallest sounds; and these sounds and the beating of their own hearts became their own world, and it was warm and good. Icicles outside the window began to drip. Someone went whistling up the street in the mild evening.

It got warmer in the room. In some nearby house a baby cried and cried, and a dog began to bark, then another dog, and when the baby stopped crying there was only the barking of one dog. Someone came in the front door and moved around in the room overhead. "Mrs. Agnew was out late," Peggy whispered. He kept her folded in his arms because he knew she wanted to feel important to someone and be comforted and be held there until she could believe she belonged to someone and yet was herself. He wanted to soothe away her fear and shame. Then suddenly he felt her lips on his neck. "You're very sweet," she whispered. As he caressed her, he could feel her heart beating against him; he could hear nothing but the beating of her heart growing louder, and it stirred up the old ache in him.

"Remember when I first came in?" he asked.

"Yes."

"You seemed to be expecting somebody. Were you?"

"I didn't know."

"Who else could have come?"

"I wasn't sure," she said candidly. "It might be you. It might be Ronnie Wilson."

"Wilson. Why Wilson?"

"He tried to help me."

"So he did," he said, and it troubled him, for he remembered that not only had Wilson rushed to protect her; a Negro waiter had defended her; other Negroes had fought believing she belonged to them.

"Oh, Jim!" she said, tightening her arm around him impulsively. "Don't ever leave me, will you?"

"Never?"

"No, never."

"May I stay here tonight?"

"If you want to, Jim."

But he could hardly believe she was willing to abandon herself to him, and he hesitated, remembering the night she had pushed him away, having no desire for him.

"Maybe you're just lonely," he said, not really to her, but to explain to himself the loss of her will to resist. If she were too lonely to resist it could mean… But the dull ache in his brain told him what it could mean. Some of those café Negroes had used her as a scapegoat; they had all let her be driven away alone. She believed that they had all turned on her, and that they now despised her, and she was heartbroken. But if one of them had got to the room before he had, and could be there now comforting her, how grateful she would be to him for showing her she could still count on their gentle affection, how moved she would be and how anxious to show him they could still have all her love! For hadn't she truly belonged to them? They had taken the happiest part of her childhood. That naked Johnson boy, Jock, had been the one who first stirred her. And if one of them were beside her now caressing and reassuring her, how much more it would mean to her! But, instead, he himself was there, and she was left with him, feeling despised by the others; and her love, which she could deny him when she had respect, he could now have if he wanted it.

In an agony of doubt he hesitated, his hand on the button of her blouse, and while he hesitated his head was filled with the mocking laughter of everyone he knew in the city; they rushed into the room, they shouted out their coarse accusations, then snickered and scoffed at his belief that she had been coming closer every day to a realization of her love for him; they jeered at his insight, drowned out his own inner voice, and he could hear Rogers cry, "Will the poor dope never get wise to her?"

"In the beginning," he said, "you didn't want me, did you?"

"I liked you from the first, Jim."

"But not to lie with me like this. Not me."

"Not like this – at the start. No."

"Not in the way you liked…"

"Liked who?"

"Well, Wagstaffe, till he turned—"

"No, with you it was different, Jim."

"That's right. Different," he agreed, feeding his doubt by deliberately misunderstanding her. But his thoughts were whirling wildly. It was the others who clamoured for his attention, insisting he listen: they had got into the room and were dancing around in his mind; Foley, his best friend, and Gagnon and Jackson and Wolgast – and they all twisted and tortured his thoughts, digging out of the depths of his mind the suspicions he had so resolutely suppressed.

"You'd think Wagstaffe would have remembered that first night he took you home, and he was so gentle," he said, making it sound sympathetic.

"No one could have been gentler."

"It's a touch. Some have it with a woman. Yes, you knew he had it," he said softly. He had gotten her to admit something. But he had hardly heard what she said. The others were all in his mind yelling, To hell with Wagstaffe! Ask her about Wilson!

"Wagstaffe wasn't like the trumpet player," he said reflecting, keeping his tone sympathetic. He could hardly bear to go on with it. A few more words and he would deepen his own agony, he would expose her to a more terrible hurt, yet he had to go on: "Wilson got a little closer to you," he said, trying to disarm her with his mild tone.

"Well, his ways were different, Jim."

"Ways that were different. Sure."

"I knew I could count on him."

"Sure you did," he said. And in the tormenting darkness of his mind all the others were yelling, Different way, sure, the way of the dark meat she goes for. Why else did she call Jackson a white bastard?

His hand on her head, he looked down at her face. She smiled, waiting, and he had to turn away and avoid her eyes.

"What's the matter, Jim?" she asked.

"Nothing. I mean... Well..." he began. "Am I the one? Are you sure, Peggy?"

"Yes, Jim."

"Tonight we're excited. We're all mixed up. Will you feel this way tomorrow, Peggy?"

"I know I will."

"And you'd go away with me?"

"Yes, Jim. Anywhere."

But she knew he was troubled, for he got up slowly. "What is it, Jim?" she asked, sitting on the side of the bed.

"Well, tomorrow," he began, hesitating, "if any of your Negro friends should talk to you, would you feel the same as you do now, Peggy?"

"You've a right to ask that," she said. "But I know how I feel."

"I want you to feel sure, Peggy. Not be driven into something because of what's happened tonight. I want to be fair to you. Tomorrow you won't feel lonely. You'll be yourself. I want you to feel free." With these consoling words he tried to hide from her the doubt that had entered his mind. If he could only get away from the night, see her again in the morning, see her aside from this room and its place in the night! His humiliating doubt was only a part of the night's humiliation, he told himself; if he could come upon her freshly in the morning he would have his own view of her back again; he would see her as he had always seen her. If he touched her now, drew her to him, took her love when he was struggling to keep his faith in her, he would be cheapening her and taking her for what they said she was. "To have anything that happens between us," he began, but he had to stop; his voice shook, and the sound of his own words was a bitter torment. "I mean it would be wrong to have it a part of this night. Don't you understand?" he said shakily. "It wouldn't be good. Not fair to you." And he put out his hands to her and she stood up and took them.

"I understand," she said gently. There was a silence. With a compassionate understanding, she was letting him keep his belief in his good faith.

But she had a new calmness. She raised her head with a shy dignity. The loneliness in her steady eyes and the strange calmness revealed that she knew he had betrayed himself and her, and that at last she was left alone.

In the moment's silence he tried to grasp what was revealed in her eyes; he almost felt it, but it was lost to him in the anguish of deeper uncertainty about her acceptance of the honesty of his belief that he did not want to cheapen her.

"You're tired and troubled, aren't you, Jim?" she said quietly. "Well, there's tomorrow."

"Will we have a late breakfast tomorrow?" he asked.

"I'll be waiting."

"I'll come down here."

"Fine, Jim."

"Maybe my shoes are dry," he said.

He put on his shoes and they faced each other. When he kissed her, the touch of her lips filled him with a nameless ache that was unbearably painful. "Be sure you lock the door," he said.

"I will."

"Good night. Good night, Peggy."

"Good night, Jim," she said, and she gave him a little smile.

Outside, he stood in the shadow of the steps, his mind still whirling. He had left her at peace with herself, yet what about her faint smile when she said good night? It worried him. He stood there leaning against the outer door. How do I know, he thought, she will look any different in the morning? It was like listening to someone else prompting him. It was his own inner voice, but it seemed to come from someone else: How do you know that in the morning you'll be able to believe in her again? If you let go, can it come again? It's now. Now. It's what you have now that you'll keep. How do you know that in the night she won't get further beyond the reach of your faith? If you go back in there – even if you're suspicious and nasty and brutal – what does it matter whether you're fair to her? Wavering, he would have gone back; but when he was turning in the shadow under the steps he stopped, startled, for there on the sidewalk was a Negro boy, not more than sixteen, coming in.

It was Al Jones, the Negro shoeshine boy, who had often laughed and joked with Peggy.

"Hey, you! What do you want?" McAlpine asked harshly. The Negro boy had appeared there like an apparition to justify all the jealous doubts already tormenting him. He strode toward the boy, who had backed away, and grabbed him by the shoulder.

"I was going to…" Al tried to explain. "I was going to see…" Then he grew frightened; it was McAlpine's eyes. He tried to jerk away.

"You little bastard – hanging around for what?" McAlpine grunted, twisting his arm. "Get the hell out of here – fast, do you hear?" And he shoved him savagely. The Negro boy, lurching away, went limping down the street. McAlpine watched him sombrely. Then he glanced at the door. Tonight – like this – I could only humiliate her, he thought. Turning, he strode up the street, looking at the ridge of the mountain against the sky; the lights glittered on the ridge, and he seemed to be walking right against it, and it had never been so dark or so high.

TWENTY-FIVE

In the bright morning the whole city steamed and sparkled in the thawing sunlight. Ice-coated trees on the mountain made glittering, lacy patterns with their sunlit branches, and the banked, melting snow on the hills turned a thousand sidewalks into rivulets that twinkled and twisted in the sunlight on their way down the slopes. Icicles on the sloping roofs sparkled like chandeliers, and on the house on Crescent Street three giant icicles had formed on the steps and were dripping over the basement entrance to Peggy's apartment.

Mrs. Agnew, standing at her front window, looked out at the melting snow with satisfaction. She wanted to go up to Sherbrooke Street to one of the little hat shops. When it was bitter cold she hated those windy corners. She believed they were the coldest corners in Montreal. You climbed right into the wind when you got to Sherbrooke, and it really took hold of you.

Through her window she saw two Negroes, who had been coming up on the other side of the street, stop before her house and look over.

Elton Wagstaffe and the grim, bony-faced café manager were inspecting Mrs. Agnew's house, making sure they had the right number. Wagstaffe usually wore a camel-haired tan-coloured coat, but today he had on a double-breasted dark coat and a black fedora, and the manager also had on a dark coat and dark fedora. Both the same height, they both had the same solemn, sedate air. They turned to consult each other before crossing the street in step. To Mrs. Agnew they looked like a couple of Negro undertakers or solemn emissaries who were carrying out an important mission. As they climbed her steps, they had a lordly air. Without waiting for the bell to ring, she hurried out to the hall and waited for them.

"How do you do?" she said uneasily when she had opened the door.

"How do you do?" Wagstaffe said, his tone formal.

"How do you do?" the manager repeated in the same tone.

"What can I do for you?" Mrs. Agnew assumed their own solemn tone and held her kimono tight across her chest.

"A Miss Sanderson lives here?"

"Well, she lives downstairs. It's the other door, just below."

"Thank you, ma'am," said Wagstaffe, bowing, and they both raised their hats.

"But she wouldn't be in," Mrs. Agnew added quickly because she had become very curious. "Have you a message for her? I could give her the message."

Glancing at each other, they hesitated cautiously. "Are you by any chance the landlady here?" Wagstaffe asked.

"I'm Mrs. Agnew, the lady of the house."

"You would know if Miss Sanderson had left town?"

"Left town? Of course I would. Why would she leave town?"

"She has said nothing about getting out of town?"

"Why, no! What is this?"

"Our apologies, Mrs. Agnew," said the manager.

"What'll I say to her?"

"Just tell her we were here."

"And that you asked if she had got out of town?"

"Exactly, ma'am, and thank you," they said. Again they raised their hats, bowed, turned together, and left her standing there mystified. They descended the steps and went down the street with their measured stride without once looking back. Only then did she realize that she hadn't asked them their names.

"Well! Well, what do you know?" she said. She had been extraordinarily impressed by their dignity. And they had really expected to find that Peggy had left town. In that case there must have been some talk about her leaving town. But Peggy had borrowed ten dollars from her a week ago. She counted on Peggy repaying her that night when she came home from the factory; she was planning to advance herself the ten from her own purse and go up to that Sherbrooke hat shop. She wanted something new that night when her grinning, bald, inexhaustible little man from St. Agathe came to see her. She liked Peggy. She couldn't believe the girl would skip out without paying her. It wasn't like her at all. But the girl's Negro friends might know a lot more about her. Above all, Mrs. Agnew wanted to count on getting the money for that hat.

It was easy to find out if the girl had left. In two minutes she could tell if she had taken her things. She wouldn't leave in her overalls, and her dresses and things should be in her room. So she went along the hall and down the back stairs and tapped on Peggy's door. "Peggy, Peggy," she called, not expecting an answer, but protecting herself in case the girl was home, sick. There was no answer, and she opened the door.

The strong morning sunlight was all on the front of the house, and it had not yet reached the window of Peggy's room. Anyway, the curtain was drawn and the light was burning.

"Oh, there you are, Peggy," she said when she saw one bare foot dangling over the edge of the bed. "Are you asleep, dearie? You had two callers, Peggy. I should have made sure you weren't at work. I say, dearie, wake up."

Taking a few steps toward the bed she raised both her hands and opened her mouth wide to scream; but her throat was paralyzed. She couldn't call out; she couldn't run. The girl lay naked on the bed. Her torn white blouse had been thrown on the floor. Her black skirt was on the floor, and sticking out from under it was a drawing of a girl in overalls; and the skirt could have been poured on the drawing. Peggy's wide-open eyes stared horribly at the ceiling and her mouth gaped. Around her throat were big bluish welts, and on her left breast was a heavy dark bruise. Her head was twisted a little to one side, her arms straight at her sides, the palms open and twisted back. She looked small, round, and white. Only her hair had any life in it, for the ceiling light touched the side of her head and there were gleams of gold in the fair hair.

The strangling tightness around Mrs. Agnew's own throat made her own eyes bulge as horribly as Peggy's; then it snapped and she cried, "Murder! Murder! Help!" She ran out of the room, turned back idiotically to slam the door after her, and staggered frantically up the stairs, still screaming.

McAlpine slept until ten and had to send a boy down to the St. Antoine for his coat and hat. When the boy returned a half-hour later McAlpine made a joke about the necessity of avoiding places that had to be deserted too quickly. He hurried out, and in the good strong sunlight on Sherbrooke he thought, It'll be all right. It was just that for a few moments I lost faith in her. She may not have noticed it. I won't even tell her. It got away from me. But only for a little while.

Coming down Crescent, he glanced at his watch. It was a few minutes after eleven, just the right time to go down to the La Salle and have an early lunch and make their plans. When he was still some distance from Mrs. Agnew's house, he saw the small crowd gathered around the entrance; he thought there might have been a fire, but he couldn't see any smoke or any firemen; then he saw a policeman circling around the fringe of the crowd and he started to run.

Everyone in the crowd was watching the basement door, where a policeman blocked the way. No one paid any attention to McAlpine as he pushed his way through. "Excuse me, excuse me, I'm going in there," he said. "What happened?" he asked a solemn middle-aged man who was whispering to a woman, a neighbour, who had her coat draped on her shoulders. They gave him the blank, slightly hostile look fascinated spectators give a newcomer who wants to break into a discussion. It was provoking. He was still filled with that confidence he had felt coming out into the sunlight.

"What happened?" he insisted, looking around impatiently. The door had opened and a thin-faced detective with a little moustache and fur-collared coat came out, whispered to the policeman, then shrugged and lit a cigarette and made his way through the crowd. "What happened?" McAlpine asked as the detective passed him. The man ignored him. A tall delivery boy with a bag slung over his shoulders, nodding at the detective, whispered with a knowing, satisfied, sophisticated air to a smaller delivery boy, "That was Bouchard. I've seen him around," he added.

"Bouchard – I don't know any Bouchard," said the smaller delivery boy.

"You dope! The one who made the gambling raids."

"Oh, the one who lost his job."

"No, the one who got kicked around."

"Son," McAlpine said to the older boy, who wouldn't turn while he could watch Bouchard getting into an automobile. Little snatches of conversation came to McAlpine. "A brute. An incredible brute," a woman's voice said. "It's actually warm today. I hardly need this coat." "These things go on," a man said. "After all, it didn't happen on the street." "You don't know who you're with these days." "It's getting worse. It hardly ever used to happen." McAlpine grabbed the tall delivery boy by the arm. "What happened, son?" he asked.

"The girl in there," the boy said impatiently. "She was killed."

"Yeah, raped and killed," whispered the smaller boy. "And left naked, they say. Gee whiz! A girl named—Was it Salmonson?"

"Naw, more like Sanderman."

"Yeah, worked in a factory."

Raising their awed faces, the boys blinked their eyes in the sunlight. A stout woman in a green coat who had listened to the boys turned to McAlpine, expecting more information from him. He lurched against her. He was trembling; there was no strength in his arms or legs. He believed he was walking out of the crowd, but he was only turning around slowly with no words, no thoughts, just the physical tremor he could not control, which made them all stare at him. "Excuse me," he said, putting out his hand and shoving the delivery boy gently out of his way. He began to go slowly down the street.

As he approached the corner everything he saw began to hurt him: the corner store, the passing streetcar, the melting snow, the sound of the traffic, the width of St. Catherine Street; it was a pain like the physical wrenching away of a part of his body. "Oh, my God!" he groaned. "Oh, Peggy – oh, my God, no!" All that was the matter, he thought, was that he had been a little late; she had to be still there to talk to.

And that corner – there was something wrong with that corner. In a nervous tremor he looked around and it came to him, the sudden recollection of having stood up the street a piece looking down at this corner in the snow, watching that one furtive figure vanishing among the snow-covered, ghostly figures who had drifted like evil spirits roaming the streets; and Peggy, herself, had come out and faded into that cold pallid world behind the curtain of snow. Filled with a fantastic primitive terror, he whispered crazily, "They got her. They got her." And he trembled all over.

He went away from the corner, going on mechanically to the La Salle Hotel, where he had planned to go for lunch with Peggy, and he ordered a drink, spilling a little of it because his hand trembled, then ordering another one, whispering, "If I had only stayed with her all night, to the end of the night."

In a little while he realized that he had been intending to sit in this place at this hour with her but she would never sit there again; and he got up, tossed a bill on the table, and fled. He went across the street to the basement bar on the corner. There the young sandy-haired bartender couldn't help watching him. Every time he took a drink he leaned back on the stool, his head tilting back, his chin coming up, his eyes always closed. "Do you want another one?" the worried bartender asked. McAlpine opened his eyes, and they were so lonely and desolate that the bartender stared at him. Why does he stare at me? McAlpine thought. He was afraid the bartender was going to ask, "Why didn't you stay with her last night?"

In the darkness of his mind he reached out after her; he sought her in the darkness with a mumbled prayer. My God, no, I won't take it! he thought. He tried to send his spirit winging after her across the world of the dead so he could take her by the hand, confront her guardian angel and shout, "Where were you last night? To let this happen! – I left her with love. You know I did, out of respect, out of a feeling for what was good. To let what was good be the cause of her death… Where were you? Where were you!"

While he could keep on protesting, he could hide from his loneliness. But the sandy-haired bartender, who had been watching his head go back a little farther each time he drank, said, "Anything the matter, pal?"

"What?"

"Aren't you feeling well?"

"Nothing's the matter with me," McAlpine said. He didn't like the bartender's accusing glance, and he paid for his drink and left, but the glance of the bartender followed him into the street. He wandered around, but he was always on a street or corner where he had been with Peggy; it became unbearably painful, and he wanted to run from those streets. He went back to the Ritz, and for a long time he sat by the window in a stupor. When the telephone rang he went to it; someone spoke to him, but he put it down, not hearing anything. Later the phone rang again. It was Foley complaining, "What's the matter with you, Jim? You hung up on me. Take it easy. I've seen the papers. It's splashed all over the front page. Now listen to me..." It was important, he said, that McAlpine shouldn't get mixed up in Peggy's story and get his name in the papers while the police were hunting for the killer; he shouldn't be around for people to question him; he should get out of the hotel. He made him promise to check out and go to his own apartment on University Avenue and wait there for him. The janitor would let him in, he said.

McAlpine packed his bag, his movements all detached and mechanical. Forgetting to phone the porter's desk he carried the bag down to the lobby. The charming desk clerk looked up in surprise. "Leaving us, Mr. McAlpine?"

"A message from home," McAlpine said, and he waited for the cashier to make out his bill.

"Not bad news, I hope."

"Yeah," McAlpine said vaguely.

"We are always pleased to have you here, Mr. McAlpine," the clerk said, and he put out his hand. McAlpine had to shake hands, and the clerk held his hand too long. Why was he trying to keep him? A taxi was at the entrance.

In ten minutes he was in Foley's apartment, where he lay down on the bed. Closing his eyes, he wanted to weep, but the tears wouldn't come. Underneath the steady throbbing of his heart was a great emptiness, and he whispered, "Oh, my God,

Peggy! Oh, my darling, where are you?" and he knew he could not stay there. Getting up, he went out and began to walk the streets. He walked in the bright, hard sunlight along St. Catherine. It was only two o'clock and the girls flowed past with their coats open, their bright scarves fluttering, enjoying the liberating warmth of the noonday sun, and he looked at each one, feeling lonely. The sidewalks were wet and steaming. At Peel and St. Catherine he stopped uneasily, for in the face of each passing young girl, in each fresh face, he saw Peggy's; all the young girls drifted by in a long noonday procession, and he had to wheel away, shaken, feeling they were all staring at him with the same mournful reproach.

✺ TWENTY-SEVEN ✺

Catherine had been out shopping and came in just before dinner. Laying her parcels on the hall table, she knocked off the evening newspaper. She picked it up and read the headlines about the death of Peggy Sanderson.

There was a picture of Peggy on the front page. With great enterprise, the city editors had got hold of copies of Peggy's college graduating class. There she was, an innocent looking schoolgirl; the long story and the interviews they wrote didn't seem to be quite right for the picture; they told of the brawl in the St. Antoine Café, and how she had been found in the morning in her room, stripped naked and raped, her assailant's marks on her throat. Beyond a doubt she was a questionable character who led a peculiar life. Catherine gathered that those from St. Antoine who were questioned about her were worried and cautious, for what was there to say about such a perverse white girl who was pretty and attractive? Yet they grudgingly declared that they liked her, and because they had liked her they resented her provoking solitude. The trouble was that too many of them liked her. When a young pretty girl was liked by so many it meant trouble. Only a Mrs. Agnew spoke well of Peggy. This Mrs. Agnew said it didn't matter to her whom Peggy had brought to the house; she had always been quiet and ladylike about it and had asked nothing from anyone.

The firmness of the alibis established by some of the St. Antoine people was satisfactory to the police, Catherine read.

When the café had closed for the evening Wilson, the trumpet player, had gone to Wagstaffe's apartment, where they had a sharp and at times heated discussion that had lasted until dawn. As for Wilson's wife, three of her neighbours who had been with her in her apartment had been trying to soothe her, they said, because she hadn't known where her husband had gone.

A prominent newspaperman, Walter Malone, had talked freely to the police. "That old drunk," Catherine said to herself. Of course he had to talk freely, for he had been involved in the café brawl. But he had left with Wolgast, who affirmed that Malone had sat in his bar until he had fallen asleep. Such awful people would hang around that Chalet Restaurant, she thought.

It had been established that the girl had been strangled at about three o'clock in the morning. Mrs. Agnew had declared that she had heard someone moving around the girl's apartment shortly before that time, and later had heard someone with a slow heavy step going along the hall. She had looked out the window; a heavy-set man had gone down the street. He didn't walk like a Negro, he didn't look like a Negro. As far as she was concerned he certainly wasn't a Negro.

And alongside the girl's picture they printed the drawing of her in overalls with its title, "Peggy the Crimper," which had been found beside the bed. Who drew this picture? they asked. Whoever drew it or whoever had been looking at it with her was the one, no doubt, who had lulled her into feeling secure and had then attacked her.

When Catherine first glanced at the drawing it had no meaning for her. A curtain was deliberately lowered across her mind. The story of the girl's wandering around St. Antoine was disgusting. "Ugh!" She made a face and tossed away the paper. Yet the fact that the names of Wolgast, Gagnon, and Malone had been mentioned pleased her. Surely Jim would be revolted now by the company he and Foley kept around that slum of a bar in the Chalet Restaurant.

At dinner with her father the girl's death was mentioned; one word led to another, and soon they were having an exasperating argument. Mr. Carver was appalled to think that a girl who had had a university education could become so depraved in her tastes and habits. It was a reflection on the whole trend of modern education. Teachers were no longer concerned with the development of moral character; but it was not to be wondered at, for look at the kind of men who were permitted to mould the minds of the young; look at a scamp like young Sloane, he said, growing eloquent and willing to put the blame for the girl's death squarely on the shoulders of young Sloane. As she tried to argue with him she became unreasonably resentful. The girl was obviously cheap and loose by nature, she insisted. A little pervert. There were such women, and men recognized them instinctively. It was utterly irrational to blame university professors because he disliked young Sloane, she said vehemently.

"I'm getting at the cause of the thing," he insisted.

"Oh, rubbish!" she cried. "You ride that poor horse to death." Words wouldn't come to her, she was so excited. She made awkward motions with her hands, glaring at her father. "Your mind is always on the one track, Daddy," she cried, banging down her coffee cup. "Oh, for heaven's sake, stop, stop! Please stop. I'm tired of this silly argument. What do we care about the girl?" And she strode out of the dining room, leaving her father looking helplessly at Jacques, who offered him a consoling shrug.

What had really been exasperating her, she told herself, was not having heard from McAlpine. It made her feel restless and vague about everything she was doing, and even now, when she started to go to her bedroom, she turned absent-mindedly and went back to the drawing room where her father had been sitting before dinner, and where, on the little green lacquer table by the chair, lay the newspaper he had been reading.

Glancing at it idly, she picked it up. She wanted to take another look at the girl's picture. Instead she found herself studying the drawing of "Peggy the Crimper." Then she wandered into her own bedroom. But even there everything, even her actions, became unfamiliar. From her clothes closet she took out two dresses, a blue one and a brown one, and laid them on the bed, wondering which one would make her look more desirable to McAlpine. She had seldom worn the brown one for him, and, if she had, why, things might have been different, for a dress of the right colour, the little extra touch, the right tone, might have surprised him. But when she had taken off her suit and was in her white slip, she forgot about the dress.

Going to her dressing table, she sat down and looked at herself in the mirror, pushing her hair back slowly with her right hand. Her shoulders and arms were bare, the curve of her breasts deep; she was assessing the fairness of her own image, longing for a splendid objective judgment of her attractiveness. The clock by her bed ticked loudly. The grandfather clock in the hall chimed the hour of nine. And still she was alone. An unfamiliar sense of dread and anxiety bewildered her. In a dream she felt herself being compelled to do something she had been trying not to do; she got up slowly, dreading each step, yet going on with a strange apprehensive expression.

The maid in the hall, seeing her emerge in her white slip, coughed, because Catherine never wandered around the apartment half-dressed, and Jacques, who had come out of the dining room, stepped back against the wall. She didn't notice him. Like a sleep walker she entered the drawing room where her father was sitting with his whisky and soda, reading the financial page. She simply reached for the paper, drew it out of his hands, and as he stood up, incredulous, she walked back to her bedroom.

From her bureau, where she kept those little objects that had a sentimental attachment for her, she took out the drawing McAlpine had made of her the night he had met her at the radio studio. She put it beside the drawing of "Peggy the Crimper" in the newspaper. On her own drawing were the words "Madame Radio." The handwriting on both drawings was clearly the same, and each showed the same touch in the free line and the careless ease of the lettering. He might just as well have signed his own name. "Oh, my God!" she whispered, sinking into the chair. Her head began to throb with a sharp pain that was like an attack of migraine she had had years ago, and she was scared, desolate, and lonely.

Yet she couldn't believe it. It was too incredible. She walked up and down with her long stride, protesting to herself that McAlpine had been the soul of gentleness with her, had even been shy of touching her, and, since no one would call her unattractive, it was therefore incredible to suggest that he would be found tearing the clothes off a worthless girl. What had probably happened was that he and Foley had met someone with the girl in that awful Chalet bar and McAlpine had amused them by drawing the picture.

But she was frightened by her pounding heart. It filled the room. With its steady loud beating it denied her easy explanation. How could she make these rational explanations when her heart throbbed so loud? What did she really know of McAlpine? His deep, careless, warm laugh and his impulsive gestures suggested a passion he had never shown to her; he had kept his secret, withdrawing from her night after night and probably sneaking off to the girl's room. Now she had that secret that she had longed to possess. She could see him in the room with the girl, going mad with passion for her; she saw it all so vividly she had to clamp her palm tight against her mouth for fear of screaming.

But she had to listen to her pounding heart, and it made her remember a stocky, redheaded young fellow who had struggled with her one night on a beach when she was eighteen. They had struggled on the sand in the moonlight, and she had been terrified as he held her down; but she had been strong enough to get away, and afterwards she had not hated him. Years later, when she had been married, she had wondered about the redheaded young fellow sometimes, even wishing she had not got away from him. That boy had really wanted her; with all his heart he had wanted her as McAlpine must have wanted this girl. Now she could feel again the grip of the boy's hands on her wrists, and she got all mixed up, looking around and wondering where she was, not knowing whether she was remembering the night on the beach or imagining she could feel McAlpine struggling with the slut of a girl.

She felt wild and confused. She started to pace up and down again, full of hatred for the girl. Yet never before had she hated anyone. She had been proud of being free of malice, of having a well bred sense of sportsmanship, and it had never been necessary for her to be envious of her friends. They had nothing she needed. But she could have given McAlpine everything he wanted: she longed to cry it out. And he knew it, oh, surely he knew it. And if so he could not possibly have touched the girl; there was some explanation; if he could hear her voice he would offer the explanation. She clutched eagerly at the phone on the table by the bed and called the Ritz, but they said Mr. McAlpine had checked out that afternoon. And she trembled and felt cold with fright.

Her eyes began to ache, and she turned out the light. A shaft of moonlight fell across the room. Striding back and forth across this strip of light, she wrung her hands. Gradually, she became aware of the moonlight. She looked at the window. The strip of moonlight reminded her of the redheaded boy. She strode to the window, trembling all over, and slashed the curtain across the light. Then she stood still, trying to make a plan. Outside, the taxis purred along Sherbrooke Street. The whole city hummed while she thought intently. But the plan wouldn't come, for she remembered how she had lain awake at night wanting McAlpine to touch her as he must have touched the girl. She felt unclean. She hated herself. She made washing motions with her hands. She hated McAlpine. He had only wanted to use her to worm his way into her father's business. He had involved her in his sordid affair with the drawing he had given her; it was a piece of evidence against him. It would identify him, but it would humiliate her publicly. Her father, too, was involved as were her friends and her whole life. The consequences of her identification of that drawing of the girl in overalls could be appalling.

But she was a strong-minded girl, proud of her own self-respect. Turning on the light, she put on her brown dress, moving slowly and gaining control of herself so her father would have respect for her.

She looked for her father in the drawing room. She found him in the library.

"What's this?" he asked when she handed him the newspaper and her own drawing. She was so pale and worried that he leaned forward to examine the drawing. "What's this, Catherine?" he repeated.

She only pointed at her own drawing. "Jim – McAlpine did it for me," she said nervously. Then she had to sit down and wait while he studied the drawing.

"I still don't understand," he said.

"Oh, can't you see?" She pointed to the handwriting. Even then for a while it had no meaning. A slow flush mounted to his forehead.

"Good God, Catherine, you don't mea—" Again he looked closely at the drawing, and, begging for an explanation, he turned to her. "These drawings," he said. "Why, there's no doubt they were done by the same hand. If McAlpine did them…" Sinking back in the chair, he protested, "But I liked that young man, Catherine."

"Yes," she nodded, holding onto herself beautifully, watching him finger his solid blue tie. Then he looked confusedly around his library. Neither spoke. They both shared the same astonishment that their home and their lives could be smirched by the sordid passions of the meanest neighbourhood in town. She told him that she had been uneasy for some days about McAlpine. She had been aware that he had some secret. She was much calmer than her father. Her self-control astonished him and made it hard for him to realize what had happened.

"But – but it must be awful for you, Catherine," he said, sighing.

"Of course," she said crisply. "Just the same, Jim couldn't really have done it, you know," she added.

"Why couldn't he?"

"Well, why didn't he ever – well – attack me or molest me?"

"Because – well, you're who you are, of course, Catherine."

"Yes, that's true."

"Just think," he said, wanting to be comforting, "how much worse it would be if you were more committed to him – if you had thought of marrying him."

"He hadn't asked me to marry him. I doubt if he wanted me to." In spite of herself her voice faltered.

Her tone aroused him, and he sat up, catching a glimpse of her suffering in her averted eyes. He understood her deep humiliation and he hated McAlpine. So they sat there rigidly, very close together in their wounded pride, yet still finding it incredible that a man they had liked, whom they had offered a chance to share their lives, should have preferred to be mixed up in the life of a debauched girl who drifted around St. Antoine.

"Catherine," he said, "it's not only this drawing of yours that involves us in this horrible mess."

"No?"

"The man was wearing my hat."

"Yes. Why, yes, so he was," she said.

"And my initials are in that hat."

"It won't matter, will it?"

"Why, the police will look at everything he has. He'll tell the police it's my hat. To give himself prestige around here."

"The police, you say—"

"Of course, Catherine. We have an obligation."

"But will we go to the police?"

"What else can we do?"

"It won't end there. People will talk."

"Yes. Yes, let me think, Catherine." His neck reddened, his face was angry. "I would have given my right arm for him," he complained. "I wanted him to get along." And as he fell into a monolithic stillness he sought words that would express the necessity of a certain course of conduct, words which would give them both some dignity. "We have to have a sense of responsibility about this, however painful it may be," he said.

"Yes, a sense of responsibility," she agreed, knowing all her training was at stake and everything they stood for would be tested by their action at this moment.

"We have here a piece of evidence," he said.

"Yes."

"We can't possibly suppress it."

"I don't know."

"Catherine," he said sternly, "we're not cheap little hysterical people who hide in the dark. This is our town. People respect us. We're not furtive. We're not ashamed of being involved – if we can be of some help."

"I understand," she said faintly.

"It will be painful, Catherine."

"I know it's necessary," she said. "We're entitled at least to keep our self-respect – to act as if we respected ourselves."

"You're a fine girl, Catherine. Just a minute." And he got up and strode out of the room to the phone. It was only when he was at the door that she looked up and noticed how burning-red the back of his neck was.

In twenty minutes a detective came, a French Canadian, Paul Bouchard. Forty-two years old, with a respectful elegant manner. He wore a black coat with a brown fur collar. He had a sharp face and a little moustache. Both Mr. Carver and Catherine conducted themselves with dignity. The detective, who was wise and shrewd, admired her manner very much. After he had compared the newspaper drawing with the one that belonged to Catherine he smiled a little. With extravagant respect he questioned Catherine about her relationship with McAlpine. If McAlpine had left the Ritz, where might he be at this hour? he asked. And she said he would probably be at the Chalet Restaurant. Only when she named the restaurant did her eyes glow with hatred. "I'd like you to come along with me," he said. "Not only to pick him out – but to identify this drawing."

"Is it necessary?" she asked, her face ashen.

"I think so."

"Very well." She hesitated only momentarily.

"I'll go with you, Catherine," her father said. "We'll see this thing through together."

"You are most helpful, sir," Bouchard said as he picked up Catherine's drawing and put it carefully in his inside pocket. "I have a car outside."

It was like a spring night out. The ice and snow on Sherbrooke Street had been cut by car wheels, and the flowing water in these tracks gleamed in the street lights. Passing cars sprayed sheets of water at the pavement.

⚘ TWENTY-EIGHT ⚘

Early in the evening McAlpine was in Wolgast's bar sitting with Foley at the corner table. The bar that night was a cheerless spot. Three strangers, salesmen from out of town, who had been advised to come there and enjoy the cheerful insults they would get from Wolgast, were expressing in whispers their profound disappointment with the place, for Wolgast ignored them. His arms folded and a cigar in his mouth, he leaned against his cash register morosely.

Foley had been trying to think of a comforting observation, but as he looked up his voice trailed off. He realized that no one could console McAlpine. His sickly pallor and the nervous twitching of his hand on the table suggested that he had been drinking. He also had the aloof, untouchable unawareness of a drunk. And yet he wasn't drunk. All afternoon he had been drinking, but his eyes showed that he was agonizingly sober and would remain so even if he lost control of his limbs. All his grief showed in the worried loneliness of his eyes.

When Bouchard came in, no one even looked up. But when he was followed by Catherine and her father McAlpine noticed them and stood up slowly. Mr. Carver looked like an aloof ambassador. Catherine, raising the collar of her beaver coat, stared blankly at McAlpine. He wore a blue suit, an inch of white cuff showing at the sleeves. He looked very clean and distinguished despite his pallor. He even smiled, for it flashed into his mind idiotically that many years ago when he had been a boy he had dreamed of the Havelocks and people like the Carvers seeking him out, and now they had come.

"Mr. McAlpine?" Bouchard said.

"Of course. You want to see me?" He came from behind the table. "I've been half expecting you."

"Wait a minute," Foley said sharply. "What's this about?"

"About? Well," McAlpine began, glancing at Wolgast, "you might say, in a sense, it's about Wolgast's white horse."

"What? What's this about me?" Wolgast demanded. But McAlpine was on his way to get his coat and hat.

"Take it easy, Jim," Foley said excitedly. "Nobody's going to push you around."

"I know, Chuck."

"Don't think you're pushing him around," Foley said belligerently to Carver. "Nor you either, lady. I, too, own a piece of this town."

Catherine turned her head away, and Mr. Carver made a gesture to Bouchard.

"Nobody's pushing your friend around," Bouchard said to Foley.

"Where are you taking him? I'll have fifteen lawyers there. Can he phone me?"

"Of course he can phone you," Bouchard said.

"I'll be sitting right here by the phone. Just remember he's got friends," Foley said.

When McAlpine had put on his coat and his hat and had joined Bouchard, who was talking quietly at the entrance with Catherine and her father, he suddenly took off the hat. "This is your hat, sir," he said apologetically to Mr. Carver. "I had intended to return it before."

"Sir," Mr. Carver said, glancing around, sure McAlpine was trying to humiliate him.

"Thanks for the loan of it."

"As you say, sir," Mr. Carver said coldly because Bouchard was watching him.

"I shall use the phone," Bouchard said mildly. "I think Mr. McAlpine would like a cup of coffee."

When they went out, Bouchard told Catherine that he would like her to come down to detective headquarters in about an hour; in the meantime, he would try to sober McAlpine up. She could identify the drawings in McAlpine's presence. He bowed to her. But when he took McAlpine by the arm she whispered, "Jim," and she put out her hand. Her father caught her arm sternly and she straightened and turned her head away, ashamed.

In the car McAlpine waited for Bouchard to speak. All that concerned Bouchard was that passing cars were spraying slush on the windshield.

"I'm under arrest, of course," McAlpine said.

"Who said you were under arrest?"

"Have I made one statement calculated to deceive you, sir?"

"It is a fact. You haven't."

"Why then should you deceive me? I'm under arrest."

"When you are feeling better we will have a talk."

"I am upset," McAlpine agreed. "But I am aware of my situation." And then he lay back in the cab in a stupor, the lights flickering on his face. Bouchard, believing he was drunk, wondered whether he should let him sleep or keep him awake and moving until his mind cleared. He had a mild impersonal manner and was proud of having no rancour for any of the criminals he arrested; he was also proud of being a cultivated citizen with sophisticated perceptions of his own. McAlpine obviously was a cultivated man, and therefore, within a certain sphere, his intellectual comrade. It was possible McAlpine would have emotions about the girl that would be stimulating, if corrupt. Bouchard had been Chief of Detectives but had made himself too difficult; he was unforgivably impartial in his arrests. He was on the way down in the department and knew it.

"Try and keep awake, my friend," he said, shaking McAlpine. "It will be easier. You are doing fine."

McAlpine, raising his head, looked out the window. "I wasn't sleeping. Where are we?" They were on their way to the Champ de Mars, Bouchard said. "Of course," McAlpine said with great understanding, recognizing the appropriateness of a ride through the old financial district where he had had his dreams of influence. "I would not like anyone to get the impression I drink too much. I never show the effects of liquor," he said stiffly. "I've been upset all day. I don't think anyone should drink who can't hold it. Excuse me." And he concentrated.

Going into Headquarters, then into the detectives' room, he was erect, and only when he sat down and leaned back with a sigh did he look around miserably.

It was a bare, shabby brown room with a long table. A stenographer, a plump dark young girl with glasses and a severe expression, brought in two cups and a quart jar of coffee. When McAlpine saw the coffee, he asked, "Would you mind, sir, if I washed my face with some very cold water?" "Not at all," Bouchard said with equal politeness. He took him to the washroom; he waited and even handed him a towel.

They returned to their coffee. McAlpine's hands were trembling; he drank the coffee greedily. When he was taking the third cup he saw Bouchard drop the drawing of "Madame Radio" on the table.

"If you please – if you please," McAlpine said in a lofty tone. "Never mind the ritual. Please don't be clever about this. I did that drawing. I also did the drawing you saw in the newspapers. I know how I'm in this. I know what I'm saying. I know it's my fault, but didn't want it. It shouldn't be like this. It's all wrong."

"And you killed the girl?" Bouchard said doubtfully.

"The way it is, it's my fault she's dead."

"And you were with her last night?"

"Of course I was."

"And you were involved in her death?"

"I told you it's my fault she's dead."

"What time did you get back to your hotel?"

"At twenty-seven minutes after two. Why is that important?" McAlpine asked impatiently. "Who's trying to fool you?"

"No one. I like to know these things. I'm curious. Drink some more coffee. I'll join you in a moment."

Bouchard's tone was sympathetic; he gave McAlpine a friendly pat on the shoulder and, his eyes bright with curiosity, he went out. Left with his coffee, McAlpine put his head in his hands and sighed. It was awful to be left there alone. All day long he had tried to avoid being alone. Bouchard, of course, was playing with him by leaving him alone. Yet there was the black coffee; but he pushed the mug away. More of it would make him sick. He felt bloated. It was better to concentrate on the scratches on the long table and realize he was to be left there endlessly shivering with the pain of his own recollections because they believed he wanted to conceal something.

When Bouchard returned, McAlpine scowled at him. "You don't have to leave me alone. Understand?"

"Excuse me," Bouchard said gently as he sat down. "I was merely doing some phoning. You will understand I wanted to check with your hotel. Abut the hour of your return."

"I've told you it's irrelevant."

"You say it is your fault. I still would like to know the one who actually killed her. Unless you know. No? One of her Negro friends?"

"Who it was is – is," McAlpine began, his voice breaking, "also unimportant."

"I am not asking now for a statement, understand, Mr. McAlpine. Maybe you would like to tell me how you were involved."

"How I was involved? That's very funny. Why, I loved her. I loved her and wanted her to be sure of herself."

"I want to know how you were involved in her death."

"I don't know what you'd call it," he said so softly he could hardly be heard, for he had put his hands over his face.

Bouchard was stirred by his protesting worried tone; it was interesting. He eyed him shrewdly, helping himself to some coffee. Then he leaned forward, bright-eyed, ready to offer his understanding of those hidden impulses that had intellectual interest for him. He knew he had been right in recognizing in McAlpine an intellectual equal who could quicken his curiosity.

"You say you loved her," he said sympathetically. "Well, it is understandable. A pretty girl. But that daughter of Mr. Carver is also handsome. Now, this Sanderson girl, they say, led a loose life, she had peculiar tastes. She hung out in strange places. You are a man of refinement and education. A professor. I must know why you went after her. Something about her piqued your curiosity, eh? Is it not so? Something elusive, strange, perhaps a discontent in your own life – boredom." He became absorbed himself and pleased with his own insight. "Around St. Antoine," he went on while McAlpine stared at him, drugged by the flow of words, "when the white and the black get mixed up, there is a field of many strange, perverted tastes for a white girl to develop. Of course you were interested. Something outside your own experience, eh? I myself understand that craving for novelty. You know the works of André Gide?"

"Sure. Sure."

"Gide. The French novelist. No?" he asked as McAlpine, straightening up, glared at him. "No?"

"All this backwoods talk about Gide," McAlpine jeered at him brutally. "It's all talk. I don't think anybody around here reads Gide."

"But just the same—"

"Just the same – what?"

"I say Gide has a fine style."

"Oh, my God, we all have a fine style! Where am I?" McAlpine looked around, then stared blankly at Bouchard, the colour draining from his stricken face. He made a desolate gesture, dropped his head on his arms, and began to weep.

It was very embarrassing for Bouchard, whose eyes had been glittering with intellectual sympathy. He didn't like it. It was primitive to weep. He got up and walked around the end of the table.

"All right. All right," he said roughly. He hadn't cried publicly himself since he was a small boy. "Come on now." But McAlpine ignored him.

The solid stenographer came in, leading the way for Catherine. "Have some dignity," Bouchard whispered, and now he was truly annoyed.

"I'm sorry. Excuse me," McAlpine said.

His reddened eyes and the misery in his face shocked Catherine; she backed against the wall and wounded Bouchard by looking at him reproachfully.

"Ah, madame," he said, bowing. "Very good of you to get here. Do sit down. Here at the table. Thank you," he added as she approached the table.

"Mr. McAlpine," he said genially, "I did some phoning – really for you. That Mrs. Agnew helped you anyway with her story about the man she heard after you left. I have phoned your hotel, and the night clerk remembers you coming in. He looked at the clock. It was a late hour for a man to be out without a hat or coat. The time checks right – for you…" Then he turned to Catherine. "But Mr. McAlpine admits he was involved, and you, madame, think so, too."

"I don't know," she said nervously. "I only said—"

"I was involved," McAlpine said. "Catherine, you have a right to know how I was involved."

"If you didn't do it – I mean—" She was so troubled she couldn't speak for a moment. "If – if you had called me – if only you had explained—"

"Wait," he pleaded.

"Let him talk," Bouchard said impatiently. "I want to know how long he has been mixed up with this girl."

"Ever since I came here," McAlpine said.

"Oh, no, Jim!" Catherine whispered.

"That's the truth," he insisted. Trying to keep his voice steady, he concentrated intently on one table leg. Their presence didn't embarrass him. He only hoped they would understand his anguished protest. He wanted to get it all straight for them.

He began with his first meeting with Peggy and the growth of his curiosity, how she had troubled him, and the growth of his own insight into her nature and the growth of his faith in his insight. All he wanted was that she should be herself. He loved her. Yet everyone he knew wanted to destroy her. They had resented her. He knew their resentment meant trouble, and he could feel it coming as you listen in the dark and hear someone creeping after you. His own faith, he said, couldn't be broken by his friends, nor by the appearance of things, or the fact that she courted destruction. He had known that he was drawing her away from a life that did not become her, and he had waited patiently for her to realize she could love him.

Sometimes he faltered, forgetting they were listening to him, the words coming slowly. He would pause, searching his memory for an illuminating incident, then begin again. His voice choked as he spoke of the hours he had passed alone in her room dreaming of seeing her in other places, in other clothes, with other people; he spoke of the pleasure he had got watching her being affectionate and laughing. He looked up, wondering if Catherine understood his suffering. The compassion in her face gave him a melancholy eloquence.

She was fumbling in her purse for her handkerchief, because the story of his devotion had filled her with sad regret that she herself had never stirred him, and yet she understood with generosity. A feverish glow was in her eyes as she listened. He's what I thought he was, she told herself. Loving and passionate and reckless and impulsive and faithful. No wonder I loved him. It could have been me. Over and over again she kept thinking painfully, it could have been me; and she waited, hearing the words she had always wanted to hear from him, hearing them about another, but glowing ardently as she identified herself with the other girl. When he described the trouble in the café and his struggle to be with the girl she could feel him struggling to be with herself, and when he told of rushing wildly up the street to get to the room, and of what had happened in the room, she was breathless with a strange, painful, yielding ardour, waiting for him to possess her.

"I could have stayed with her all night," he said. "She was mine. There and then she was mine. But when I looked back on the way it had been – the others – all the others – I could not believe she wanted only me. She was alone, rejected by everybody. I happened to be there. She was feeling grateful. I wanted to be fair to her. I wanted to give her a chance to be sure. To make staying with her a part of that awful night – it wasn't right, was it? She needed respect above all, didn't she? Wasn't I right in wanting to be fair to her?"

For an apprehensive, silent moment Catherine and Bouchard dwelt on that night and what it could have meant.

"And so you left her?" Bouchard asked.

"Until the morning. Only till the morning when she could feel free, understand," he said, longing for absolution from the silence of their profound disappointment, and from the look in Catherine's eyes. But Catherine stood up slowly. "I see," she said. In her thoughts she was left in the girl's room, left there without that gesture of reckless, ruthless devotion she could understand and forgive because it would be worthy of him. And she stared at him resentfully. "Catherine," he said, coming around the table toward her apologetically, "I know I was unfair to you."

"What?" she asked, all her disappointment showing in her face. "Unfair?" She was confused by what had happened to her and what hadn't happened, and what she had wanted and what she hadn't wanted.

"I know how you must have felt." Longing to make a friendly gesture, he took her by the arm.

"Oh, don't touch me now," she said fiercely, and she slapped him across the face.

Bewildered, he backed against the table. His hand went up to his face. Catherine waited tensely, expecting Bouchard to interfere with her. She tried to smile disdainfully, but she was shaken by her own violence and its meaning, and what it might have revealed of her.

"Do you need me anymore, Mr. Bouchard?" she asked nervously.

"No, madame. Not anymore."

"Thank you," she said in her clipped cool tone, and she walked swiftly to the door.

He still felt the blow on his face, but it was the expression he had seen in her eyes that tore at his heart; and he wanted to cry out.

"Why did she slap me? Why?"

"Women have odd impulsive resentments," Bouchard said philosophically. "I don't think you quite lived up to her expectations."

❦ TWENTY-NINE ❦

Slumped in the chair, his face burning, he remained silent for so long that Bouchard in his embarrassment offered him a cigarette, which he took and put in his mouth. His movements were slow and deliberate. He lit Bouchard's cigarette for him and then his own. But his train of thought was not broken by these movements.

"Well, who do you think did it?" Bouchard asked abruptly.

"I don't know."

"No one in your mind?"

"No." McAlpine had sunk into lethargy. He wasn't interested.

It irritated Bouchard. "How does Wolgast come into it?" he asked, trying again.

"I don't think he does."

"I heard what you said to your friend in the Chalet. He asked you what it was about when I came in. You said it was about Wolgast and a horse."

"Oh, that!" McAlpine said in a dull tone. "It was a general ironic remark."

"Wolgast has an alibi anyway."

"Everybody has an alibi."

"Maybe we'll never find out who did it, Mr. McAlpine. You know why?" Bouchard asked, insisting on getting his attention. "What if we all did it? The human condition. That has truth, don't you think?" When he didn't answer, Bouchard was wounded and wanted to jolt him. "Well, at least you'll never know whether the girl was a slut or an innocent, will you?" Then he was embarrassed by the desolation in McAlpine's eyes. "But in the way she died, resisting someone who thought she was a slut... Well, there you are. I think she really loved you," he said blandly.

"Can I go now?"

"Indeed, yes," Bouchard said. "I know you'll be anxious to help if I need you." He got McAlpine's coat for him. But McAlpine lay inertly in the chair, his neck resting on the back, one leg curled under the chair, the other sprawled out stiffly. "I wouldn't have any regrets if I were you, Mr. McAlpine," Bouchard said, wanting to be friendly, for the discovery of a little human weakness in a cultivated man was always a consolation to him.

McAlpine didn't answer. Bouchard waited, watching him, then smiled, believing he understood why he didn't get up and march out: he couldn't bear to go out; he didn't want to be back among his friends who might learn his story and then look at him as that girl had done, wanting to scratch out his eyes. The darkness, the dizzying, stupefying darkness after the alcohol and the exhaustion was all he wanted. His breathing grew heavier. He was asleep. Bouchard went to shake him, then pitied him and put the coat on the table and went out.

When McAlpine woke up, his neck aching, his legs cramped, he couldn't remember where he was. Then he stood up and put on his coat. In the corridor he hesitated, as if expecting to be called back or find the way barred. No one spoke to him. Outside, in the thin, cold dawn light, he shivered and turned up the collar of his coat. The sky was leaden, the hard lines of the buildings were beginning to emerge out of the night shadows. It was between the dark and the dawn. The grey limestone buildings in that light looked cold and bleak. A few lights still shone in office windows where the charladies scrubbed the floors. Water trickled along the gutters. All night the snow had been melting. Parts of the city were still shadowed by the heavy mountain darkness against the sky.

He wanted to walk for hours until he could understand that what had happened was not a stupid irrational mockery of his love. He had to know truly, and no matter how it lacerated his heart, what had prompted him to draw back in that fatal moment in her room instead of abandoning himself impulsively and going headlong with her and never leaving her no matter what she was. Oh, what had compelled him to put her beyond him? Always the high dark hedge, the black barrier. The lights and the laughter and the singing on the other side of the hedge. He had to figure it out.

It was getting a little lighter; the elephant grey of the limestone buildings dissolved in shafts of light. Trucks began to rumble down the streets. He was cutting down through the warehouse district, heading for Bleury. Pale lights in a few office windows were turned out. The doors of buildings opened and charwomen came out. In the dawn silence voices sounded loud and important. Noises came from the harbour, which hadn't been touched yet by the sunlight. A yawping ship's whistle was answered by a foghorn, like a moan, from another ship. But the noises were isolated; the small trickling sound of running water from the melting snow was still a night sound made in the morning.

Suddenly McAlpine thought, "Bouchard was right. It's the human condition. Why did I make that remark about Wolgast?" Wolgast was not the only one who had a grudge against Peggy. All the best people could get behind Wolgast on his proud white whose. Not the magic horse of his childhood though! That was gone. In his own way, Wolgast now was a big success. He had got established. He had his pride.

McAlpine slowed down, for he didn't want the sound of his own footfalls to protect and spare him from another painful glimpse of himself in that room last night with Peggy. "Oh, no, no!" he whispered. Yet he had made the remark about Wolgast. Even if he had been a little drunk, being there with Wolgast he must have thought, When I knew I had her and could keep her, maybe I remembered that I, too, had come to Montreal to ride a white horse. Maybe that was why I was always trying to change her. That was the sin. I couldn't accept her as she was.

In the sky over the mountain a faint pink streak appeared. The rim of trees was a dark fringe against the pink light. On the mountain slopes the great homes and massive apartments were still in the grey shadow. As sunlight to the east glinted on the canal and touched church spires and towers, the city began to stir with a faint low hum. Monastery bells chimed clearly. The streetcars rattled along St. Catherine, a train pulled into the Windsor Station; all the new morning noises blended into a low rumble, getting louder until the night sound of the trickling water in the gutters was lost in the sounds of the morning.

As the sun touched the top of the mountain and suddenly brightened the snow, McAlpine stopped, watching it intently. He had a swift wild fancy: the streets on the slopes of the mountain were echoing to the pounding of horses' hoofs. All the proud men on their white horses came storming down the slope of the mountain in a ruthless cavalry charge, the white horses whirling and snorting in the snow. And Peggy was on foot in the snow. She didn't own a white horse. She didn't want to. She didn't care. And he was beside her; but he drew back out of the way of the terrifying hoofs and they rode over her. And now he was left alone on the street, and the young women who knew his story were staring at him sorrowfully, all saying the same thing.

Then he heard a voice saying, "What do you care what they say?" It was her voice, and he whispered, "Oh, Peggy, Peggy, wherever you are, be always with me." And as he uttered this whispered cry he reached out desperately to bind her to him. Stopping, he watched the morning light brightening the snow on the slopes until the whole rich mountain glistened. His shoulders were hunched a little, his collar turned up, his face raised, as he regarded the sloping city with fierce defiance. Yes, what they say is unimportant, forever unimportant to me, he thought. I know what happened, Peggy. I know why you're gone. In a moment of jealous doubt his faith in her had weakened, he had lost his view of her, and so she had vanished. She had vanished off the earth. And now he was alone.

Yet he would keep her with him. In some way he would keep her with him. Wondering where he was, he looked around for Bleury Street. He had a plan in mind, and everything quickened. He found Bleury and began to climb the long slope. He hurried along eagerly, believing he had found a way to hold on to Peggy forever.

He wanted to find the antique church she had taken him to that day they had walked in the thick falling snow. When he got to St. Patrick's the tolling bell called the people to early mass. An old woman carrying a prayer book hurried by, and a gaunt bearded man holding a small boy by the hand. Prayer beads dangled from the boy's overcoat pocket. While the St. Patrick's bell clanged loud and close to him he looked up, alert. Soon the bells would ring in that little church nearby. He could get his bearings from the bells. Then he heard it, coming from the west and only a little way off, quick light chiming bells calling, softly calling, and he hurried in that direction; but the ring-ing faded away. He stopped and waited. Again he heard the light silver chiming. He followed where it beckoned, back to the east now and tantalizingly close; then it was gone. Another bell chimed from the mountain, monastery bells called from St. Catherine, and he wandered around confused, not knowing which way to turn, tormented by the soft calling bells...

But he went on with his tireless search. He wandered around in the neighbourhood between Phillips Square and St. Patrick's. He wandered in the strong morning sunlight. It was warm and brilliant. It melted the snow. But he couldn't find the little church.

COMMENTS BY EDMUND WILSON

The Canadian Morley Callaghan, at one time well known in the United States, is today perhaps the most unjustly neglected novelist in the English-speaking world. In his youth, he worked on the *Toronto Star* – Toronto is his native city – at the time when Ernest Hemingway had a job on the same paper, and, through Hemingway, who took his manuscripts to Paris, some of Callaghan's early short stories were accepted by Ezra Pound for his little magazine *Exile*. Maxwell Perkins of Scribner's was impressed by these stories and had them reprinted in *Scribner's Magazine*, which later published other stories by Callaghan. His novels were published by *Scribner's*. Morley Callaghan was a friend of Fitzgerald and Hemingway and was praised by Ring Lardner, and he belonged to the literary scene of the twenties. He appeared in *transition* as well as in *Scribner's* and he spent a good deal of his time in Paris and the United States. But eventually he went back to Canada, and it is one of the most striking signs of signs of the partial isolation of that country from the rest of the cultural world that – in spite of the fact that his stories continued to appear in *The New Yorker* up to the end of the thirties – he should quickly have been forgotten in the United States and should be almost unknown in England. Several summers ago, on a visit to Toronto, I was given a copy of the Canadian edition of a novel of his called *The Loved and the Lost.* It seemed to me so remarkable that I expected it to attract attention in England and the United States. But it was never published in England, and it received so little notice in the United States that I imagined it had not been published here either.

I want to… speculate first on the reasons for the current indifference to his work. This has no doubt been partly due to the peculiar relation of Canada to England and the United States. The Canadian background of Morley Callaghan's stories seems alien to both these other countries and at the same time not strange enough to exercise the spell of the truly exotic. To the reviewer, this background has much interest and charm. Montreal, with its snow-dazzling mountain, its passionate winter sports, its hearty and busy bars, its jealously guarded French culture, and its pealing of bells from French churches, side by side with the solid Presbyterianism of its Anglo-Scottish best people, is a world I find pleasant to explore. It is curious to see how much this world has been influenced – in its language, in its amusements, its press – by the "Americans," as they still call us, and how far – in, for example, its parliamentary politics and its social and moral codes – it rests on somewhat different foundations. But Mr. Callaghan is not writing about Canada at all from the point of view of exploiting its regional characteristics… he does not even tell the reader that the scene of the story is Montreal. The landscapes, the streets and the houses, the atmosphere of the various milieu are known intimately and sensitively observed, but they are made to figure quite unobtrusively; there are no very long descriptions and nothing like "documentation." We simply find ourselves living with the characters and taking for granted, as they do, their habits and customs and assumptions, their near-Artic climate and their split nationality. Still less is Mr. Callaghan occupied with specifically Canadian problems. The new and militant Canadian nationalism – in these novels, at least – does not touch him; he is not here concerned with the question of "what it means to be a Canadian." And the result of this has been, I believe, that a public, both here and in England, whose taste in American fiction seems to have been largely whetted by the perpetrators of violent scenes – and these include some of our best writers as well as our worst – does not find itself at home with, does not really comprehend, the more sober effects of Callaghan. In his novels one finds acts of violence and a certain amount of sensuality, but these are not used for melodrama or even for "symbolic" fables of the kind that is at present fashionable. There are no love stories that follow an expected course, not even any among those I have read that eventually come out all right. It is impossible to imagine these books transposed into any kind of terms that would make them acceptable to Hollywood.

The novels of Morley Callaghan do not deal, then, with his native Canada in any editorial or informative way, nor are they aimed at any popular taste, Canadian, American or British. They center on situations of primarily psychological interest that are treated from a moral point of view yet without making moral judgments of any conventional kind, and it is in consequence peculiarly difficult to convey the implications of one of these books by attempting to retell its story. The revelation of personality, of tacit conflict, of reciprocal emotion is conducted in so subtle a way that we are never quite certain what the characters are up to – they are often not certain themselves – or what the upshot of their relationships will be... These stories are extremely well told. The details, neither stereotyped nor clever – the casual gestures of the characters, the little incidents that have no direct bearing on their purposes or their actions, the people they see in restaurants or pass on the street – have a naturalness that gives the illusion of not having been invented, of that seeming irrelevance of life that is still somehow inextricably relevant. The narrative moves quietly but rapidly, and Mr. Callaghan is a master of suspense... The style is very clear and spare, sometimes a bit commonplace, but always intent on its purpose, always making exactly its points so that these novels are as different as possible from the contemporary bagful of words that forms the substance of so many current American books that are nevertheless taken seriously. Mr. Callaghan's underplaying of drama and the unemphatic tone of his style are accompanied by a certain greyness of atmosphere, but this might also be said of Chekhov, whose short stories his sometimes resemble... one's tendency, in writing of these novels, to speak of what the characters "should have" done is a proof of the extraordinary effect of reality which – by simply presenting their behaviour – Mr. Callaghan succeeds in producing. His people, though the dramas they enact have more than individual significance, are never allowed to appear as anything other than individuals. They never become types or abstractions, nor do they ever loom larger than life. They are never removed from our common humanity, and there is never any simple opposition of beautiful and horrible, of lofty and base. The tragedies are the results of the interactions of the weaknesses and strengths of several characters, none of whom is either entirely responsible or entirely without responsibility for the outcome that concerns them all. But in order to describe his book properly, one must explain that the central element in it, the spirit that pervades the whole, is deeply if undogmatically Christian. Though it depends on no scaffolding of theology, though it embodies an original vision, there is evidently somewhere behind it the tradition of the Catholic Church. This is not the acquired doctrine of the self-conscious Catholic convert – of Graham Greene or Evelyn Waugh. One is scarcely aware of doctrine; what one finds is, rather, an intuitive sense of the meaning of Christianity... The reviewer, at the end of this article, is now wondering whether the primary reason for the current underestimation of Morley Callaghan may not be simply a general incapacity – apparently shared by his compatriots – for believing that a writer whose work may be mentioned without absurdity in association with Chekhov's and Turgenev's can possibly be functioning in Toronto.

November 26, 1960

Questions For Discussion And Essays

1. Many anglophone Canadian writers have envied the strong sense of national and cultural identity that is shared by Quebecois storytellers. For Callaghan, as the critic Ray Ellenwood has pointed out, the whole issue is a red herring. There is no doubt that he is rooted in Toronto, but his novels are not in any way nationalist or regionalist. Though the city in *The Loved and the Lost*, the world of the mountain and the world of the river, are accurately described with feeling, Montreal is never named, suggesting to the dismay of some that Callaghan has been deliberately "continental" from the beginning. Political questions arise in his novels, but mostly as elements of a specific situation between two or three people, their character and not the politics being at stake. Does this mean that Callaghan is a profoundly Canadian writer, so secure in his own identity that he need make no issue of national or regional matters, or is he, this creature, a so-called insecure continentalist?

2. Callaghan's Catholicism expresses itself in unorthodox ways. He is, perhaps, a kind of miscreant, "on the fringes of a religion and yet dependent on it." He once told an interviewer: "At the end of your life, the whole question should be, 'How did you manage to get along with people?' If you say, 'Well, I lived my life in the desert, loving God,' to my temperament that doesn't mean anything. Okay kid, you've dropped out, you're a saint in the desert, you're a hermit... but you know nothing about human beings. From my view, you know nothing about love. And if you know nothing about human love, to me, in my stupidity, you can't know anything about divine love. I hate the person who loves the idea, you know. I don't believe in that

kind of love." If *The Loved and the Lost* is to be read as a love story, discuss it as such in light of Callaghan's remarks.

3. Self-discipline does not appear to be one of Callaghan's values. He presents it as the enemy of passionate intensity and human involvement. He himself has said about McAlpine: "He made a mistake; I think he should have stayed with the girl. There should have been something in his heart that would override any attitude. When you're really good you don't have to think. The trouble is, he thought." In other words, a reason for doing something need not be reasonable. Discuss.

4. The critic Milton Wilson wrote: "The special talent of Morley Callaghan is to tell us everything and yet keep us in the dark about what really matters. He makes us misjudge and rejudge and misjudge his characters over and over again; we end up no longer capable of judgment, but not yet capable of faith." Which, of course, leaves the reader uncertain about what moral stance to take toward a given character, leaves the reader in a state of ambivalence and ambiguity. Is this a strength or a weakness in Callaghan's work?

5. Does Callaghan's prose style, his determination that prose should "be like glass" – that the writer himself should not be there, should not in any way stand between the reader and the word – only serve to deepen that ambiguity, that ambivalence – for the reason that the author is never there to instruct or direct? The reader is on his or her own. And is this "being on your own" not, finally, the state of all his so-called "criminal-saints" – his heroes and heroines, and if this is true, is it possible that that is the bond he seeks, a bond between reader and character as criminal-saints? And does that imply that the reader who does

not get this, is simply too tied to conventional narrative needs, the conventional wisdom, always remembering that today's avant garde is tomorrow's academic staple? Discuss.

6. Around the time of publication, 1951, several reviewers, suggested that Callaghan, in *The Loved and the Lost*, was attempting to solve the so-called "race problem" – and that having tried, he had failed. Discuss how this is a complete misreading of the novel.

7. Callaghan more than once declared that the great sin that preoccupied him the most was a man or woman's failure to realize their potential. "The great trick in life," he told Robert Weaver, "is to remain on an even keel – and somehow or other be able to draw yourself together and realize your potentialities as a man. And the great sin is to not realize your own potentialities." McAlpine begins, as a tolerant liberal, by supposing that he can maintain the integrity of his character and develop his potential while operating among men and women who would exploit and corrupt his talent, corrupt him. He suffers, as does Peggy, from what some call innocence, but if it is innocence, it is innocence as unawareness. Would it be true to say that it is Peggy's unawareness that beguiles McAlpine and that it is his unawareness that leads him to betray her – (which is why who actually killed her is of no consequence to the story) – so that the potentialities inherent in their lives are lost? Discuss.

Related Reading

Callaghan, Barry. *Barrelhouse Kings*. Toronto, McArthur & Company, 1998.

Callaghan, Morley. *A Literary Life. Reflection and Reminiscences 1928-1990*. Holstein, Exile Editions, 2008.

Conron, Brandon. *Morley Callaghan: Critical Views on Canadian Writers, No. 10*. Toronto, McGraw-Hill Ryerson, 1975.

Cameron, Barry. "Rhetorical Tradition and the Ambiguity of Callaghan's Narrative Rhetoric." The Callaghan Symposium, University of Ottawa Press, 1981.

Ellenwood, Ray. "Morley Callaghan, Jacques Ferron, and the Dialectic of Good and Evil." The Callaghan Symposium, University of Ottawa Press, 1981.

McDonald, Larry. "The Civilized Ego and Its Discontents: A New Approach to Callaghan." The Callaghan Symposium, University of Ottawa Press, 1981.

McPherson, Hugo. "The Two Worlds of Morley Callaghan: Man's Earthly Quest," Queens Quarterly, LXIV, 3 (Autumn 1957). 350-365.

Orange, John. *Orpheus in Winter: Morley Callaghan's* The Loved and the Lost. Toronto, ECW Press, 1993.

Snider, Norman. "Why Morley Callaghan Still Matters," The Globe and Mail, 25 October, 2008.

Walsh, William. *A Manifold Voice: Studies in Commonwealth Literature.* London: Chatto & Windus, 1971.

Wilson, Edmund. *O Canada: An American's Notes on Canadian Culture.* New York, Farrar, Straus & Giroux, 1964.

Of Interest on the Web

www.editoreric.com/greatlit/authors/Callaghan.html
— *The Greatest Authors of All Time site*

www2.athabascau.ca/cll/writers/english/writers/mcallaghan.php
— *Athabasca University site*

www.cbc.ca/lifeandtimes/callaghan.htm
— *Canadian Broadcasting Corporation (CBC) site*

www.bookrags.com/morely callaghan
— *The Morely Callaghan Study Pack*

Exile Online Resource

www.ExileEditions.com has a section for the Exile Classics Series, with further resources for all the books in the series.

THE EXILE CLASSICS SERIES

THAT SUMMER IN PARIS (No. 1)
MORLEY CALLAGHAN
Memoir 6x9 247 pages 978-1-55096-688-6 (tpb) $19.95

It was the fabulous summer of 1929 when the literary capital of North America had moved to the Left Bank of Paris. Ernest Hemingway, F. Scott Fitzgerald, James Joyce, Ford Madox Ford, Robert McAlmon and Morley Callaghan... amid these tangled relationships, friendships were forged, and lost... A tragic and sad and unforgettable story told in Callaghan's lucid, compassionate prose.

NIGHTS IN THE UNDERGROUND (No. 2)
MARIE-CLAIRE BLAIS
Fiction/Novel 6x9 190 pages 978-1-55096-015-0 (tpb) $19.95

With this novel, Marie-Claire Blais came to the forefront of feminism in Canada. This is a classic of lesbian literature that weaves a profound matrix of human isolation, with transcendence found in the healing power of love.

DEAF TO THE CITY (No. 3)
MARIE-CLAIRE BLAIS
Fiction/Novel 6x9 218 pages 978-1-55096-013-6 (tpb) $19.95

City life, where innocence, death, sexuality, and despair fight for survival. It is a book of passion and anguish, characteristic of our times, written in a prose of controlled self-assurance. A true urban classic.

THE GERMAN PRISONER (No. 4)
JAMES HANLEY
Fiction/Novella 6x9 55 pages 978-1-55096-075-4 (tpb) $13.95

In the weariness and exhaustion of WWI trench warfare, men are driven to extremes of behaviour.

THERE ARE NO ELDERS (No. 5)
AUSTIN CLARKE
Fiction/Stories 6x9 159 pages 978-1-55096-092-1 (tpb) $17.95

Austin Clarke is one of the significant writers of our times. These are compelling stories of life as it is lived among the displaced in big cities, marked by a singular richness of language true to the streets.

100 LOVE SONNETS (No. 6)
PABLO NERUDA
Poetry 6x9 225 pages 978-1-55096-108-9 (tpb) $24.95

As Gabriel García Márquez stated: "Pablo Neruda is the greatest poet of the twentieth century – in any language." And, this is the finest translation available, anywhere!

THE SELECTED GWENDOLYN MACEWEN (No. 7)
GWENDOLYN MACEWEN
Poetry/Fiction/Drama/Art/Archival 6x9 352 pages
978-1-55096-111-9 (tpb) $32.95

"This book represents a signal event in Canadian culture." –*Globe and Mail* The only edition to chronologically follow the astonishing trajectory of MacEwen's career as a poet, storyteller, translator and dramatist, in a substantial selection from each genre.

THE WOLF (No. 8)
MARIE-CLAIRE BLAIS
Fiction/Novel 6x9 158 pages 978-1-55096-105-8 (tpb) $19.95

A human wolf moves outside the bounds of love and conventional morality as he stalks willing prey in this spellbinding masterpiece and classic of gay literature.

A SEASON IN THE LIFE OF EMMANUEL (No. 9)
MARIE-CLAIRE BLAIS
Fiction/Novel 6x9 175 pages 978-1-55096-118-8 (tpb) $19.95

Widely considered by critics and readers alike to be her masterpiece, this is truly a work of genius comparable to Faulkner, Kafka, or Dostoyevsky. Includes 16 Ink Drawings by Mary Meigs.

IN THIS CITY (No. 10)
AUSTIN CLARKE
Fiction/Stories 6x9 221 pages 978-1-55096-106-5 (tpb) $21.95

Clarke has caught the sorrowful and sometimes sweet longing for a home in the heart that torments the dislocated in any city. Eight masterful stories showcase the elegance of Clarke's prose and the innate sympathy of his eye.

THE NEW YORKER STORIES (No. 11)
MORLEY CALLAGHAN
Fiction/Stories 6x9 158 pages 978-1-55096-110-2 (tpb) $19.95

Callaghan's great achievement as a young writer is marked by his breaking out with stories such as these in this collection... "If there is a better storyteller in the world, we don't know where he is." –*New York Times*

REFUS GLOBAL (No. 12)
THE MONTRÉAL AUTOMATISTS
Manifesto 6x9 142 pages 978-1-55096-107-2 (tpb) $21.95

The single most important social document in Quebec history, and the most important aesthetic statement a group of Canadian artists has ever made. This is basic reading for anyone interested in Canadian history or the arts in Canada.

TROJAN WOMEN (No. 13)
GWENDOLYN MACEWEN
Drama 6x9 142 pages 978-1-55096-123-2 (tpb) $19.95

A trio of timeless works featuring the great ancient theatre piece by Euripedes in a new version by MacEwen, and the translations of two long poems by the contemporary Greek poet Yannis Ritsos.

ANNA'S WORLD (No. 14)
MARIE-CLAIRE BLAIS
Fiction 5.5x8.5 166 pages ISBN: 978-1-55096-130-0 $19.95

An exploration of contemporary life, and the penetrating energy of youth, as Blais looks at teenagers by creating Anna, an introspective, alienated teenager without hope. Anna has experienced what life today has to offer and rejected its premise. There is really no point in going on. We are all going to die, if we are not already dead, is Anna's philosophy.

THE MANUSCRIPTS OF PAULINE ARCHANGE (No. 15)
MARIE-CLAIRE BLAIS
Fiction 5.5x8.5 324 pages ISBN: 978-1-55096-131-7 $23.95

For the first time, the three novelettes that constitute the complete text are brought together: the story of Pauline and her world, a world in which people turn to violence or sink into quiet despair, a world as damned as that of Baudelaire or Jean Genet.

A DREAM LIKE MINE (No. 16)
M.T. KELLY
Fiction 5.5x8.5 174 pages ISBN: 978-1-55096-132-4 $19.95

A Dream Like Mine is a journey into the contemporary issue of radical and violent solutions to stop the destruction of the environment. It is also a journey into the unconscious, and into the nightmare of history, beauty and terror that are the awesome landscape of the Native American spirit world.

THE LOVED AND THE LOST (No. 17)
MORLEY CALLAGHAN
Fiction 5.5x8.5 302 pages ISBN: 978-1-55096-151-5 (tpb) $21.95

With the story set in Montreal, young Peggy Sanderson has become socially unacceptable because of her association with black musicians in nightclubs. The black men think she must be involved sexually, the black women fear or loathe her, yet her direct, almost spiritual manner is at variance with her reputation.

NOT FOR EVERY EYE (No. 18)
GÉRARD BESSETTE
Fiction 5.5x8.5 126 pages ISBN: 978-1-55096-149-2 (tpb) $17.95

A novel of great tact and sly humour that deals with ennui in Quebec and the intellectual alienation of a disenchanted hero, and one of the absolute classics of modern revolutionary and comic Quebec literature. Chosen by the Grand Jury des Lettres of Montreal as one of the ten best novels of post-war contemporary Québec.

STRANGE FUGITIVE (No. 19)
MORLEY CALLAGHAN
Fiction 5.5x8.5 242 pages ISBN: 978-1-55096-155-3 (tpb) $21.95

Callaghan's first novel – originally published in New York in 1928 – announced the coming of the urban novel in Canada, and we can now see it as a prototype for the "gangster" novel in America. The story is set in Toronto in the era of the speakeasy and underworld vendettas.

IT'S NEVER OVER (No. 20)
MORLEY CALLAGHAN
Fiction 5.5x8.5 190 pages ISBN: 978-1-55096-157-7 (tpb) $19.95

1930 was an electrifying time for writing. Callaghan's second novel, completed while he was living in Paris – imbibing and boxing with Joyce and Hemingway (see his memoir, Classics No. 1, *That Summer in Paris*) – has violence at its core; but first and foremost it is a story of love, a love haunted by a hanging. Dostoyevskian in its depiction of the morbid progress of possession moving like a virus, the novel is sustained insight of a very high order.

IRREALITIES, SONNETS AND LACONICS (No. 21)
W.W.E. ROSS

Fiction 5.5x8.5 262 pages ISBN: 978-1-55096-158-4 (tpb) $21.95
The poetry of William Wrightson Eustace Ross spans over forty years. Ross left behind not only a great mass of unpublished manuscripts, but a reputation as the first modern Canadian poet – years ahead of the *automatistes* in Quebec – he was a translator, and a sonneteer of formal excellence. Through him, modernist poetry in Canada must now be looked at with an entirely fresh eye.

AFTER EXILE (No. 22)
RAYMOND KNISTER

Fiction 5.5x8.5 246 pages ISBN: 978-1-55096-159-1 (tpb) $21.95
This book collects for the first time Knister's poetry. The title *After Exile* is plucked from Knister's long poem written after he returned from Chicago and decided to become the unthinkable: a modernist Canadian writer. Knister, writing in the 20s and 30s, could barely get his poems published in Canada, but magazines like *This Quarter* (Paris), *Poetry* (Chicago), *Voices* (Boston), and *The Dial* (New York City), eagerly printed what he sent, and always asked for more – and all of it is in this book.

www.ExileEditions.com has a section for the Exile Classics Series, with further resources for all the books in the series.